The Binding Oath

The Binding Oath

SYBIL DOWNING

University Press of Colorado

Copyright © 2001 by Sybil Downing
International Standard Book Number 0-87081-607-1

Published by the University Press of Colorado
5589 Arapahoe Avenue, Suite 206C
Boulder, Colorado 80303

The University Press of Colorado is a cooperative publishing enterprise supported, in part,
by Adams State College, Colorado State University, Fort Lewis College, Mesa State
College, Metropolitan State College of Denver, University of Colorado, University of
Northern Colorado, University of Southern Colorado, and Western State College of
Colorado.

The paper used in this publication meets the minimum requirements of the American
National Standard for Information Sciences—Permanence of Paper for Printed Library
Materials. ANSI Z39.48-1992

Library of Congress Cataloging-in-Publication Data

Downing, Sybil.
    The binding oath / by Sybil Downing.
        p. cm.
    ISBN 0-87081-607-1 (alk. paper)
    1. Women journalists—Fiction. 2. Ku Klux Klan (1915–)—Fiction. 3. Police corruption—
Fiction. 4. Denver (Colo.)—Fiction. 5. Racism—Fiction. I. Title.
PS3554.O9348 B56 2001
813'.54—dc21
                                                                    00-012080

Text design by Daniel Pratt
Jacket design by Laura Furney

10 09 08 07 06 05 04 03 02 01   10 9 8 7 6 5 4 3 2 1

This book is dedicated to my husband.

Acknowledgments

The list of people who offered their expertise and support is long. Among them are Margaret Coel, Ann Ripley, Karen Gilleland, Elizabeth Downing, Elaine Long, and Beverly Carrigan; Ann Hagemeier, director, and the staff of the Overland Trail Historical Museum of Sterling, Colorado; the Western History Collection staff of the Denver Public Library; the Stephen Hart Library staff of the Colorado Historical Society; the dedicated volunteers of the Grover, Colorado, Depot Museum; Judy Hoxey, former director, and Sybil Barnes, local history librarian, of the Estes Park, Colorado, Public Library; Richard N. Hall, Allen Main, and Jim Pilkington; and the reference librarians of the Colorado Supreme Court Library. Thanks also to Darrin Pratt, Laura Furney, Jane Jordan Browne, and Luther Wilson, former director of the University Press of Colorado, for their belief in this project.

The Klan oath and prayer that appear in the novel are quoted from Wyn Craig Wade's *The Fiery Cross: The Ku Klux Klan in America* (Simon & Schuster, 1987). Finally, special recognition must be given to the doctoral dissertation of Robert Alan Goldberg, *Hooded Empire: The Ku Klux Klan in Colorado, 1921–1932* (University of Wisconsin, Madison, Wisconsin, 1977).

The
Binding
Oath

1

L iz O'Brien rapped sharply on the door to the suite and waited. Annoyed at her own uneasiness, she glanced up and down the elegant hallway, where a uniformed maid bustled about like a bit player in a movie, the sound of her movements muffled by the deep carpet. She placed a fresh bouquet on a table at the far end of the hall, and Liz breathed in the lilies' sweet fragrance. The hotel was an odd choice for a Ku Klux Klan press conference.

With its air of gentility, the Brown Palace was the epitome of refinement, so important to post–Great War Denver's struggle to shed its cow-town image. White-sheeted cross burners would be obscenely out of place here.

Liz remembered reading accounts of the Klan in the South. Keeping Negro voters away from the polls, burning houses, and driving families out of town—that was only part of it. Klan members whipped, castrated, and lynched people. She could hardly imagine such hate.

The KKK had first surfaced in Denver last year when white-robed and -hooded members roared down Sixteenth Street in an open car to the Rivoli Theater, demanding a rerun of a movie that showed the Klan riding to the rescue. Management meekly complied. The Klan had disappeared. Or so Liz—and everyone else in town—had thought, until earlier this morning, when the call came into the *Post's* newsroom. Apparently, the Grand Dragon of Colorado—otherwise known as John Locke—had an important announcement to make. And Liz had smelled a story, maybe a big one.

She'd wanted the assignment in the worst way. She resented being stuck reporting on the inconsequential of Denver's suburbs, in what was known as the "Neighbors" section. Recently, something called "Bright Sayings of Children" had been added to her plate. And, occasionally, the city editor sent her out to do a theater review.

A woman didn't cover hard news at the *Post*. Just before the war, she'd been hired to cover Society. Then, when the men were called up, other women were brought in to replace them. Now she and the Society reporter were the only ones left. Liz was well aware that she had to watch her every step: smile, work fast, keep her mouth shut, and pretend not to hear the smutty comments about single women. As far as everyone else in the newsroom was concerned, interviewing the KKK Grand Dragon clearly belonged to the city beat, Charlie Collier's job.

Sure enough, she was there when the city editor had called Charlie over and given him the assignment, naming the time and the place. She had nothing against Charlie. She liked him. He let her do her job and treated her with respect. Skinny, with sandy hair and a beaked nose, he was an easygoing family man who never questioned orders. Yet as he listened to the city editor's instructions, Liz had noticed an uncharacteristic frown knit his forehead.

When he returned to his desk to retrieve his hat, his washed-out brown eyes were desperate. She had followed him out of the newsroom.

"Anything I can do?" she had asked.

"Alice. She telephoned an hour ago. The baby's on the way. But Ware wants me to do this interview."

"Tell you what. I'll handle the interview, write it up, and have it on Ware's desk by this afternoon. Nobody'll be the wiser."

Charlie had smiled his relief. "You'd do that?"

"You can pay me back later."

Now, half an hour later, Liz stood in front of the hotel suite's door, about to knock again, when it was opened by a young, buxom woman dressed neatly in a white maid's uniform. Liz introduced herself as the reporter from the *Denver Post*. Judging from the girl's confused look, Liz realized a woman reporter wasn't expected. Almost reluctantly, she asked Liz to come in.

Standing in the doorway, Liz had a clear view down a short hall to a sitting room—mahogany furniture, a framed Watteau print over the desk, an oriental rug. She didn't hear any voices. The possibility that she'd be the only reporter present hadn't occurred to her.

"Dr. Locke's in there, waitin'. I guess you can just go right in, ma'am," the maid said.

Wary, Liz swallowed hard and entered the sitting room.

She wasn't certain what she'd expected. Locke had lost his license to practice medicine several years ago. His seamy reputation was well known. Yet the title of Grand Dragon conjured the image of a big man, larger than life, nothing even vaguely resembling the person seated in the crewel-embroidered wing chair across the room. His feet barely touched the floor. His thinning black hair was carefully combed to cover a bald spot on his bulbous head. His large, dark eyes contrasted starkly with his pasty skin. Several diamond rings adorned his pudgy fingers. He reminded her of an oversized toad.

"Yes?" he asked imperiously.

"Miss O'Brien from the *Post*."

Locke scowled. "Since when has the *Denver Post* employed women reporters?"

Liz met his disdainful gaze with a steady look and flashed her most professional smile. "Fifteen years, give or take."

Locke drew in a deep breath, as if resigning himself to life's vagaries, and waved her summarily toward the couch opposite his chair. She chose the far end near the open windows, pulled a pencil and her notebook out of her pocketbook. To her dismay, she noticed that her hands were shaking.

He settled into the high-backed chair. Before she could pose her first question, he launched into his prepared remarks. "We have just fought a great war to end all wars. Our men faced untold dangers to protect the ideals of our forefathers, which are being destroyed before our very eyes. Papists and the Hebrew syndicate have taken over the banks. Socialists invade our schools." He went on for another five minutes.

So far the diatribe was boilerplate of speeches she'd read in the Chicago and New York papers. Nothing new.

"Right here in Denver, the Queen City of the Plains, crime runs rampant because the district attorney is in the pay of the Dago underworld."

Liz ignored the offensive slur on Italians. She'd heard it often enough. But his accusation against the D.A. caught her attention. Phil Van Cise made news. She glanced up from her notebook with interest.

"The man has hoodwinked the entire city. But not for long. Once he is replaced with a true native-born, white, gentile American . . ."

Liz knew Phil—born and raised in Denver, of good English stock. If he didn't qualify as a true white gentile, no one did.

"The good citizens of Denver cannot wait another three years to elect a district attorney with the necessary moral fiber to return law and order to its streets, a man who will wipe out the prostitutes, the gamblers, the drug traffickers, the bootleggers. At the same time, here and across the state, we must flush the foreigners from our midst. By this November, God-fearing Christian men will be elected to every office. And Colorado will once again be in the hands of leaders dedicated to making the state a fit place in which to live and raise children."

"By 'we,' you mean the Klan?"

The Toad offered a smug smile.

"Exactly how many members does the Klan have in Colorado?"

"That is privileged information."

"An estimate, then. A thousand? Two thousand?"

He placed his small hands majestically on the armrests. "Multiply by ten and you will come closer."

Twenty thousand? In Colorado? Liz's eyes must have shown her surprise. Then a disturbing thought hit her. She must have passed Klan members on the street. Did they carry membership cards, have tattoos? How would you know a Klan member if you saw one? Maybe you wouldn't. Maybe that was the point.

She pushed aside these random thoughts and drew herself up an inch. "A point of clarification. Mr. Van Cise was elected not more than a year ago on a platform of law and order. Yet you say the Klan—"

"Apparently, you weren't listening, young woman, so I will repeat. The district attorney is in the pay of the underworld. His talk of law and order is nothing more than subterfuge. Let me assure you that once the voters are confronted with irrefutable facts, they will cast him out of office in a matter of months."

Liz sensed the Toad's "facts" were not unlike those that had hounded loyal German-Americans from their homes and jobs all over the country during the war. She took a long, slow breath to curb her anger and made a show of consulting her notes. "You said the Klan intended to 'flush out foreigners.' I believe those were your words."

"They were indeed. Italians, Greeks, socialists, and Bolsheviks, of course. Catholics and Jews. And niggers."

Liz had to give him credit. He understood Denver's underlying bigotry well. Negroes and Jews were expected to stay in their own parts of town. Even the wealthiest Catholics couldn't buy their way past certain gates. White Anglo-Saxon Protestants made the rules and ran the show, firmly believing equality was a fine idea if it wasn't taken too far. On the record, the high-minded would cluck disapprovingly at the Toad's venom, but the sickening truth was that in private, they'd probably eat up every word.

The Grand Dragon's eyes glittered. "Did I mention that we've opened headquarters? On Glenarm, just off Fourteenth."

She scribbled the address: in the heart of Denver's downtown, convenient to the city's power brokers and mainstream shoppers. She suppressed a shiver. "One last question."

The small man nodded as a king might acknowledge a subject.

"The God-fearing Christian men who will be elected to office . . . any names?"

"I'm afraid that for now they must remain between the Klan and the candidates. But when the time is right, the *Post* will be the first to know."

Liz kept a straight face. She'd bet her paycheck that any candidate confronted about being supported by the Klan would deny it. The success of their entire agenda depended on lies, deception, and secrecy.

"Well." He rose, reached for several sheets of paper lying on a nearby table, and handed them to her. "Press releases. In case you missed something." The interview was over.

❦

Squinting in the bright June sun outside the hotel, Liz pulled on her only pair of white cotton gloves without holes in the fingers. Since that night last year when the touring car full of Klansmen had blatantly dared Denver to stand up to them and it hadn't, she should have known they'd be back. The Toad's announcement was just the opening salvo of worse to come. She had to do what she could to derail it. She set out for the D.A.'s office. But on the way, she decided to take a look at the KKK headquarters.

As she strode across Seventeenth Street, careful to avoid the tar bubbles dotting the asphalt, soft beneath her feet, she saw a wave of men in seersucker suits and secretaries wearing smart straw hats pour out of an office building ahead, perhaps heading for lunch. Nice-enough-looking, ordinary people who probably went to church and paid their taxes. Could any of them be Klan members?

Liz ducked under awnings and dabbed with her handkerchief at the perspiration trickling down the sides of her face. The next block was Glenarm. Without an exact address, she had to guess which building held Klan headquarters. She surveyed the offices and storefronts on either side of the street. Her eye was caught by a large plate-glass window that had been curtained off to obscure any view of the interior. There was no sign above the door to indicate the building's purpose or ownership. It smacked of Klan.

Still she hesitated. Maybe she'd have to give a password. She took a deep, calming breath and walked over to the door. To her surprise, it was open, and she went in.

Closing the door quietly behind her, she found herself in a small entryway that opened into a larger room, which appeared to be a clinic. Four rows of neatly made iron cots that resembled hospital beds. Glass-fronted cabinets containing what looked like surgical instruments against the far wall. In spite of a strange, musty odor about the place, there was nothing even vaguely sinister about it.

A door opened.

"Hey, you there!"

She spun around to see standing in the doorway a giant of a man with cropped brown hair and a red birthmark smearing one side of his face. The sleeves of his long, sweat-stained underwear were rolled up to expose muscled, hairy arms.

"I was looking for the headquarters of the Ku Klux Klan," she said.

"It's closed." He moved to bar the entrance.

"Yes. Well, I can see that." She was tempted to ask him about the hospital-like surroundings but decided against it. Summoning all the dignity she could muster, she turned and left.

Outside, she stood in the doorway of the neighboring building, trying to make sense of what she'd seen. Though a clinic and the former doctor Locke fit, it was the last thing she'd expected. But if deception were the objective, the menacing guard ruined the effect.

❧❀❧

The fifteen-block walk to Phil Van Cise's office at Speer and Colfax reduced Liz to a puddle of sweat. Everything she had on, down to her silk stockings, was soaked. Phil's secretary brought her a glass of water. Liz ran a comb through her hair, flattened by her hat and perspiration, and dabbed her face with a powder puff to repair the damage as best she could before Phil emerged from his office.

Tan and slim, in shirtsleeves and loosened tie, the district attorney looked the part of a crime fighter. The effect of his brown hair combed straight back, emphasizing his cheekbones, led some to describe him as handsome. To her, he was just an okay-looking guy with a decent build.

"Liz, I've been meaning to call you." Their paths hadn't crossed since the Good Samaritan picnic last September in City Park. She'd known and liked Phil and his wife for ten years, and had worked hard on his election campaign. Phil tended to be caught up with himself, and she didn't agree with some of his politics, but his pledge to return law and order to Denver outweighed his flaws.

"Then you've already heard?"

He cocked a quizzical eyebrow.

"The Klan's back in town. I just came from an interview with the Grand Dragon himself."

"The infamous Dr. Locke."

"The same."

He led her into his office. "Then that explains the recall petitions taken out against me. Seems three guys representing something called the Law Enforcement Association came into the Elections office this morning. The charge against me is dereliction of duty, failure to enforce the law. Purposely vague, of course." Phil pulled a chair over to his desk.

"Take a look at this," Liz said grimly as she sat down, handed him the press release, and waited as his eyes skimmed the page. "You can see that on the surface, it's the usual diatribe. But the crime angle is new. As is the business of electing their people to office."

"Makes sense, if you think about it. The average candidate can be easily manipulated. I can't. I'm the stumbling block. They have to get rid of me to make their plan work. And the Klan knows damn well that a recall is their only chance." He settled into his high-backed leather chair, seemed to relax. "But, hey. The voters love me. The papers are with me."

"I wouldn't count on it at this point, Phil. Sure, Charlie Collier and maybe Harry Teaks will be assigned to stay on top of the story. But don't forget: officially, the *Post* avoided endorsing either you or your opponent. And public sentiment can be very fickle."

"You worry too much." Phil smiled and tossed a pencil onto a stack of papers. "I'll survive just fine."

Liz frowned, disturbed by his nonchalance. "I wish you'd take this more seriously. The Klan must think they have something on you that'll stick if they've taken out recall petitions." Liz paused, hesitant to bring up his Achilles' heel, but plunged ahead. "Police corruption might be it. You made a big point of getting rid of it in your campaign."

"The commissioner and I are working on it," he said defensively.

"Fine. But 'working on it' is a far cry from a clean police force." She leaned forward. "Phil, this isn't a popularity contest. You said it yourself. Their scheme won't work unless they get rid of you. You may not be worried, but I am. Just take another look at that press release.

"The Klan is sprucing up its image. Starting with a news conference in Denver's best hotel. They're going legit on us, trying to show the world they're upright, law-abiding citizens. They're not riding you out of town on a rail. They're doing it through legal channels—or trying to—circulating petitions."

Phil tipped back, hands laced behind his head, and stared at the ceiling for a moment. "The worst of it is that the Klan has a certain appeal."

"You're joking."

He righted his chair. "Think about it, Liz. A man puts on a hood and robe, recites a bunch of mumbo jumbo, and he's no longer just a clerk in a shoe store. A secret handshake and he's part of the mystical, invisible empire. That's a powerful motivator."

"I can't believe you're saying this."

"Liz, calm down. It takes eight thousand signatures to get an election called."

"Locke told me they have twenty thousand members."

"All in Denver? I doubt it very much. And even if it were true, it'll be the middle of the summer. People go to the mountains, work in their gardens, play ball. Politics is the last thing on their minds. And the petitions have to be signed in eight weeks," Phil said.

Liz held up a hand. "Okay. I hope you're right. But let's just say the Klan does have something on you—something bad enough to discredit you and grab the headlines. Maybe having to do with police corruption. They'll get those signatures in a heartbeat. The recall vote will be mid-August. If the Klan carries the day, you'll be gone, and the Klan will have their ready-made issue come November. They'll get their candidates nominated. They'll wage an all-out campaign. Their boys will win. And the Klan will take over the state."

"Jesus." Phil slumped in his chair, sighed. "It's like a timetable."

Liz nodded. The more they talked, the worse the scenario became.

"You don't suppose this is happening in other states, do you?" he asked speculatively.

"I haven't picked anything up off the wire, but it could be. Though Colorado seems like a strange place to start."

Phil leaned his elbows on the desk. "Strange or not, here they are. And you're telling me that they have something on me big enough to make headlines."

"Like a neighbor kid stumbling across a carload of whiskey stored in a warehouse. I can hear Harry Teaks now. 'Mr. D.A., how is it that you and the cops missed the whiskey? Could you tell us, sir, is someone on the take?' "

"Oh, come on," Phil said. "You're not giving the people of Denver enough credit. They'll smell a rat."

"May I remind you bootlegging is no longer just a state crime but a federal one, too."

"Your example's way off. I'm telling you, I'm on top of the bootlegging."

"You've closed down *all* the speakeasies? Run *every* bootlegger out of town?"

Phil sat forward, defiance in his eyes. "Okay, you've convinced me. Almost. In fact, the minute you leave, I'm going to call the police commissioner, see if he's heard anything."

"He won't know any more than you do. He's your man. You talked the mayor into appointing him. What you need is someone who isn't associated with you or with the police. Like me."

"Oh, for God's sake, Liz, you're no detective. Stay out of this."

"I'm a reporter, a good one. And I want this crowd stopped."

"Last I heard, you were assigned to 'Neighbors.' "

"There are ways around that." She rose, tucked her pocketbook under her arm, and headed for the door before he could argue.

"Your boss will never go for it," Phil called after her.

She looked back over her shoulder. "I'll call you."

〜

Outside the *Post* building, the oversized thermometer advertising Coors Golden Near Beer had already topped the ninety-eight-degree mark. Liz shook her head. Colorado wasn't supposed to have heat like this. She doubted even a good rainstorm would help.

Inside, it wasn't much cooler. She passed the business office and Classifieds. The display board of lodging ads reminded her that she still hadn't rented the two back bedrooms. Her grandfather's big house, where she'd lived since she was ten, was her refuge. It was also a treasure she couldn't afford, but one she wanted desperately to hang on to.

After Granddad's death seven years ago, her life had changed dramatically. Shaky finances had dictated she go to work. And she'd been confronted with the care of a huge house—she who'd never so much as cooked a meal or washed a window. So she'd proposed a deal to Greta Kuhlmann, one of several maids from the halcyon days: a little cleaning and cooking in exchange for free room and board. It had proved to be a viable arrangement. The house had been saved from wrack and ruin. They had both scraped by. Then, last year, after Greta left, Liz had rented out several rooms to schoolteachers, doing the light housework herself and letting the rest go.

But with the end of the school year, the teachers had moved on. The fifty dollars in rent was more than she could afford to lose. After turning in the Locke story, she'd get right on it and run another ad.

Liz climbed the stairs to the second floor. The large windows of the newsroom were wide open. Rows of sweating reporters hunched over typewriters, talked on telephones. Not one looked up as Liz made her way through the labyrinth of desks toward the slight, balding city editor seated at his desk across the room.

With his collar open and his tie askew, Ed Ware looked more harassed than usual. Maybe it was the oppressive heat. Yet she'd noticed lately that he seemed to have shrunk, grown older. Though they'd had their share of disagreements since she'd first been hired, he had kept her on after the men came back from the war. As frustrating as it was to see the few hard news stories she'd occasionally been assigned become things of the past, she still had a job. She wanted to think Mr. Ware would give her a fair hearing.

He looked up as she approached, put down his pencil, and peered at her over the top of steel-rimmed glasses that had slipped to the end of his nose. "Miss O'Brien. As I live and breathe. Your buddy Collier called in. It was a seven-pound girl."

Her heart skipped a beat. In her agitation over the Klan, she had completely forgotten how she'd maneuvered her way onto the story.

"A devious woman doesn't belong in this newsroom."

"No, sir."

"I trust you can explain."

Deep down she'd known Mr. Ware would eventually figure out the switch. Now it didn't seem to matter. She dragged a chair over to his desk, sat down, and handed him the remaining copy of the press release.

"Mr. Ware, I have reason to believe the Ku Klux Klan is attempting to take over this state." Her voice was quiet and firm, professional as she told him about the strange, frightening interview, about the petitions taken out under the name of the Law Enforcement Association to recall the D.A. "I think they'll create some kind of scandal to discredit him."

Mr. Ware scanned the press release with a dour expression. "Pshaw. Those bigots aren't worth wasting ink on." He tossed the press release on the nearest pile of papers; then, to further signal his assessment of the matter, reached into the wire out-basket at the front of his desk for a cardboard fan imprinted with "Niagara Falls" and began fanning himself vigorously. "Lousy, hot day," he grumbled.

"You are going to run the interview, aren't you?"

"An inch."

"Mr. Ware—" Liz stopped herself. She had to play her cards right. "How about the recall petitions against the D.A.?"

"Now that'll sell papers." He gave her a stern look. "In either case, the story will have Collier's byline."

"I understand." Liz wiped a bead of perspiration from her hairline with her index finger. "Charlie might want to know that I was the only one who showed up at the press conference."

The editor's eyebrows shot up. "The *News* wasn't there?"

"No, sir. Which would make the story an exclusive."

The editor sighed. "O'Brien, give it up. Collier does the story, such as it is. I'll give him this cockamamy press release and you can fill him in."

Liz gave him a subdued smile.

"But while you're here, you might as well tell me about your chat with Van Cise."

She straightened, seeing her chance, and told the editor what she knew. "We figured that the Klan might be looking for a scandal to nail him on. Like a bootlegging operation over in Five Points or Little Italy. Or the Bottoms. Places with Negroes and Italians and Greeks. Denver's lowlife, as the Klan sees it."

"A story for the police beat." Mr. Ware shouted toward the center of the room. "Hey, any of you get a call from Teaks about bootleg action in Five Points or Little Italy or the Bottoms?"

"Haven't heard from Teaks all day, boss," the rewrite man yelled back.

Liz wasn't surprised. Newsroom gossip had it that Teaks spent more time in speakeasies than following the police beat. He was the last person who should follow a story with a Klan connection.

She racked her brain for an angle. "Mr. Ware, it occurred to me . . . the *Post's* going to be giving away free operetta tickets to needy children in Five Points and the Bottoms again, right?"

The editor eyed her warily.

"And we really haven't carried a good 'Neighbors' story on either of those areas for quite a while."

"You've lost me."

"The kids who live in places like the Bottoms, Five Points and Little Italy, even Jew Town—I could go over there, hand out tickets, then write up the kids' reactions. It'll make a great human-interest story."

His eyes narrowed.

"Mr. Ware, I know what you're thinking and I don't blame you. The D.A. story is Harry's. But it couldn't hurt if I happened to hear something that he might want to follow up on."

The city editor gave her a long look, weighing the risks. He knew her better than she wanted to admit. "Okay. A feature story on kids and the operetta." He jerked his head toward the stairs. "Pick the tickets up downstairs and get out of here."

She tried to stifle a grin. She wanted to kiss the top of his balding head. Whether or not he'd intended to, he'd just given her another chance at hard news.

✈

Outside in the blinding sun again, Liz walked around the building to her aging black Buick. The windows were down, but the heat hit her like a blast oven when she settled behind the wheel. A wad of operetta tickets in her purse on the seat beside her, she headed for the Bottoms, less than a mile from the *Post*. Not five minutes later she passed the first of the shabby little houses.

Tucked along the west side of the South Platte River beneath a viaduct, this neighborhood—a dozen blocks of weed-filled yards and broken-down houses—was a part of Denver most people pretended didn't exist. Liz slowed nearly to a stop. Now that she was here, she wasn't sure what to look for.

Down the powder-dry dirt street was a group of barefoot girls playing hopscotch. Otherwise, the neighborhood appeared deserted. She looked about for a garage or a warehouse, some likely spot to stash whiskey, but saw only one-story shacks and a few adobe houses.

She lifted one hand from the steering wheel and wiped the back of her neck, feeling damp strands of bobbed hair beneath her hat. The brilliant sun intensified the bleakness of the yards, bare of grass and littered with trash. She drove on, smiling at the girls as she drew even with them. The tallest had flaming red hair and a belligerent look on her freckled face. She appeared to be about twelve, older than the others. She wore a stained and faded blue cotton dress. Hands on her hips, she demanded to know who Liz was.

"I'm a reporter for the *Denver Post*," Liz said, smiling, but the girl didn't smile back.

Liz turned off the engine and got out. In her stylish navy blue straw hat and matching two-piece cotton knit, she suddenly realized she looked every inch the outsider. Without even stepping beyond the first dilapidated fence, she'd encounter the code of silence that was almost a religion in this part of town. She beckoned to the girl.

After a few whispered words with her friends, she sauntered toward Liz with the confident air of an experienced snitch.

"I'm working on a story, and I need to know what's going on around here." Liz held out half a dozen tickets. "These'll get you into the *Denver Post* operetta at Cheesman Park next week. It's a lot of fun . . . music, a wonderful story."

The girl eyed the tickets without interest. "Me, I like the picture shows."

Liz dug a dime out of her change purse and handed it to the girl. She couldn't believe she was bargaining with a street urchin.

The girl pocketed the dime. "I dunno whatcha mean by 'goin' on,' but the ladies in that house over there vamoosed yesterday. Cleared out in a hurry, took a bunch of stuff with 'em."

Liz shot a glance at the row of houses. Eviction wasn't the story she had in mind. "Nothing else? No strangers stirring up trouble for you girls or your families?"

"Ain't seen nothin' like that."

Liz looked back at the houses. The girl had said she'd seen women on the run. They could have been Catholics. A forced eviction could be intimidating enough to frighten them into leaving town. "Which house are you talking about?"

"The one with the green door and the shades down."

"They all just up and left?"

The girl sighed in obvious disgust. "Look. A big old black rattle-trap of a car that I wouldn't be caught dead in drives up. The ladies pile in. Except . . . come to think, I didn't see Emma with 'em."

"So Emma might be at home." Liz could interview her.

The girl shrugged.

Liz studied the house with the green door more closely. The windows were closed. Some people shut their houses up against the heat, but staying at home on a day like this with the windows down would be like being locked in a trunk. And the place had a distinctly abandoned look. Still . . .

She looked back at the girl. "My name's Miss O'Brien. What's yours?"

"Ginger."

Liz smiled. "Ginger, how about introducing me to Emma?"

The girl gave her a calculating look and Liz said, "Ice cream cones for you and your friends, and another dime. *After* we meet Emma."

"And if she ain't there?"

"It still goes."

The girl eyed her, uncertain whether to trust her. Then with another shrug and a casual wave toward her friends, she led Liz through the opening in the fence toward the green door. Almost to the front stoop, she suddenly stopped and held her nose. "Jeez! What's that stink?"

Liz sniffed and nearly gagged. She couldn't imagine anyone inside enduring that stench. Something wasn't right. She knocked on the door. No answer. She tried the knob and found it locked. "I'm going around back."

With the girl dogging her heels, Liz skirted rusting tin cans and refuse as she trudged through the weeds between the house and its drab neighbor. As she rounded the corner, she saw a window cracked open. Like an evil presence, the smell seeped out into the hot air. She felt her breakfast lurch. Holding her breath, she leaned down and looked in, saw nothing.

She straightened. Chickens cackled somewhere down the street. A train whistle sounded. Otherwise, the neighborhood was unnaturally quiet. Liz moved to the back door, knocked, and waited. With growing uneasiness, she strained to catch some sound of movement inside, but heard nothing. She tried the doorknob. This time it turned.

She looked over her shoulder at the girl. "You stay here a minute while I take a quick look." Liz could be accused of breaking and entering, but she'd cope with that later if she had to. Her fingertips tingled with fear as she pushed open the door and stepped inside.

The foulness hit Liz full force, and she swallowed hard to keep from retching. The smell of death was unmistakable. She should leave this minute and call the police. But she went on, across the room, past a kerosene stove and a dilapidated table piled with dirty dishes, to a doorway that led to the front of the house. Her heart pounding in her ears, she entered the room. It was empty save for a couch and two overstuffed chairs with torn upholstery. On the other side, two doors stood ajar.

Trying not to breathe, she jammed her sweat-soaked handkerchief against her nose and mouth, went over to the first door, hesitated for a split second, and looked in. A bedroom. Two narrow iron cots, their stained mattresses bare, had been pushed together in the tiny space. The chiffonnier drawers were open, empty.

Sweat poured down the sides of Liz's face and from beneath her arms, yet her skin felt cold and clammy. Seized by a violent shiver of apprehension, she pushed open the door to the second room.

Sprawled across an unmade bed was the body of a woman in a white dress, covered with blood. Maggots swarmed out from under her. Her skin was a ghastly greenish-brown, her features bloated beyond recognition. More maggots were consuming her from within, causing her dead body to pulse with movement.

2

L iz let out a gasp and gagged. A wave of dizziness washed over her. She leaned against the door frame for support, her gaze riveted to the dead woman who must be Emma. Could this be the work of the Klan?

She quickly surveyed the room: blood-smeared walls, a lone chair tipped over, one leg broken off. A shattered mirror over the chiffonnier. Clothes strewn on the floor between the bed and the far wall. She shuddered at the image of Emma, standing off God knows what intruder, fighting for her life in this tiny room, only to be left to rot, alone.

Swaying like a drunk, Liz retraced her steps through the little house and finally gulped in fresh air, never guessing the Bottoms could smell so good. She looked around for the red-haired girl, eager to ask her more questions, but she had disappeared.

A grocery store blocks away was the first place Liz found that had a telephone. By the time she returned to the house, she might as well have yelled "Murder!" from the middle of the street: the neighborhood was a ghost town—not a car, not a person anywhere. Liz suspected the news was out, and the Bottoms had hunkered down against the world.

Still shaky, Liz sat on the running board in the shade of the Buick and waited a good half hour before a uniformed cop, his face flushed and sweaty, rolled up on a motorcycle with an empty sidecar. She stood and walked over to him, pointed out the house where she'd found the body, then returned to her car. Too edgy to sit, she began to pace.

A few minutes later, a Ford coupe with the Denver Police Department symbol on its doors and an ambulance drew up. Behind them was a two-door Rambler. She recognized it at once and cursed softly. Harry Teaks, her police-reporter colleague. She should have realized he'd show up. He'd probably been hanging around the station when she called in.

The two men in the Ford coupe were probably detectives—one well over six feet and thickset, in a rumpled brown suit, the other at least a head shorter, with a pockmarked face, smoking a cigar. They got out and walked over to the Rambler. At their approach, Teaks, a thin man with a sallow complexion, climbed out, a straw hat tipped back on his brown hair.

The big detective took off his sweat-stained brown fedora and mopped his face and neck with a handkerchief as he talked to Harry. Afterward, the detective turned to her, told her to stay put, and motioned to the beat cop. Following the ambulance driver, the officer and the detectives disappeared through the back door of the little house.

Harry leaned against the fender of the Rambler and made a show of lighting a cigarette, all the while pretending he didn't see her. It suited her fine. The less she had to explain, the better. She fanned away flies with shaky hands and contemplated the house. The interior had been meager at best. Whatever the rent, it had been too much.

The image of the woman's body returned. Blond hair cut in a bob. Plain, white dress caked with blood. It could have been a waitress's uniform. Liz began to formulate a scenario in her mind. Living on tips, Emma had been forced to find the cheapest lodging available and ended up sharing the rent with three other women in similar straits.

The landlord, figuring lone women were good targets for intimidation, might have come down to frighten them into paying more money. Or, if the women were prostitutes, their pimp might have showed up to demand more than his share of their earnings. Frustrated when he found only Emma at home, the killer started shoving her around, then the beating got out of hand. Emma's three companions returned later, discovered her body, and fled, not daring to call the police. But what if the women had left before Emma had been killed? The red-haired girl may have seen Emma after the other three women left, even if she hadn't said anything about it.

Whatever the scenario, it was common knowledge that violence—even murder—was no stranger in the Bottoms. Exactly the type of thing the Klan would use against Phil.

"Hey, Liz."

Startled out of her thoughts, she looked over at Harry Teaks, who was walking her way. His husky voice had a distinctly nasty edge to it.

"What I wanna know is what the hell you're doin' here?" He flipped his cigarette butt into the dirt, every inch the in-control male reporter.

She offered what she hoped passed for a smile, ignored his rudeness, which was legendary. "I was doing a story about the operetta." Normally, she did her best to get along with Harry, but at the moment she didn't give a damn. He was a hard-core drinker, undeterred by Prohibition, the kind of man whose tongue loosened when he'd had too much.

The beat cop and the ambulance driver came out of the house, bearing a stretcher with Emma's body beneath a sheet and followed by the detectives. They slid the stretcher into the rear of the ambulance with practiced dispatch. The driver got in and drove away.

Leaving the beat cop, the big detective and his sidekick came toward her. The second man had a deeply pitted face, perhaps the aftermath of smallpox.

"Miss O'Brien?"

She nodded.

"The name's Bentliff," said the larger man, his voice whiskey-rough. He nodded toward his partner. "Neihouse. Northside Station." They pulled out their notebooks and asked what had brought her to the Bottoms. Harry Teaks stood behind them, listening. She repeated what she'd told the beat cop, leaving out the part about the girl named Ginger, but including the victim's possible first name.

Apparently satisfied, Bentliff said she was free to go. Liz climbed into the Buick. Harry Teaks was talking to the detectives as she drove off.

Rolling along the dirt street, Liz looked from one side to the other, hoping she'd see Ginger, who might remember when she'd last seen Emma, or the license plate of the mysterious black car. But the yards were empty, the windows vacant.

Liz glanced at her wristwatch. Likely, Harry would go back to the station and wait to see what the police turned up before he phoned in his story. Which gave her a little time. She wanted to talk to Phil Van Cise before news of the murder hit the headlines. She drove back to the grocery store, telephoned his office. From Phil's sober tone, she could tell that he, too, was shocked by the turn of events. She told him about the red-haired girl and the women who had fled, perhaps just hours before the murder.

"You might have a problem," she said. "I didn't get a very good impression of the two detectives, Bentliff and Neihouse. If they hold out on you about the murder weapon, motive, suspects, and autopsy results, you're going to come off looking like an incompetent."

"The entire force isn't crooked, Liz."

"I realize that. But just to be on the safe side, don't you think you should have a man you can count on?"

"I suppose you have someone in mind."

"As a matter of fact, I do. Tim Ryan. As honest as you could hope for. He was a friend of my granddad's."

Liz sensed Phil's hesitation. "And you'll tell him what, exactly?"

"That I need to find out what the police know at this point."

"Liz, I'm not sure—"

"Trust me on this, Phil. I'll get back to you just as soon as I have anything." And she hung up.

❦

Liz pulled up to Tim Ryan's buff-colored brick duplex and parked. She'd known him since she was a kid. An Irishman right down to his thick brogue, he and her granddad had been friends from the time Mr. Ryan was a rookie and her grandfather had first been elected to the state senate. Granddad had died broke, defending noble causes. In all his years on the force, Mr. Ryan had never risen above patrolman. They'd each paid a price for their integrity.

Carrying a pot of salmon-colored geraniums she'd picked up at Elitch's hothouse, Liz crossed the porch. The front door was open. She knocked on the screen door and waited, enjoying the aroma of fresh bread that came from inside, admiring the bank of red and white petunias that edged one side of the manicured grass. The postage-stamp backyard, she knew, supported a garden that had to be the envy of neighbors for blocks around.

A moment later, she heard muted footsteps. Through the screen she made out the round figure of Margaret Ryan coming down the hall from the back of the house. Liz took a step back and smiled as the white-haired woman peered at her through the screen.

"Elizabeth O'Brien," Liz said, not sure Mrs. Ryan recognized her. "I hope I haven't interrupted anything."

Mrs. Ryan squinted more closely at her, then a smile spread across her wrinkled face. "Oh, my dear Lord. Of course. I'd know those O'Brien eyes anywhere. And the black hair. How I remember those beautiful, long braids of yours." Mrs. Ryan pushed open the screen door. She had on house slippers. "Come in, for heaven's sake. I'll get us a nice glass of cold lemonade. The iceman came by just yesterday."

"That sounds wonderful, but I came on a matter of business. I'm afraid I can't stay." She held out the geraniums. "For you."

Mrs. Ryan stepped out onto the porch, examined the pot of flowers with an appreciative eye, and looked back at Liz. "What kind of business, dear?"

"Is Mr. Ryan here?"

"Oh, my, no. Not at this time of day."

"Then would you ask him to telephone me at home." Liz took her notebook out of her purse, tore off a page, scribbled down her name and number, and handed it to Mrs. Ryan. "I need some information I can't get myself."

The older woman's forehead knit into a worried frown. "Not on a police matter?" she asked, dubiously.

"Just a little background."

Mrs. Ryan's frown deepened.

"I'd really appreciate it." Liz took a step back, smiled, and pulled out her ace. "Granddad was proud to count you and Mr. Ryan as friends."

"And sure the senator was a wonderful man. But I can tell you this, Elizabeth O'Brien: he would turn over in his grave if he knew you were mixed up in police business."

Mrs. Ryan's solemn, clear blue eyes reflected wisdom accumulated through years of hard times. Liz had heard her granddad's stories often enough. About Tim Ryan, who had never taken a penny of graft. Mrs. Ryan gazed pointedly at the flowers in her hands, then back at Liz as if to say she wasn't any more prone to bribes than her husband. "The geraniums are very nice."

"I hope you enjoy them." Liz turned, gave a little wave.

Back in the Buick, Liz glanced in the rearview mirror as she pulled away from the curb. Mrs. Ryan, arms folded over her breasts, was still standing on the porch, her disapproving eyes following the auto. Even with the pull of old loyalties, Liz wasn't at all sure she'd ever hear from Tim Ryan.

3

As Liz returned to the *Post*, a gold and pink haze edged the mountains on the western horizon, but she took no joy in the beautiful sight. Climbing the stairs to the newsroom, she could barely put one foot in front of the other. Emma's murder had caught her unawares. She'd gone in search of a bootlegging operation, not a murder. Her instincts told her the Klan was behind it. If she was right, it meant the KKK hadn't changed its spots after all.

Liz crossed the newsroom to Mr. Ware's desk. In shirtsleeves, he was hunched over several sheets of paper, reading.

"Mr. Ware—"

He looked up at her. "Collier just phoned this in to Rewrite," he said, holding up the typewritten sheets.

"I thought Charlie was with his wife at the hospital."

"Was. I told him about the recall petitions and he followed up on it." Mr. Ware looked down at the sheets. "Listen to this. From the D.A. himself. I quote: 'The Law Enforcement Association is camouflage for the underworld, the real force behind this recall. Since I have taken office, the underworld has been all but put out of business. I am cramping their style, and they want me out.'"

Liz hid a smile. Phil knew how to use the press.

"The Law Enforcement Association is the group that took out the petitions against Van Cise," the editor said.

"I think I mentioned that to you earlier."

The editor cocked an eyebrow and returned to the sheets before him. "Here's another doozy. Again I quote: 'Not even the underworld's attempt to remove me from office by recall will dissuade me from my battle against crime and restoring the rule of law to the Queen City of the Plains.'"

Mr. Ware shook his head as his eyes traveled down the page. Finally, he looked up at her again. "Well. How did the kids like the tickets?"

"Actually . . . I found something, Mr. Ware." Liz told him about the murdered girl. "It could have been connected with an eviction, or even prostitution. The Klan is bound to jump on it." She paused. "You should also know that the police asked me some questions."

The city editor scowled.

"And Harry showed up."

Heaving a great sigh, Mr. Ware pushed to his feet and headed for the water cooler. Steeling herself for a royal chewing-out, she waited as Mr. Ware filled a paper cup, swallowing its contents in one gulp. Absolute quiet held the newsroom. No one wanted to miss the fireworks. This wasn't the first time Liz had tested the confines of her beat.

But without so much as a word, her boss returned to his desk, pawed through the papers jamming his in-basket, pulled one out, and handed it to her.

"Tomorrow morning the Denver Garden Club is dedicating a new rose garden in Washington Park," he said. "Ten o'clock. It's all there."

In his way, he had forgiven her. Without even turning around, Liz could picture the good old boys exchanging looks of disgust at the missed entertainment.

Mr. Ware lowered himself into his ancient swivel chair. "One Mrs. J. B. Means is president of the Denver Garden Club. She expects a photographer. I'll send Smith."

His gravelly voice held a resentment Liz had never heard before. She wouldn't have thought the tough old editor could be fazed by the likes of Mrs. Means. Liz knew her, and she was a pain, but Mr. Ware had dealt with snobs like her hundreds of times. The years were taking their toll. Liz felt an unexpected surge of tenderness toward him.

❧❧❧

It was eight-thirty and the sun had dropped behind the Rockies by the time Liz left the newsroom, went downstairs, and stepped into the growing dark. She was tired clear through. She hadn't eaten since breakfast, and not much then. But the gruesome events of the day had stolen her appetite. Still, she knew she should probably eat something. She'd fallen into the bad habit of stopping off at a café for a quick supper, and the cost was adding up. Determined to be more frugal, she drove up to the Marion Street Market just as it was closing, bought a loaf of bread, a quarter pound of calf's liver, a medium-sized white onion, a half-pound of bacon, and a half-pound of green beans. The makings of a healthy meal. And Liz's mouth actually watered at the prospect of the liver pan-fried in butter with slivers of onion and crisp bacon, the way Grammy's cook used to fix it.

Back in the car, she turned south on Marion toward Eighth. The streets were nearly empty. She drove for several blocks, pretending she didn't feel the car jerk, and hoping it would go away. But the jerk became a sputter, then a cough. The carburetor might be clogged. It could be bad gas.

Granddad had bought the stately Buick sedan shortly before his death seven years ago. She'd kept it up, but the car had gone twenty thousand miles, mostly over roads unworthy of the name. It was showing its age. She probably ought to sell it and buy something new, like a Nash coupe, but the six or seven hundred dollars was money she didn't have, and couldn't spare if she did.

She shifted gears. The cough disappeared. Relieved, she vowed she'd take the old car to McFarland's Auto for a thorough overhaul. She liked to drive. More importantly, without the Buick, she couldn't do her job.

Liz was eager to get home to the three-story gray stone house to which her grandparents had brought her more than twenty years ago after her father had unloaded her like so much extra baggage. "An even swap," she remembered him saying with a straight face: his inheritance—to pay for the fashionable women and racehorses he kept outside Paris—in exchange for his motherless child of five. He'd probably been killed in the war—she didn't know for sure. What she did know was that she'd come out with the better end of the deal.

Over the years, nothing about the house had changed. The nursery walls were still painted yellow. The antique cherry rocker where Grammy had soothed away her fears still stood by the window. Granddad had taught her to type in his green-shaded study, had helped perfect her putting game in the back garden, had taught her to play billiards in the vast, paneled basement billiard room. Even if she rented out some of the nine bedrooms, the taxes were killing her. But at the moment, she had the luxury—and anxiety—of having the place to herself.

She imagined a long, cool bath. She'd soak, sip a little Irish whiskey left from Granddad's stash, and cook her dinner. She'd have her energy back, ready to talk to Tim Ryan when he called. If he called.

Liz turned in at the driveway and parked the car in the garage, which had originally served as the carriage house. Sack of groceries in one arm, she was pulling the heavy door closed when she noticed a light in one of the basement windows. Odd. She was usually good about turning them off.

She began to feel uneasy. Had someone in the Bottoms seen her talking to the detectives and followed her home? She contemplated the window and told herself not to be stupid. Then the lights in the kitchen went on. And the back door opened.

4

The instant Greta Kuhlmann stepped outside and recognized Liz's slim figure in the driveway, she was set to give her what-for. Locking up had never been something Liz cared about. As much as she claimed to love the big house, she'd always treated it like an old sweater. Last year when Greta had announced her departure and Liz had given her a key, Greta had crossed her fingers and hoped she'd change her ways. But this afternoon Greta had arrived to find the house wide open.

"Greta! Thank God it's you! I saw the lights and—" Liz ran toward her.

"Ya promised ya'd lock up." Greta automatically took the grocery sack from her.

"What in the world are you talking about?" Liz said distractedly. "You won't believe what's going on!"

Greta frowned. There was no talking to her friend right now. "Come on." And she led Liz inside.

Greta put the groceries on the kitchen table and Liz sank into one of the high-backed wooden chairs. Her face was ashen. Whatever had happened had obviously terrified her. Greta was glad she'd showed up when she did.

She missed Liz, more than she'd realized. Greta had grown up with five sisters and brothers in a house no bigger than a freight car. Until she'd come to work in this house, she'd never had a bed of her own. Company was not something she craved. But Liz was a friend.

Over the nine years they'd known each other, Greta had given considerable thought to the bond she and Liz shared, but never quite figured it out. Greta had come to work for the old senator as a maid, bringing nothing but calluses from working the sugar-beet fields, and four years of schooling in a one-room schoolhouse. After a few disasters, she'd caught on to serving the fancy people who came for dinner, and to using carpet sweepers, a gas stove, and even a washing machine. But when the senator died broke, Liz had been forced to let her and the cook and the chauffeur and the gardener go, and get a job herself.

So Greta had moved into a rooming house and gone to work as a waitress at the Union Station café. But on her very first day off she couldn't help but go back to the old place to check on Liz, who hardly knew how to use a broom, much less take care of a nine-bedroom house. That same afternoon, after Liz carried on about the weather for a while, they sat at the kitchen table and made a deal. Greta would move back in and keep an eye on the house in exchange for free room and board. She wouldn't get rich, but it beat the rooming house all hollow. They hadn't been friends at the time, just two women who needed one another's help.

Liz took off her hat with hands that no longer shook. The color was returning to her face.

"Okay. Now just who the Sam Hill did ya think I was?" Greta asked.

"It's a long story." Liz gave her a weak smile. "Right now, all I want is to get rid of some of these clothes."

"Suit yourself." Greta was willing to wait. "Meantime, I'll get supper started."

Liz eyed the sack of groceries. "I'm afraid it's liver and onions."

Greta made a face. German Russians were known to eat everything except the pig's squeal, but she drew the line at liver. "Don't worry yourself. I'll find somethin' else." She took the package of liver out of the sack, opened the refrigerator door, and shoved it to the back, out of harm's way.

A quick survey revealed a half-empty bottle of milk, a glass pitcher of tea, a head of lettuce whose outer leaves were wilting, a couple of tomatoes, the remains of a roasted chicken, a few oranges. She guessed that the bread was probably molding in the breadbox. Liz hadn't changed. Greta figured it was too hot to eat much anyway.

In half an hour, dinner—for what it was worth—was ready. Liz came down, wearing a loose-fitting dress that reminded Greta of a nightgown, and they took their trays out to the screened-in porch overlooking the garden. The only light came from the dining room. A moth batted against the screen. Greta took her usual spot in the fan-backed rattan chair and breathed in the heavy scent of honeysuckle. The elm trees edging the walled backyards of the big houses on either side towered like shadowy sentinels. A dog barked in the distance. Living as she did now on the prairies, she'd almost forgotten this soft-edged world of trees and grass and flowers. She had to admit there was a comfort to it.

Liz settled on the aging, flowered chintz cushions of the rattan settee. Balancing the tray of food on her lap, she told Greta about her interview with the Grand Dragon of the Ku Klux Klan, his plans, the D.A. Then, saving the worst for last, she told about the woman she'd found murdered in the Bottoms.

"God almighty," Greta murmured, shaking her head.

"Today isn't one I'd care to repeat."

Greta studied her friend. "I figured whatever it was had to be bad."

Liz took a sip of iced tea. "I just wish I knew for sure who she was."

Greta thought about it for a moment. She knew Denver. "She could've been a whore. It's the right part of town."

"I'd thought about that, but she had on a white dress."

"She mighta been a nurse, or somebody's maid."

"Or a waitress."

"Possible."

"If only I could find those women she lived with, or that little red-haired girl. She might have caught the license plate number of the car they drove off in."

They ate in silence.

Greta speared her last piece of chicken and looked over at Liz. "Ya thought the Klan had broken in here, didn't ya?"

"It crossed my mind."

"If I was you, I'd get out the senator's pistol."

Liz shrugged off the idea, as Greta knew she would.

"Did ya hear me? Go hunt it up. While you're at it, get the bullets that go with it."

"I'll think about it."

"You do that," Greta said, knowing Liz would do nothing of the kind—unless it suited her.

Liz took a last swallow of tea and set the tray on the floor. "Enough about me. Tell me what's going on in your life."

Greta had known Liz would ask, but the answer wasn't any easier to come up with. "We were talkin' about the murder."

"Were." Liz tucked her feet under her. "So. Tell me. You don't write letters."

"Stamps cost money."

Liz gave her a crooked smile. "You're avoiding my question."

Greta took a deep breath and plunged in, feeling a little like she had as a kid diving into the frigid waters of the lake by the sugar factory. "All in all, everything's pretty good," she said, putting aside her tray.

As Greta had expected, Liz looked at her doubtfully.

A year ago when Greta had finally saved enough money to buy a deserted homestead claim in the northeast part of the state, Liz had put up one objection after another. Mainly it boiled down to the isolation, and managing by herself as a lone woman.

"Well, see, it's taken me some longer to get settled than I thought. But soon as the girl I'm pickin' up gets to goin'—"

"What girl?" Liz broke in, her voice suddenly sharp.

"Didn't I tell you? I'm hirin' a country girl like me who's not afraid of hard work. Well, not hirin' so much as tradin' room and board for work. Like you and me did." She crossed her legs, sat back, like she was discussing the weather. "I hired a fella once, but it took cash, and he wasn't much count."

"Besides," she continued, "with me bein' single and livin' out there alone, I couldn't very well keep a fella on regular, even if I could pay him. It wouldn't look right."

"Since when do you care what people think?" Liz asked coolly.

"Since livin' by myself. People talk."

"I know," Liz said.

And Greta suspected she did. Her boyfriend, Frank Capillupo, was too handsome and his visits too steady to go unnoticed by the neighborhood busybodies.

"Anyway, it's different now," Greta said. "I wrote to one of the places here in Denver that takes in girls who get themselves knocked up. Asked if there was someone who'd be interested in room and board in exchange for givin' me a hand with the work. Sure enough there was. Tomorrow I'm gonna go over and pick her and the baby up."

"The baby? She's going to bring along a baby?"

"Why not?"

"I thought the girls who go to those homes put their babies up for adoption."

"Most do, I guess. But it's not a worry, we're gonna do okay." Greta liked how convinced she sounded.

"Bunk! A girl with a baby? Out in the middle of nowhere?"

"It's where I live," Greta said defensively.

Her face set, Liz swung her feet to the floor, leaned forward, resting her elbows on her knees. "Greta, that country up where you live is hard enough on strong men. But for two women?"

"When was the last time you was up there?" asked Greta, rankled by the criticism. "Listen, I'm tellin' ya, it's gonna work fine."

Liz's expression didn't soften. She got up, her tray in her hands. "You can talk till you're blue in the face, and it's still the most insane idea I've ever heard."

Greta folded her napkin. "Maybe, but it's what I decided on."

"Damn it, Greta. Why do you have to be so stubborn? You're like a stone in the middle of the road that can't be moved, no matter what."

"It takes one to know one." Greta got to her feet. "Let's do the dishes. Then I'm gonna go up and get some shut-eye."

"You go on. I'll do the dishes. I'm expecting a call."

Greta looked at her hard.

"From Tim Ryan. You remember. The cop who was a friend of Granddad's. Like a big bear with a brogue. Phil Van Cise, the D.A., needs someone he can trust who's on the inside. I asked Tim's wife to have him call me."

"You want a cop to snitch on other cops?"

Liz looked injured. "Did I say that? All I want is the victim's identity, her full name. And what's being done on the case."

Greta let it go. The requests seemed harmless enough. Later on, as she lay on top of the sheets in the narrow bed that had been hers for nine years, she was glad she'd saved her breath. The instant she'd walked in the front door this afternoon, she had picked up the lingering odor of the old senator's Cuban cigars. After all this time, he might as well still be sitting in his study or at the dining room table, he was that much alive in the house. He'd been a man who would stop at nothing if he thought he was right. Liz was just like him. A fighter who would plunge in with both fists swinging. And yet, as innocent as it sounded, Liz still was asking the old cop to stick his neck out.

If Greta knew anything, it was that justice was skewed in favor of the rich. The one cop in her hometown of Windsor had treated German

Russians like so much dirt. She was sure Denver cops were no different. To them, the murder of a woman from the wrong part of town
was not worth any extra effort or attention. Unless another cop started
asking questions. It was bound to spell trouble.

❧〰❧

The next morning, at the first sound of the sparrows' soft calls, Greta
threw her legs over the side of the bed. She hadn't slept well. In
different ways, she and Liz were both on edge, like two people who
had to cross a fast-flowing river with hidden holes deep enough to
drown in.

Greta's stomach was already in knots over the day ahead. She
wanted to look capable, confident. Not like some worn-out soul barely
hanging on, which was nearer the truth. She got up, grabbed the towel
and washcloth off the rack by the closet, and walked down the short
hall to what once had been the servants' bathroom. In the months
since she'd been gone, the room had stood empty. She doubted Liz
ever set foot in this part of the house. Last night Greta had found
dead flies and moths in the tub and sink and washed them down the
drain.

She snapped on the bathroom light, blinked in the sudden light.
The linoleum floor felt cool beneath her feet. The air was still warm,
and she left the window open, not bothering to pull down the shade.

The claw-foot tub was small, but still big enough for a good soak.
This would be the last time for she didn't know how long that she
could just turn on a tap and have hot and cold running water. She
pulled her cotton shift over her head, turned on the water, and sat on
the commode to relieve herself while she waited. Outside the window, she could see what looked like a robin's nest half-hidden in the
high reaches of an elm tree.

The water continued gushing out of the taps, but she didn't turn
it off until the tub was nearly full. She climbed in, easing down into
the tepid water, leaned back and stretched her legs until her toes
touched the end, closed her eyes.

Lying very still, she heard the early morning sounds of the city—
the distant clink of milk bottles being delivered, a barking dog, the
slap of a newspaper as it hit a front stoop. This time tomorrow she
would be back home, milking. Opening her eyes, she reached for the
washcloth and dipped it in the water, then spread it across her breasts.

The girl from the home had better be strong, a good worker. If her baby was one of those fussy kids that bawled, they'd all be in trouble. Greta stuffed the worry aside. Sitting up, she reached for the bar of soap.

After a good scrub and a rinse, she climbed out, dried herself off. Wrapping the towel around her, she padded back down the hall to her room. Her blue skirt hung in the closet. Next to it was the extra blouse she'd brought. Her saved-for-best blouse. She'd been ironing out the wrinkles when Liz had arrived last night.

Once dressed, Greta glanced in the mirror as she brushed her wiry brown hair into place. Sunburned skin the color of saddle leather. A stubby nose. Full lips. She was on the hefty side. She grimaced and rubbed an index finger to polish her teeth—straight and white—which she considered her best feature. Squaring her shoulders, she was as ready for the day ahead as she was going to get.

Downstairs, over a breakfast of toast and oranges and coffee, Liz commented on how nice she looked. She seemed more relaxed. Greta asked if the cop had called.

"No, but he will," Liz said, smiling, as she slathered jam on her toast.

Greta took a sip of coffee. She couldn't let it go. "Ya know, I've been thinkin'. As old as he is . . ."

Liz glanced across the kitchen table. "Greta, we went over this last night."

Greta concentrated on finishing her orange. Under the circumstances, she should feel relieved, knowing Liz had a cop who was a family friend to turn to. But this cop surely had his own problems.

"You should listen to yourself. You're beginning to sound like a stuck record," Liz said.

"Ya said it yourself. The Klan could have a stake in this murder. They're a bad bunch."

Liz leaned forward, her eyes bright with intensity. "That's exactly why it's so important for Phil to find the killer as soon as possible. If he could rely on the detectives on the case, he wouldn't need Tim Ryan."

"He's the only honest cop?"

"The only one I know."

"Seems like you're takin' on what rightly is the D.A.'s business."

"Are you saying I should just sit back and do nothing?"

Greta gave her an even look, took a last gulp of coffee, wiped her hands on her napkin. "Well. I gotta go."

"I wish I could make you see how it is," Liz said.

"I said my say, my valise is packed, and it's time to go." Greta got to her feet.

"I'll drive you." Liz pushed back from the table.

"Thanks, but the home is way east, out of your way. And the Colfax trolley runs right by it."

Liz carried their dishes over to the sink. "It's just a phone call."

Greta came to stand beside Liz. She didn't want to leave things as they stood. "Liz, it's your business and I had no call to butt in."

Liz smiled, just enough to move the corners of her mouth. "Friends can butt in any time they want."

"Yeah. Well, that depends." Greta took a few steps backward. Their gazes met. "Thanks for lettin' me camp out last night."

"I'll walk out with you." And Liz threw an arm around Greta's shoulders.

They were standing in the driveway when the telephone rang in the front hall. Liz put a hand on Greta's arm. "Wait a sec. It may be Tim Ryan."

"Listen, I got a streetcar to catch." But Liz had already run into the house.

A few minutes later she was back, a big smile on her face. "That was him. He was calling from a grocery store." She paused for a moment, considering. "Doesn't that strike as you as odd?"

"It's probably on his beat." Greta picked up her valise.

"All I had to do was mention the murder in the Bottoms. He knew the woman's name right away. Emma Volz, he said."

"A good German name," Greta observed.

Liz wasn't listening. "She and three other women had been picked up at a speakeasy at Twenty-second and Broadway the day before and taken down to the station house on charges of prostitution. A clerk from Mildred Loggin's office got them out. White dress or not, it looks like my Emma was a prostitute after all."

Greta caught the "my Emma," as if the dead woman were family.

"Lord. Why couldn't she have been a maid?" Liz moaned. "I can just see the headlines now. 'Prostitution ring operating out of speakeasy.' The public will eat it up, Greta. Phil's really going to have his hands full now."

And you'll be right there with him, Greta thought ruefully. "Listen, before I forget. I think I remember seein' the senator's pistol and the box of bullets in the top drawer of his desk."

"And that's where they'll stay."

"At least lock up."

"That I'll do." Liz gave Greta a little hug. "And you send me a postcard—let me know how everything works out with the girl. And the baby."

"If I have time."

5

Liz closed the door, the big house instantly empty without Greta's presence. She tried to push aside the tug of disappointment at Greta's negative reaction to the phone call. If only Greta had heard the conversation, she would have picked up the eagerness in Mr. Ryan's voice, how glad he sounded to be of help.

Liz walked back to the kitchen to wash up the dishes, her thoughts still on the call. Mr. Ryan's news about the women at the speakeasy was a bombshell. She wanted to call Phil to be certain he knew. She glanced at her watch: eight fifty-five. She'd wait another five minutes till the office opened.

Liz was intrigued that the Loggin law office was involved. Unlike the dozen or so other women attorneys in the state who represented mothers and children or handled real estate matters, Mildred Loggin specialized in criminal cases and was known to have clients from among the underworld. The owner of the speakeasy must be one of them.

Liz had first met Miss Loggin during the final push for ratification of the women's suffrage amendment, when they'd served together on a committee. She'd been practicing law since before the turn of the century. Yet, even now, she was considered a curiosity.

Liz checked her watch and put in a call to Phil, but he was out. Liz left her name and a message that she had urgent news. She had a speech to cover for the paper, but she would call back later.

Liz pinned on her hat, gathered up her notebook and purse. At the last minute, remembering Greta's orders, Liz turned the latch on the inside of the front door, found her house key in one of the kitchen drawers, and locked the back door behind her. Her grandfather's pistol would remain where it was.

❧❧❧

Notebook and pencil in hand, Liz leaned against the elm tree at the edge of the Washington Park rose garden, where she had retreated for shade. Occasionally, she jotted down a phrase of Mrs. Mead's dedication speech, but her mind was on the murder case. The happy shrieks of children playing in the lake, the steady hiss of sprinklers arching streams of water through the dry air, and the heady scent of roses all might as well be a million miles from the Bottoms.

She thought about Emma. Emma Volz. Knowing her full name gave Emma a reality beyond that of brutally slaughtered victim. From the very first, Liz had felt a growing urge to know the living woman Emma had once been. Liz knew what it was to be a woman, trying to get by on half wages in a man's world. Where had Emma come from, what had she dreamed of? Had she been married, borne children? Had she really been a prostitute? Liz was as determined to find the answers as she was to learn who had killed her. The white dress might be a lead.

A smattering of applause jarred Liz back to business. She saw the photographer get out of his car, and headed over to introduce him to Mrs. Mead. Her obligations fulfilled, Liz was anxious to get on with her search.

Thick, dark clouds were beginning to form. Moving fast, they were the kind that could dump an inch of rain in fifteen minutes. As she drove back to the *Post*, she thought of the white dress again. It wouldn't hurt to stop at St. Joe's and St. Luke's. But neither hospital had records of a nurse named Emma Volz. Later Liz might call the employment agencies that handled domestics. As a last resort, she could ask around at the city's restaurants and cafés.

It was midafternoon before Liz walked into the office. Spying a pile of the day's first edition at the bottom of the stairs, she picked up a copy. There it was. Just below the headline story predicting a rail strike was Charlie Collier's article on the recall petitions, including Phil's crazy quote about the underworld. But not a line about the murder. Odd. Murders routinely got front-page coverage in the *Post*.

Liz combed the first section, finally spotting Harry Teaks's byline over a two-paragraph story on the bottom of page twenty-two, above the day's "Gasoline Alley" comic strip. Either he hadn't found out anything new, or he was saving it for later.

She walked upstairs. Drops of rain as big as dimes smacked against the closed windows of the newsroom. A spear of lightning sliced through the clouds to the west. A clap of thunder echoed. Water came down in sheets.

Liz plunked herself down in front of her typewriter and made short work of her rose-garden story. Before she turned it in, she reached for the telephone and called the D.A. again, only to learn Phil still hadn't returned.

She glanced toward the windows, saw that the rain had stopped as abruptly as it had started. One of the other reporters opened the windows. Liz dropped her copy on the rewrite desk and walked over to breathe in the pungent odor of the damp air.

Leaning on the windowsill, she gazed down on Champa Street. From the corner of her eye she could see shoppers coming out of Woolworth's five-and-dime, a few waiting for the light to change on Sixteenth Street. Four blocks to the west was Market Street, once home to the largest prostitution business in the Rocky Mountain region. The law had officially closed it down before the war, but business continued to operate out of rooming houses and apartments, even speakeasies—like the one where Emma and her friends had been picked up. The police must have intended just to hassle them, or the women would have been formally arrested and booked.

Turning back, Liz noticed that Harry Teaks had come in. He was standing by his desk, hat still on, chatting with one of the sports reporters.

She wandered over. "Any news on the Volz murder?"

"Read tomorrow's first edition," he drawled, fixing her with bloodshot eyes.

The sports reporter, slouched against the adjoining desk, chuckled appreciatively. Several other reporters laughed. The good old boys were in their element. She'd been messing around Harry's beat: if there was a way to put her in her place, they'd jump on it.

🦋

The sun was poised on the tips of the mountains when Liz pulled the Buick into the garage. Closing the door, she noticed the grass in the garden looked as if it had grown a good three inches. She sighed, vowing to get up early tomorrow and cut it. Then she'd put another ad in the paper for a roomer, preferably someone who liked yard work.

Just as she unlocked the back door, she heard the shrill ring of the telephone. Phil might be trying to track her down. She dashed through the kitchen and pantry to the front of the house to answer it.

"Hey, stranger."

She grinned at the sound of Frank Capillupo's deep baritone. The Klan, the murder, and money problems suddenly took a backseat.

"Have you missed me?"

"What do you think?" It had been three weeks since she'd seen him. She leaned against the antique refectory table, her heart lurching just as it had that day he'd walked toward her across the city newsroom with the long, sure stride of an athlete.

She'd met him nearly six years ago, when he'd been the *Post's* sports reporter and she the society-page columnist. She was a nobody. He was the former star pitcher for the Denver Bears. They fell in love. Everyone said they made a great couple, but the timing was wrong. War was coming. And when the country jumped in, Frank joined the American Expeditionary Forces. She'd always believed the war was Frank's great adventure. For him, it certainly had nothing to do with politics or righting a wrong.

Though four inches taller and ten pounds heavier than AEF regulations allowed, he had managed to talk his way out of the mud-filled trenches and into flying airplanes. The instant he climbed into the flimsy trainer on the hard-packed dirt field in Texas, flying became his obsession. After the war, Frank was one of the first pilots to sign up for the airmail runs. At the moment, his route was between Chicago and Cheyenne.

"I thought we could have some of Papa's rigatoni. A little *vino* to go with it," he said.

"I like a man with the right connections." Liz had always marveled at how the Capillupos, whose restaurant in Little Italy essentially depended on wine for its existence, had managed to get around state and now federal Prohibition laws. Fortunately for the Capillupos, enforcement was uneven at best. And she'd always suspected half the Treasury men in the region ate there regularly.

"How does seven sound?"

She glanced at her watch. She wouldn't have much time to bathe and change clothes. But, eager as she was to see him, she didn't want to make it later.

"Seven it is, then," he said, without waiting for her answer.

Still smiling, she hung up the phone and started up the stairs.

🐦

Dressed in a peach-colored silk, with a long string of crystal beads around her neck, Liz sat beside Frank in the shiny roadster that still smelled of new car. It had been long enough since she'd seen him for the pressure of his thigh against hers to set her afire, pushing every other thought out of her mind.

He sniffed, glanced at her in the fading light, and grinned. "Is that a new perfume?"

"It must be the bath oil you gave me." In another second they'd be wrapped around each other like gift paper and never make it to dinner. She decided to change the subject. "Nice car. Delivering mail must pay better than I thought."

"It belongs to the boss." He placed a hand on the back of her neck and kneaded it.

"That feels delicious." She closed her eyes, surrendered to the feel of his hand. She was tempted to suggest they forget dinner and go back to her house.

"Not the U.S. postmaster. The other one. Bud Humphreys. You know—the rich guy with the airline." Liz immediately caught the familiar excitement in his voice. Someday, some way, he intended to own or at least fly passenger planes on regularly scheduled trips.

"A real airline? For sure?"

He took his hand from her neck. "Not quite. But close. I've got three days off, so I'm going to fly some of Humphreys's influential buddies from a bash in Estes Park down to the Broadmoor Hotel in Colorado Springs. He wants to impress them. I persuaded him to buy a DeHavilland, like we fly for the mail runs. His old Jennies can't handle the extra weight of passengers at that altitude."

"Buddies like who?"

"Blackmer, Ben Stapleton. With his gold mines and investments, Blackmer's got the bucks. Stapleton has the political connections from his years in the Speer administration. Folks may remember the parks Speer built, but the politicos remember the arm-twisting—and Stapleton was the one who did the twisting." He glanced at her. "What about you? Anything exciting?"

"More than you'd believe." And she described her interview with the Grand Dragon and the murder in the Bottoms. "I have no proof, but I'm convinced the Klan is mixed up in it. Locke wants Phil Van Cise out and won't stop at murder to get his way."

"Seems like those would be Collier or Teaks's stories."

"They are. But I pushed my way in. And now Harry Teaks is upended about my butting into his business. I don't know about Charlie. This really isn't his kind of story. He's the sort of guy who generally takes people at face value. When the D.A. told the press that the underworld was after him, I think Charlie actually believed him. He probably couldn't care less if I'm involved."

Frank shot her a glance. "And Ware?"

"I don't know. He won't let me off 'Neighbors,' but I keep hoping. Depending on what I bring in, he may or may not relent. He knows I'm a good reporter."

"You are."

Liz studied Frank's profile. She thrived on his praise, which he did not give lightly. He pulled the car up in front of his family's restaurant, cut the engine, and turned to her. "Just don't go off half-cocked. Okay?"

"Never."

His black eyes warm with love, he reached out and touched her cheek. "You could marry me and stay clear of all this, you know."

She smiled, tilted her face into his hand. Her love for Frank frightened her. She found herself distrusting it, like a summer day too perfect to last. She could handle grief, but the risk of love withdrawn as it had been when her father walked away was not worth taking. "We've been over that a time or two, remember?"

"I keep hoping."

She kissed his fingertips. "Isn't being engaged enough?"

"You tell me."

She laughed lightly, loving him. "Oh, you Italians are a wily bunch."

He pulled her toward him. "We try."

🪶

The moment Liz walked through the restaurant door, she heard a woman's sobbing above the buzz of chatter.

Frank glanced at Liz, worry in his dark eyes. "It's Mama. Wait here a minute. I'll find out what's going on."

Liz stayed by the front door, out of the way of scurrying waiters, balancing trays filled with plates of steaming pasta. Breathing in the inviting aroma of garlic and onions and basil, she realized how hungry she was. Capillupo's had been a favorite in north Denver's Little Italy, just west of the labyrinth of railroad tracks and Mt. Carmel Church, for as long as she could remember. Frank's family had converted a vacant store into a restaurant reminiscent of their native village of Potenza, not far from Naples. Eventually, success had forced them to take over the adjoining two-story frame house.

Ten minutes went by. Liz strained for some sight of Frank through the open door to the kitchen. His family had treated her with unfailing kindness. Yet, if they'd had their druthers, she suspected they would have preferred their only son to be involved with a nice Italian girl.

"The man is a monster. He will be sorry for what he does to my girl," came a man's indignant roar, the words thick with an Italian accent.

"Papa, don't. There's nothing to do about it." Liz recognized the reasoned, contralto of Frank's older, unmarried sister, Maria.

"This is America," her father shot back.

Liz decided then and there that the family trauma, whatever it was, overshadowed her casual dinner plans. She walked to the doorway, peered into the bustling kitchen, and saw Frank across the room, one arm around his sister's shoulders. A stolid woman with a big heart, Maria was the oldest of the five children, nearly as tall as her brother. All of Little Italy knew about her important job as secretary to the president of the Mountain States Bank. Huddled next to Frank and Maria, out of the way of the cooks, were their parents, sniffling and red-eyed.

Not wanting to intrude, Liz was about to leave when Frank spotted her in the doorway. His black eyes were brilliant with anger. "Maria got fired."

Mrs. Capillupo dissolved into tears again, and Frank handed her his handkerchief. Dabbing at her tears, she looked over at Liz. "Mr. Foster said he was sorry, but she is Catholic. There was nothing else he could do. If he didn't fire her, customers would take out their money." The older woman looked frightened, bewildered.

Frank wrapped his arms around his mother, patted her gently on the back.

"Maria's worked at that bank since she graduated from high school. Twenty years. Foster can't make a move without her. What does it matter she's a Catholic girl?" Frank's father asked no one in particular in his heavy Italian accent.

The question rang in Liz's ears as she left the kitchen, slipped out the front door, and headed toward Thirty-eighth Street, where she knew she could catch the streetcar. Maria would never be able to prove it, but, given the last two days, Liz was certain the Klan was behind the firing. If Tammen and Bonfils, the owners of the *Post*, were pressured by Klan-connected advertisers, the same might happen to her.

Footsteps hurried up behind her and she heard Frank's voice. "Liz. Hold up."

She stopped, turned. Her heart wrenched at the agony on his face.

"Mama sent me to get you. She says you need your supper."

Liz smiled, touched by Mrs. Capillupo's thoughtfulness in the face of her own worries. "Tell her thank you. Another time, but not tonight."

Frank regarded her with warm eyes. "Mama wouldn't say for you to come back if she didn't mean it. You're family, even if you are Irish."

She smiled at his little joke and put her arms around his waist. "Go back. Maria and your parents need you."

He reached behind him and loosened her arms, held her hands. "Wait here. I'll get the car and drive you home."

Liz shook her head.

"You're too stubborn for your own good. You know that?"

She smiled, and Frank gathered her into his arms. Her head against his chest, she heard his heartbeat. She drew back. Gazing up at him in the cone of light from the streetlamp, she was struck by how uncharacteristically vulnerable he looked.

6

The soft coos of a mourning dove stirred Liz out of sleep, and she turned on her side, hoping that this once Frank would still be there.

After she'd left him at the restaurant, she'd waited on the porch at home in the dark until well after midnight before she heard the distant sound of his car. He always parked around the corner to avoid neighbors' gossip. Several minutes went by. The back door opened, and she called to him softly. Not turning on the lights, she walked through the dining room to the kitchen, where he was standing by the door. She took his hand, felt the heat of it, and the sensation left her weak-kneed with desire. Without a word, they went upstairs to her bed.

Their lovemaking had been more tender than passionate. Afterward, lying in each other's arms, they talked a little of what more might happen to Frank's family and others in Little Italy. Liz got up and went to the bathroom. When she returned, Frank was already asleep.

Now Liz gazed out the half-open window at the dawn-gray sky and thought about the Capillupos. Good, decent people, they had achieved a certain success with hard work and a little luck, and basked in their children's triumphs. Frank had once been the idol of baseball fans. Then readers had followed his sports column in the *Post*. He'd come home from the war a local hero. But apparently none of that was enough to protect his family from the Klan. First and foremost, the Capillupos were Italian Catholics with dark, foreign looks and outgoing ways that apparently didn't fit the Klan's image of tight-lipped true Americans.

Liz threw off the top sheet, stood, and padded barefoot to the bathroom. She flicked on the overhead light and peered in the mirror above the sink. Blue eyes, dark hair. Pure Irish. Beyond the occasional snub from Denver's old guard, though, Granddad's money and position in politics had sheltered her from much of the prejudice.

She turned on the tap and watched the ribbon of hot water snake across the stark white porcelain and slither down the drain. As she had dozens of times in the last few days, she asked herself why the Klan had chosen Colorado in which to surface.

She reached for a washcloth and rubbed it with the last of the Pears soap a friend had sent her from New York. As she slathered her face and neck and washed under her arms, Liz thought back on the self-righteous citizens' groups that had mobilized during the war on the pretext of rooting out disloyalty. In reality they were conducting a witch hunt. Last year's emergency immigration law had seriously restricted the number of southern and eastern Europeans who could enter the country. Several years ago, a book had been published about protecting the purity of Anglo-Saxon stock; for a while it had been the topic of every dinner-table conversation in Denver. Its message could just as well have come out of the Grand Dragon's mouth.

The war had shaken the country from its isolationism, thrust it into the outside world. The song had it right: "How're ya gonna keep 'em down on the farm after they've seen Paree?" Movies, fast cars, roadhouses: young people's morals were going to the dogs. Everything was topsy-turvy and had to be put to rights. Or so some thought.

As hard as Phil Van Cise was working to clean up crime, he wasn't making much headway. How Emma's murder fit, and whether prostitution figured in, Liz had no idea. But the connection between the Klan and Maria Capillupo's dismissal was frighteningly clear.

Back in the bedroom, Liz got dressed automatically. She hurriedly ran a brush through her hair and smoothed a touch of red lipstick over her lips. Downstairs in the kitchen she put on some coffee. The refrigerator was nearly empty, but there was enough bread in the breadbox for a slice of toast. She would have to go to the market again. Her stomach growled. She'd gone without dinner last night. Yet more than food, she wanted to talk to Frank. Before she even had time to get to the phone, he walked in the back door.

"I'd hoped you'd come by," she said, hugging him.

"Come with me to Estes Park."

She smiled up into his eyes dark with worry. "You won't have room. You're taking your boss."

"I can make two trips."

"I can't, Frank. I work for a living. Besides, where would I sleep? I don't have enough money for a new pair of shoes, much less the price of a hotel room."

He kissed the tip of her nose. "How 'bout under the wings of the DeHavilland? I do it all the time. You'd love it. God, the stars you see!" He put an arm around her shoulders, hugged her to him. She smelled the Stroller cigarettes he always smoked and imagined making love in the cool mountain air.

Reluctantly, she stepped away. "I wish I could, but I can't."

Frank looked at her gravely. "I don't like the idea of your staying in town."

"It goes with the job, Frank."

"Forget the job and marry me."

She shook her head.

It was always the same. The responsibilities that kept them apart were a sticking point they couldn't seem to get past. But this morning, she knew Frank's worries went beyond the issue of her job.

As if reading her thoughts, he said, "Can I change your mind with a decent breakfast?"

She kissed him lightly on the lips. "No, but you can try."

The Blue Parrot was nearly empty when they walked in. A stout, white-haired waitress in a blue-and-white-checked uniform showed them to a window table with a view of the Capitol. The restaurant, famed for its tiny cinnamon rolls and ample portions at a reasonable price, was a favorite haunt of lawmakers and lobbyists.

Famished, Liz ordered eggs and bacon, coffee and cinnamon rolls. Frank decided on the blue-plate special—two fried eggs, sausage patties, hash browns, rolls, and coffee. After the waitress left, they played with their silverware, looked out the window, locked in an uncomfortable silence. Finally, Liz couldn't stand it any longer.

She reached for his hand. "Frank, it's not just that I have to earn a living. The integrity of the district attorney's office is at stake. The Volz murder is an important story. I have to keep on it, particularly now, after what's happened to Maria." She didn't dare stop. In a moment his steady gaze would turn her heart soft as pudding. "I know what you're going to say. It's Harry Teaks's story and Mr. Ware won't let me budge from 'Neighbors.' But it's still mine."

"Maria is exactly why you have to stay out of this." He squeezed her hands. "The folks or you could be next. I couldn't stand it if anything happened to you."

"It won't. Besides, family tradition demands I stay the course."

He gave her a level look. "I suppose you're going to tell me again about how the old man stood up to the APA back in the nineties."

"The American Protective Association was first cousin to the Klan, Frank. It intimidated Catholics."

"I don't care if they were joined at the hip. You aren't your granddad."

Liz bristled with indignity. "Are you deliberately missing the point, Frank?" She saw the spark in his eyes. "Granddad's legacy of courage—a boy on his own, who grew up seeing signs in shop windows that said 'No Irish or dogs allowed'—and your parents' legacy: that's what this is about."

Frank sat back. "Liz, it's 1922, a different ball game."

"Whatever that means." She could feel her temper rise.

"It means you're incredibly naïve if you think a woman reporter is any match for the Klan."

She drew in a long breath and let it out slowly. "Oh, so I'm naïve."

"Yes." His intense gaze met hers.

By some miracle, she managed to hold her tongue. A time might come when she'd regret saying the words that blazed in her heart. She carefully folded her napkin and placed it on the table. Frank fumbled in his pants pocket, put a silver dollar next to his cup. Without another word, they got up, breakfast forgotten, and walked outside.

"Can I give you a lift?" Frank asked, his voice carefully neutral.

Their argument had stepped beyond the usual bounds into dangerous territory.

"No, thanks."

They parted, Frank climbing into the Nash, Liz striding to the corner. It wasn't until his car rolled by and turned the corner that, too late, she gave a little wave.

❦

The awnings along Seventeenth Street provided welcome relief from the heat as Liz made her way to the Loggin law office, but she barely noticed. Her mind churned with thoughts of Frank and the morning's argument. She didn't blame him for his caution, but to expect her to back off? He should know her better than that. Besides, he was wrong. Lying low and out of sight fed into the Klan's plan of intimidation. Didn't he see that? And accusing her of being naïve: that had really hurt.

She shoved aside her anger as she strode through the doors of the Equitable Building, a Renaissance revival structure in the heart of Denver's financial district. Its elegance and location appealed to the well-heeled and influential, and those who wanted to appear that way. Liz suspected Mildred Loggin had chosen the spot to thumb her nose at the male attorneys who had done their best to put her in her place.

She found the offices at the end of the hall on the third floor. The straight-backed chairs and bare walls of the reception area were about what Liz had expected. Leather-cushioned couches and oil paintings were not Mildred Loggin's style. A harried-looking woman sat behind a desk, attempting to type and answer the telephone at the same time. A door slammed, and Liz heard a muffled exchange between two men. Telephones jangled. The law firm was doing a brisk business. Liz gave the secretary her name and asked to see Miss Loggin.

"She's in the library, but she's due in Judge Robert's chambers at noon. Go on back if you want. End of the hall. If she's busy, I guarantee she'll tell you so."

Liz walked down the hall, tapped on the frame of the partially opened door. "Miss Loggin?"

"What is it?" a brusque voice asked.

Liz stepped into the book-lined room and was assailed by the cloying smell of Turkish tobacco. A woman of average height with a square face and ruddy complexion that no powder puff had ever touched was seated at the end of a long pine table covered with neat piles of legal papers. Liz recognized her as Mildred Loggin. She wore a serviceable black suit intended for winter months, beneath it a plain white blouse. Steel-rimmed half-glasses were perched on the end of her nose. Her graying hair was cut in a severe bob, chosen, Liz guessed, for convenience rather than fashion. At her elbow was a large glass ashtray with a partially smoked cigarillo balanced on one edge.

"Elizabeth O'Brien from the *Post*, Miss Loggin. You may not remember me. I cover the 'Neighbors' section."

The attorney surveyed Liz over the top of her eyeglasses. "I remember."

Liz smiled. Mildred Loggin didn't smile back.

"Well, don't just stand there. Sit down. Time is money." She waved Liz to a chair, reached for the cigarillo. Holding it between thumb and index finger in the European manner, she took a long drag, peering at Liz through the veil of smoke. "It was the meeting on the suffrage amendment at the Cosmopolitan Hotel two years ago."

"You gave a wonderful speech," Liz said. "The economic problems women face are usually overlooked."

"Indeed." Miss Loggin sat back. Clearly, she didn't give a damn what Liz thought about her speech or anything else. Not a good start. "What's on your mind?"

"I'm doing background for a story, and I was told your office represented four women brought to the Northside substation on suspicion of prostitution day before yesterday. One of them, Emma Volz, was murdered. I was hoping you could give me the names of the other three women, and any other information you have on the four of them."

"What's your interest?"

"I don't have the facts to back it up, but I think the Klan is involved somehow in the murder. I also think they're behind the petition drive to recall Phil Van Cise."

Mildred Loggin took a final drag on the cigarillo and stubbed it out. Her dislike for Phil was public knowledge. During his election campaign, she had called him a smug nincompoop, a description that had stuck in Liz's head. "Did I read it wrong, or did Van Cise actually say that the underworld was after him?"

"Oh, he said it all right."

One corner of the older woman's mouth twisted into a cynical smile. "Given all the bull he dished out on the subject during the campaign, it almost sounds plausible. But you think it's really the Klan." The comment came out like a question.

Liz nodded. "I think they're using the Volz murder to embarrass the D.A."

"It wouldn't take a murder to do that. But go on."

Miss Loggin seemed to enjoy being disagreeable. "First, let me explain that I was the person who discovered Emma Volz. I have no idea how long she'd been dead. A girl I spoke to in the Bottoms said she'd seen three women drive away—lock, stock, and barrel—in a black car. It's possible they knew who the killer was. From the maggots, I think Emma Volz must have been killed at least twenty-four hours before I found her."

"I wouldn't count on it. Heat speeds up decay. Maggots can appear as soon as eight hours after death."

"That quickly?"

Miss Loggin nodded. "Was she shot? Knifed?"

"I don't know. There was a lot of blood," Liz said. It was time to get to the point. "Miss Loggin, would it be possible to speak to the client who requested you secure the women's release?"

"I don't think so." The tone, the look, shut that door, tight. Maybe later, after Miss Logan was convinced Liz could keep her mouth shut, she would part with the information. "However, if you want to know the women's names, Jake Steinberg, my clerk, is your man. He's in the next office. Just passed the bar. Green as grass, but smart."

Miss Loggin reached for the slim box of cigarillos and looked up at Liz. "Good hunting."

7

Liz paused at the open door. A man, whipcord thin, his curly, sandy-colored hair cut close to his head, was hunched over one of several desks jammed into the small office. Piles of legal tomes were stacked on every available surface, including the chairs. He was so engrossed in his reading that he didn't look up when Liz came in.

"Mr. Steinberg, may I have a minute?"

He started, glanced over his shoulder at her, and sprang to his feet, knocking over a chair and its contents. "Gosh. Sorry. Didn't hear you come in." He righted the chair and gathered up the papers. "Won't you sit down?"

She shook her head, smiled, and introduced herself as a reporter on a story. "Miss Loggin suggested you might be able to tell me about four clients you had released a few days ago. I understand they were picked up for prostitution at a speakeasy. The only name I have is Emma Volz, and she was murdered."

"I heard." He shook his head. "She seemed like a nice person."

"Were the women actually prostitutes?"

"Three of the ladies had priors, but Miss Volz's record was clean."

Liz was inexplicably pleased.

"The women were never actually booked. If you ask me, I'd say it was a roust. It was Monday. The nineteenth. Must have been a slow day. Anyway, I gave the lieutenant some legal double-talk, and he let them go. I've got their names here someplace." Jake Steinberg pawed through a stack of papers until he found a legal-size sheet of white paper. "Here. Mary Jessup, Rosie Steele, Burtie Bidlow. And Emma Volz. If you give this to Miss Hill, the secretary, she can type you up a copy."

"Thanks." Liz scanned the list quickly.

"Did I hear you say you'd been told they were picked up at a speakeasy?"

"On Twenty-second and Broadway," she said.

"That's not the information I had. According to the detectives and the ladies, it was a social club. One of those places with a band where people go to dance and drink near-beer. The official story is that the ladies were soliciting. They claim they were just having a good time. One—the victim—even said she'd bumped into a friend from her hometown."

"Did she say which town? Or the name of the friend?"

"Nope, and I didn't think to ask."

"What about the other women?"

"The only address I have is the one in the Bottoms they gave when the detectives brought them in." Jake Steinberg smiled apologetically. "I'm sorry. I'm afraid there's not much to go on, is there?"

❧❧❧

Armed with the list of women's names, Liz took the streetcar home and retrieved her car. Phil could stall the press with vague statements about "pursuing the case with all the forces available to him" for only so long. A fighting prosecutor—particularly one under threat of re-call—was expected to produce a credible suspect, witnesses, evidence. So far, if he was lucky and the detectives had made out an official report, all he had was the victim's name.

Her list helped: the other three women might be witnesses, or even suspects. But it might be days before the detectives even went through the motions of combing the Bottoms for suspects and evidence. Besides, Phil would be a fool to rely on the accuracy of any information they came up with. Before she called Tim Ryan again, she should poke around some more, try to find Ginger.

But just driving across the viaduct toward the Bottoms made Liz uneasy. She slowed at the house with the green door, noting the Denver Police Department warnings to keep out, but no beat cop stood guard. Nearby, three toddlers sat in the dirt, playing with a puppy. Liz fought back the flood of memories and tried to steady herself.

The sun was high in the sky, and she parked in the shade of a giant cottonwood, climbed out. As she swiped at the knife-sharp wrinkles the heat had pressed into the skirt of her pale yellow chambray dress, she surveyed both sides of the street. Where to find Ginger? Best to start at the corner and ask at each house.

More often than not, the door was slammed in her face. A few times, not surprisingly, Liz recognized the open expectation of a bribe. She'd about given up when she came to the next-to-last house on the third block.

An old, gray-haired woman with no teeth, wearing a tattered housedress, came to the door. Liz asked if she knew the whereabouts of a girl with red hair.

The woman squinted at her suspiciously. It occurred to Liz that she didn't speak English, or didn't speak it well. Liz repeated the question, touching her hair and pointing to the red trim on her dress.

"*Capelli rossi. Ah, si.*" The old woman's face broke into a broad smile. She pointed to the house next door. Liz nearly kissed the woman. A dozen questions flashed through Liz's mind as she raced across the weedy dirt yard. Did Ginger remember the number of the black car's license plate? Would she recognize the driver? But the red-haired girl turned out to be a toddler. Her mother, little more than a girl herself, said she had no other children. Liz forced a smile, thanked her, and slowly walked back to the Buick. Next stop: the D.A.'s office.

❦

Liz heard the men's voices drifting through the open door of the D.A.'s office and cringed. She knew without looking that Phil Van Cise had thrown caution to the winds and called a press conference. A quick glance from the safety of the reception area confirmed as much. The gang was all there: the city reporter and the crime-beat man from the *News*, a fellow from the *Denver Times*. An anemic-looking man from the *Denver Express* sat next to Harry Teaks.

Liz got out her sole contribution—the paper with the women's names—and scribbled an addendum that according to her police contact, the women had been picked up in a speakeasy, then handed the sheet to Phil's secretary, who took it to him.

Phil scowled as he read, and put the paper aside. Standing behind his desk, leaning casually against the window ledge, he appeared to be in complete control. He glanced Liz's way. The frown was gone, but there was no smile. No hint of what was coming or whether he would use the list. He folded his arms, cleared his throat.

"Gentlemen." He nodded in her direction. "Miss O'Brien."

Heads swiveled; annoyed gazes asked what the hell she was doing here.

Phil said, "I called you together to assure you that the Denver Police Department and my office are on top of the violent murder discovered in the Bottoms two days ago." With an appropriately grave expression, he named the two detectives in charge of the investigation.

A hand shot up. "Any suspects?"

"Not as yet," Phil said. "However, the police are tracking down possible witnesses."

"Like who?"

"I'll get to that in a minute."

"How 'bout time of death?" the city man from the *Times* asked.

"The preliminary investigation indicates estimated time of death to be the evening of Wednesday, June 20." The D.A.'s crisp, business-like tone was just right. "The autopsy report should be available by tomorrow at the latest."

Liz wondered if two days for an autopsy report was standard or if he was being stonewalled.

Phil stuck his hands in his trouser pockets, seemingly relaxed. "Investigators also know that the victim, Emma Volz, was picked up along with three companions the night before the murder at a social club on Twenty-second and Broadway."

Liz blinked. Hadn't he read what she'd written in the note? One look at the frown on Harry Teaks's face—the man who knew the location of every speakeasy in the city—confirmed her information. Phil must have his reasons.

The *News* reporter on the crime beat uncoiled his loose frame from the chair like a panther about to spring. "Mr. Van Cise, you did say social club, didn't you?" he asked in a slow drawl.

Phil flashed his between-us-men smile. "Boys, if it was a speakeasy, I would have known about it, raiding speakeasies being a specialty of mine." The anticipated chuckles rippled through the group. Liz had lost count of the newspaper photos showing Phil raiding speakeasies and wielding an ax on crates filled with illegal hooch. Like Roosevelt charging up San Juan Hill, the D.A. knew the political value of being the first into battle.

"And the charge against the women was?"

"Prostitution."

Nods, knowing smiles. Prostitution sold papers.

"However, let's hold off on that for a moment." He unfolded the paper. "I promised you names."

"Witnesses?"

"Companions of the victim. Witnesses . . . that remains to be seen." He read the women's names slowly to give the reporters time to get them down, then glanced up, surveying the group with a somber smile. "There you have it. The police chief and I are on top of it. I pledged myself to rid Denver of vice and crime. And, as you know, boys, I take promises seriously."

There was a general stirring among the seated men. Deadlines loomed.

"So unless there are any more questions . . ." He looked from man to man. The eyes that looked back were expressionless. Reporters by training and nature were a suspicious, cynical lot. And their editors were impatient.

Liz tried not to worry. Phil's charm had seen him through awkward spots before, but this was the first time the Klan had waited in the wings.

⟡

The minute the last reporter filed out the door, Phil sank into his leather chair and regarded Liz with accusing eyes. "Speakeasy?"

"That's what my contact told me, Phil."

"The commissioner swears it was a goddamn social club."

"Of course. That's what he was told. But all you had to do was look at Harry Teaks's face to know the place is a speakeasy."

"God. That miserable Teaks ought to crawl back into his hole. You wait. He'll make me out as a liar and a dupe, or worse." Phil's image was on the line, and he didn't like it. "Crooked cops. That's what this is about. The only way I miss a speakeasy is when some of Denver's finest get paid to look the other way."

For a few minutes the only sound was that of traffic beyond the open window.

"I'll tell you one thing: the detectives who say they picked up those women in a social club are going to have to look me in the eye on this." He leaned forward and yelled for his secretary to get Commissioner Barber on the phone.

While they waited, Liz, too antsy to sit, got up and walked over to the window, idly watching the stream of cars and trucks making their way along Colfax Avenue. Finally, the shrill ring of the telephone. And she turned to listen. Phil's gruff voice demanded the names of the officers who picked up the four women. A pause. Then the slam of the receiver. "Barber's going to call me back."

Liz went back to watching the traffic for another fifteen minutes before the phone rang again. Phil snatched the receiver from its cradle, glaring as he listened. When he finally hung up, his face registered near despair.

Elbows on his desk, he held his head in his hands. "It's a nightmare, that's what it is. The story is that detectives had been nosing around the neighborhood there on Twenty-second." He looked up. "One thing and another, they got suspicious of a place called the Good Times Club. So one day they went in. Found a half-dozen customers, in addition to the four women and the manager. No sign of a bar. Just tables and a little band—an accordion and a violin—playing oom-pah-pah stuff. The detectives told the manager they wanted to look around, which they did. No sign of liquor anywhere. They were about to leave when one of the detectives remembered booking a couple of the women for prostitution. They suspected all four of them were soliciting. So they brought them in."

"And you believe that?" Liz asked cynically.

"Hell, I'm just passing on what Barber told me." Phil let out a heavy sigh.

The inventive scenario pictured two detectives just trying to do their duty. They'd been after liquor and hadn't found any. But they hadn't left empty-handed. Soliciting was a misdemeanor, so they'd brought the women in. Liz had to admit that the story rang true enough to hold off further questions from the powers-that-be.

"These detectives. Do they have names?" she asked.

Phil glanced down at the pad on his desk. "Bentliff and Neihouse."

"Imagine that. The same detectives investigating the murder."

Phil gazed at her glumly. "A man's innocent until proven guilty. But I admit this is beginning to smell bad."

"You think the cops killed Emma Volz?"

"I doubt it, but anything is possible at this point."

"The motive being . . . ?"

"Who knows?"

"I could call my source in the department, ask what he knows about them."

"Liz, I appreciate your offer. But if your man doesn't hang up on you the minute you push for specifics, I'll be surprised."

"He came through before."

"That was then. This is different."

8

Frank taxied the DeHavilland over the bumpy strip of high mountain meadow that served as a runway. Coming in from Denver over ten-thousand-foot peaks, he'd had to compensate for the thin air and tricky winds. He raised his flaps, turned off the carb heat, and came to a stop in front of a makeshift hangar just big enough for a single plane. He yanked on the parking brake, pulled the mixture knob full out, flipped off the ignition and the master switches. He was pleased with how easily the landing had gone, grateful for the head wind that had checked his speed.

He thought of Liz again. Christ! When didn't he think of her—the feel of her, the scent of her? He felt himself harden. Yet even when they made love, when he was thrust deep inside her, her legs wrapped around him, she was his only for that moment. He'd figure a way to move the goddamned Rocky Mountains if that's what it would take to persuade her to marry him. But it wouldn't work. Not because she didn't love him, but because marriage meant giving up her independence. That's what her job at the *Post* was about. The pay was lousy. And she had to put up with those narrow-minded bastards. But she was free to go on acting like the reincarnation of her crusading grandfather. All fine and well, if it weren't for the Klan.

The Klan worried the hell out of him. His blood boiled at what they'd done to Maria. And he sensed that was only the beginning. Little Italy had been targeted, and he felt helpless to do anything about it. The lower his family's profile, the safer they'd be. But right now he had to concentrate on the weekend ahead and how to make his sometime boss and benefactor, Bud Humphreys, look good.

The heavyset man sitting in the front cockpit looked over his shoulder at Frank, grinned and gave him the thumbs-up. Frank shoved his goggles up onto his helmet, unbuckled, climbed out, and jumped to the ground. While Frank wedged the chocks in front of the wheels, Humphreys pried his large frame out of the confines of the cockpit and eased himself down.

He walked over to Frank and they shook hands.

"Whale of a flight, Cappy." From the first time they'd met, Bud Humphreys had been unable to get his tongue around "Capillupo" without stumbling. "You'll impress them all."

Frank grinned. "I hope so, sir." The success of ferrying Humphreys's rich cronies could determine the future of their dream—a passenger airline.

Bud Humphreys stretched expansively and glanced about. "God, but that was a beautiful flight. The air's so clear up there you can see a million miles. Makes you glad you're alive."

"You got that right, sir." Out of the corner of his eye, Frank saw a plume of dust announcing the approach of a car. "Looks like Harold must have seen us coming in."

Humphreys took off his helmet and unbuttoned his flying suit. "I told him to bring our gear. We can change in the hangar."

Frank sensed that the suggestion was an order. Appearances were important to Humphreys. He'd acquired an English valet during his trip to England last fall. Harold Jones was a good Joe who'd survived the war and taken a job at a resort hotel in the seaside town where he'd grown up. His dad had been "in service," as they called it over there, so Harold knew the ropes.

The Cadillac touring car roared up. With his usual dispatch, Harold pulled off his chauffeur's cap, smoothed his hair, stepped out, removed his employer's suitcase and Frank's rucksack, and carried them into the hangar. As Frank secured the DeHavilland and his boss changed clothes, Frank wondered how the hell he was going to find a dinner jacket and black tie for the smoker tonight. Ordinarily, wardrobe wasn't a major issue in his life. He was just one step up from Harold Jones. The minute he got into Estes Park, he'd scout around.

🦋

Frank always likened the Stanley Hotel to a queen on a hill overlooking a peasant village, in this case Estes Park, whose summer population made it a respectable-sized town with a number of streets, log cabins, summer homes, and stores. The hotel, opened before the war, was the brainchild of F. O. Stanley, inventor of the Stanley Steamer, and he'd spared no expense. A mirrored elevator, rooms furnished with antiques: it had the grandeur of some of the places Frank had seen along the Atlantic Coast. White clapboard, three stories tall, with dormer windows along the roof and a wide porch spanning the center section, the hotel boasted a bowling alley in the basement, as well as large outbuildings designed for musicales and theater productions. Behind it rose a magnificent trio of pine-covered mountains well over twelve thousand feet high.

Once Humphreys had registered and disappeared into the elevator, Frank stowed his rucksack behind the front desk and headed to town on foot. The main drag, Elkhorn Street, was jammed. Cars mingled with the bright red White Tour Company buses, packed with passengers headed up to timberline and over the newly completed Trail Ridge Road to Grand Lake. Frank elbowed his way through the crowds, amazed at the hordes of people thronging the streets. Surely this was more than the usual crush of summer visitors.

His best hope of finding a dinner jacket was in a men's store, but he soon learned that the only one in town didn't carry them. The owner suggested the Hupp Hotel gift shop. Frank was skeptical, but he had to give it a shot. Not surprisingly, the salesgirl thought he was drunk. Frank cussed himself. He'd intended to borrow a jacket from a friend in Denver, but with the mess about Maria getting fired, it had slipped his mind.

He was standing on the corner next to the High Drive drugstore, stumped, when Harold Jones came to mind. He was sure to have a dinner jacket. Maybe even a tux. Frank was a little taller, bigger in the shoulders, but it would do. He had to make the right impression. His future was riding on it.

9

L iz's blouse stuck to her back. The Buick was an oven. She circled the block three times before finding a parking place near the *Post*. The day was already going badly. Yet the moment she entered the newsroom and saw Mr. Ware, red-faced and with a ferocious frown, beckoning to her, she guessed the day's troubles had only begun.

Steeling herself, she walked toward him. "You want to see me?"

"I got a call from a Detective Bentliff at Northside. He wants to talk to you again."

"Did he say what he wanted?"

"Not a word. But I could take a guess," the editor said. He leaned across the desk. "O'Brien, I want you out of this. Today. Understand me?"

"Yes, sir." She didn't trust Bentliff and Neihouse, and was deeply uneasy about what they could want. Harry Teaks might have told them she'd been at the D.A.'s press conference, that she and Phil were friends.

☙❧

The nondescript two-story building that housed the Northside substation was in the middle of the block. If not for the barred windows and the sign over the entrance, it would have blended right in with the neighborhood stores. A police car was parked in the garage next door. There was a general commotion of police and other men, coming and going. With a certain trepidation, she went in and gave the desk sergeant her name. He nodded, as if she were expected, and directed a uniformed policeman to take her to the interrogation room upstairs.

Its bare walls were painted a dull ochre. The only furniture was a table and four wood chairs. A ribbon of yellow flypaper covered with dead flies dangled from a bare bulb that hung from the ceiling. The barred windows were wide open, but the place was stifling, and the two detectives she recognized from the day of the murder were coatless.

"Thanks for coming in, Miss O'Brien," said the towering, thickset man named Bentliff as he slowly rose.

Detective Neihouse stayed put.

Liz sat down and fixed each man with an even look.

"We hoped you could help us clear up a few questions about the Volz murder," Bentliff said.

"If I can." Liz arranged her purse in her lap with deliberate care, tried to appear calm.

They took out notebooks and pencils. She was conscious of the size of Detective Bentliff's hands as he flipped through several pages of notes.

"Let's see. You came upon the victim at approximately two-thirty on June 21." He glanced over at her.

"About that. Yes."

"You knew her?"

"Knew her? No."

"I see." The giant chewed thoughtfully on the inside of his mouth. "You didn't know her, but you were inside her house."

"I thought I explained that before. I was doing a story about kids and operetta tickets. I wanted to talk to someone in the neighborhood. I knocked on the door. No one answered. I went to the back door and smelled something horrible. I decided to go in. The door was unlocked."

"Walking in uninvited is usually considered breaking and entering," the smaller man said, running his hand over a pockmarked cheek.

"I thought something was very wrong inside. I thought perhaps I could help."

"And you found the body."

"Yes."

Detective Bentliff tilted his chair, balancing on its back legs. Liz was surprised they didn't break. "I'm curious what a nice lady like you was doin' in the Bottoms," he drawled.

"As I said—"

"You wanted to talk to someone in the neighborhood. Can you give me a name?"

Liz's heart skipped a beat. "I wasn't there to see anyone in particular. I was there for a story."

"I didn't know they sent lady reporters to the Bottoms," Ed Neihouse said.

"It depends on the story."

The thickset detective scrawled something in his notebook. "So the story you were after . . ."

"It was about kids getting free tickets for the *Denver Post* operetta. A human-interest piece, as I already told you."

"Human interest."

"Yes."

"Like 'Man Bites Dog.'" Joe Bentliff managed a half-smile.

She met his gaze, saw the stubbornness in his eyes. She might be here for quite a while. "Not exactly."

"I'm curious. Did you get the story?" asked the detective with the pit-marked face.

"No, I didn't."

"So the murder wasn't your story?"

She gave him a level look. "I already explained what my story was. As you know, Mr. Teaks is the person who covers the police beat for the *Post*," she said, trying not to show that they were beginning to wear her down.

"Harry."

"Yes." Liz felt as if she were treading water, going nowhere.

The heavyset man glanced at his partner. "You got a smoke on you, Ed?"

The smaller man reached into a pocket of his jacket, slung over the back of the chair, pulled out a rumpled package of cigarettes, and tossed it to Joe Bentliff.

"You don't mind if I smoke, do you, Miss O'Brien?" he asked.

She shook her head and checked her watch. "Detective, how much longer do you think this will take?"

"I don't blame you for wanting to wind this up. It's just that I still can't figure what you were doin' in the Bottoms that day." He winked. "Honest Injun. Between us."

"I told you. I was on a story."

He pulled a cigarette out of the package, stuck one end in his mouth, lit it, and blew the smoke toward the ceiling. "We're all grown-ups here. You ladies can vote. You smoke. Take a drink now and then." He leaned forward so the chair's four legs rested on the floor, and smiled a knowing smile. "These days, unless you know where to get it, good booze is hard to find. Know what I mean?"

"I don't believe I do."

One corner of his mouth curled into a hard smile. "You didn't come to the Bottoms for booze?"

"No."

"Okay." He examined his notes, squinting against the smoke. "And you didn't know the victim. You'd never seen her before."

"That's right."

"You're sure of that?" His tone had taken on a hard, insistent edge.

"I am." She forced herself to stay calm.

"Was there anybody who saw you that day?" the smaller man asked.

"I'm not sure I understand your question, detective."

"A witness who could say he saw you."

Something inside her tightened and warned her to use extra caution. "Detective Neihouse, am I a suspect?"

"Why should we think you're a suspect?"

"Because if I am, I wish to call my attorney."

"Look, Miss O'Brien, I'll level with you." The cigarette dangling from one corner of his mouth, the huge detective leaned across the table. "We got a case on our hands with a lot of blood, no clues but a knife, and some smeared fingerprints. We found you on the scene. The lieutenant's on our necks. We thought you could help. Know what I mean?"

Liz rose. "I wish I could, but I've told you all I know."

The two men slowly got to their feet.

"Your address is 825 Washington," Ed Neihouse said, reading from his notes.

Liz glanced at him. "Yes." Her uneasiness jumped a notch.

"The phone number is Capitol 4451."

She nodded. "May I go now?"

"You bet."

Downstairs again, Liz was walking out the front door when she almost bumped into a tall, thickset uniformed policeman. The man stepped aside and apologized. The instant she heard his bass voice, she knew it was Tim Ryan. She looked at him. He was so much older than she remembered. Not just the gray hair but the deep creases in his face, the jowls. Hesitation, as if unsure he recognized her, appeared in his blue eyes, and then that wonderful full, irresistible smile filled his broad face.

"Elizabeth O'Brien."

"The very same," she said, meeting his smile.

He shot a worried look toward the entrance of the station, took her arm protectively. "The Northside Precinct is no place for a lovely lass like yourself."

"The detectives on the Volz case asked me to come in."

His frown deepened. "And do you have a way to get home?"

"The Buick. You remember. Granddad's car." She placed a hand lightly on the sleeve of his uniform. "Mr. Ryan, I'm glad we had a chance to see one another so I could thank you in person. For everything."

He smiled, touched the visor of his cap. Anywhere else, Liz would have asked him about the detectives. Instead, she merely smiled, said good-bye, and watched him duck into the station. Without looking up, she sensed someone standing at the window on the second floor. But even if she were wrong, dozens of policemen might have seen her and Tim Ryan together. It would only be a matter of time before news filtered back to Bentliff and Neihouse.

🦋

Back at the paper, Liz told Mr. Ware about the interrogation, skipping the part about meeting Tim Ryan. The crusty editor scowled, fanned himself, listened. After she had finished, he mopped his glistening head and the back of his neck with a red kerchief and sighed heavily.

"O'Brien, I am the soul of patience."

"Yes, sir."

"So I will repeat myself." He fixed her with hard eyes. "Stay clear of the police," he said, pronouncing every word with care.

"They called me. Not the other way around."

"That means stick to your knitting," he growled as if he hadn't heard her. "Beginning with the operetta tonight."

"I haven't forgotten."

"Good." And he got up and walked over to Rewrite.

For a moment, Liz stood by his desk. She felt let down. And knew it was unreasonable. She had pushed her way into the murder story. He could have fired her. God knows, the last thing Mr. Ware needed was a woman reporter being trailed by the police. The heat was getting to her. There was nothing to do but go home, take a cool bath, change her clothes, and get over to Cheesman Park before the overture.

❧

It was after ten-thirty when she finally unlocked the back door. The temperature had dropped into the high sixties. Humming the Victor Herbert tunes, she switched on the kitchen light. The leading lady had routinely overpowered the tenor. But from the enthusiastic applause, the audience didn't care. Liz's lead was a natural: the fun of the evening—families stretched out on old blankets under the starry sky to listen at no charge, thanks to the generosity of the *Denver Post*. At the risk of overdoing it, the story might put Mr. Ware in a better mood.

Liz opened all the first-floor windows, then returned to the kitchen to pour herself a glass of milk. By now Frank was in Estes Park. The trip was an important opportunity for him to rub shoulders with the monied crowd and convince them to buy into Bud Humphreys's airline. If she'd gone, it would only have muddied the waters.

The best of any liquor a guest might want—single-malt Scotch, hundred-year-old French cognac, British gin, Kentucky bourbon—would flow like water, as if Prohibition didn't exist. The occasion, after all, was a private party. The liquor came from private stock, purchased before the ban went into effect. Or so Bud Humphreys would claim. Fortunately, he and the guests were big shots who could intimidate local law enforcement. As thin as the Treasury men were stretched in this part of the country, there was little chance one of them would be in Estes Park.

Knowing Frank, he'd nurse a bourbon along, laugh at the jokes, tell a few himself. Probably throw in a war story or two so he could work airplanes into the conversation. The older men he and Humphreys needed to finance the airline would eat it up—enough, she hoped, to invest in their dream.

Liz finished the milk, rinsed out the glass and put it in the sink, and went upstairs to her grandfather's study to write up her story. The words came easily. She wasn't the best writer in the world, but she'd had enough practice that a routine story was just that. She had her hand on the telephone, ready to call it in to Rewrite, when her thoughts turned to her chance meeting with Tim Ryan. She could picture the window above the stationhouse entrance. What she hadn't seen were Bentliff and Neihouse looking down.

Yet, before she could sleep, she felt compelled to talk to Mr. Ryan, despite the risks. He was still the key, the sole chink in what Phil claimed was an impenetrable blue wall. She picked up the receiver and asked the operator for the number.

At the eighth ring, Liz was about to hang up when the familiar deep voice said, "Hello." A voice thick with sleep. She'd gotten him out of bed.

"Mr. Ryan, it's Elizabeth O'Brien. I'm sorry if I woke you."

There was a slight pause. She could almost see him rubbing his hair, tousled from sleep, in an effort to wake up. "It was grand seein' ya today, Elizabeth."

"I wouldn't bother you again, and I realize I'm asking a great deal," she began, "but there's something I have to know about the police, and you're the only person I can trust." Liz told him about Phil's press conference, what Bentliff and Neihouse had told the commissioner, and the questions the detectives had asked her at the Northside station. "Mr. Ryan, is it possible they're on the take?"

For several seconds there was no answer. Then, "Ah, well." There was no mistaking the reluctance in his voice. Phil might be right after all. Or maybe Mr. Ryan thought the operator was listening. "It's hard sayin' sometimes. A man, if he's smart, doesn't go out and buy himself a fine new automobile. Nothin' like that."

"You mean he'd put the money in savings accounts. That kind of thing," she suggested.

"Now you have it."

"But that wouldn't show up unless the police chief were to hold a full investigation, which would take time. Time Mr. Van Cise doesn't have, with the Klan after him and a murder to solve." Liz paused, hoping Mr. Ryan would take the bait.

"I see the problem."

Liz heard his ragged breathing. She wondered if he'd had tuberculosis. Or maybe a heart problem. Seeing him earlier today had brought her up short, made her realize he was an old man. She cut the conversation short, and they hung up.

10

Back at the Stanley Hotel, Frank found Harold Jones shooting the bull with a couple of waiters in the kitchen and arranged to borrow his dinner jacket. Frank shaved, washed up in the men's-room sink, and dressed. Jones's jacket was tight in the shoulders, but it served its purpose.

The dinner was to be held in the small Georgian-revival manor house adjoining the hotel, which Humphreys had taken over for the evening. Frank mingled with the guests, nursing the bourbon a waiter handed him. It was just like the old days before Amendment 18 had passed. The talk was of the war and where he'd flown. At dinner—elk steaks, potatoes Suzette, baby peas, and chocolate Bavarian mousse—Frank was seated next to a man named Amos Middleton.

Of medium height, with graying hair and a tic in his left eye, Middleton had served his time in the backwaters of Colorado politics. By his own admission, he was ready to take the big step up. He was good-looking, one of those hail-fellow-well-met types whose jokes were directed toward spicks and kikes and dagos. He rubbed Frank wrong, but he had connections to money that Frank and his boss needed. And, if Middleton were elected governor, he'd have a say over legislation authorizing airline service. By dessert, Frank had talked him into taking a ride in the DeHavilland to Colorado Springs.

It was nearly nine-thirty, full dark, when chairs were pushed back and everyone adjourned to the porch for Cuban cigars and snifters of Courvoisier brandy. The chilly air might have a sobering effect. Frank walked to one end of the porch for a cigarette. Looking out as he lit up, he noticed a solid line of headlights moving toward the center of the meadow beyond. Too many cars for a family get-together. Whatever was going on explained the crush of traffic earlier in the day.

His dinner partner strode by with another man Frank couldn't put a name to. "Over there's where we're headed." Middleton pointed toward the stream of headlights. "Let's get a move on. I don't want to be late."

Staring at the headlights, Frank recalled Middleton's crude jokes. And the Klan came to mind.

☙☞

Frank walked fast, sticking to the side of the road, out of the way of the steady line of cars. He had changed into his boots, traded Harry's dinner jacket for the sweater he'd brought along. He wished he had a hat to hide under. If this was, as he suspected, a Klan gathering, his swarthy skin and black hair would not be welcome.

Just ahead were rows upon rows of tightly parked cars. Frank could barely make out the figures moving toward a large open space illuminated by a giant bonfire. The headlights of the arriving cars created a weird, phosphorescent glow, bleaching the faces of the people around him a ghostly white. Head down, Frank wove his way through the rows of cars, stopping short of the open space and the blazing fire. This close, he could see rising above it a wooden cross probably ten feet high. He felt the fear surge through him. He thought of Middleton and the other dinner guest out here in the dark somewhere. Until tonight, he'd supposed Klan members were only small fry, little men scrambling to get by. Every instinct told Frank to get out, leave, yet a sick curiosity forced him to stay.

Frank's eyes had adjusted to the dim light, and he surveyed the men and women standing near him. They, at least, fit his concept of the Klan: ordinary-looking, nondescript faces that would be lost in a crowd. Frank followed their gaze. What he saw made his blood run cold.

Illuminated by the bonfire were hundreds, maybe thousands, of figures in white robes. Hoods hid their faces. *Jesus.* Frank sucked in a quick, ragged breath, overwhelmed by the thought of the collective power of this invisible army. Twenty yards more, and he'd be in its midst.

Frank couldn't move. Fear verging on terror spread through him. He'd been through the war. He could take care of himself, but the evil around him was overpowering. He had the sense that if he so much as blinked, he would be discovered.

Just then a procession of a dozen robed and hooded men, each carrying a lighted torch, marched toward the bonfire and stopped in front of the cross. One man, shorter than the others, stepped forward and faced the assemblage.

"All kneel," he commanded.

For an instant, Frank panicked. If he didn't obey, he'd be singled out. He shot a glance at those around him. No one made a move. Frank breathed a silent sigh of relief.

"Our Father and our God, we acknowledge our dependence upon Thee and Thy loving kindness toward us; may our gratitude be full and constant and inspire us to walk in Thy ways. God save our Nation and help us to be a nation worthy of existence on the earth. Keep ablaze in each Klansman's heart the sacred fire of a devoted patriotism to our country and its government. We invoke Thy blessing upon our emperor, the imperial wizard, and the official family, in the administration of the affairs pertaining to the government of the invisible empire. Grant him wisdom and grace, and may each Klansman's heart and soul be inclined toward him in loving loyalty and unwavering devotion. We ask these things in the name of Him who taught us to serve and sacrifice for the right."

A chorus of amens echoed through the dark mountain air.

For a Catholic, attending the services of another faith was a sin, but this gathering had nothing to do with God. His name had been used to invoke the devil. The words of the prayer echoed in Frank's head.

A huge man, so tall the bottom of his robe stopped at his shins, stepped forward. In the faint firelight, Frank caught the glint of silver at the tips of the man's shoes. "Gentlemen, answer after me."

Frank's guts knotted with fear at what was coming. The questions began.

"Is the motive prompting your ambition to be a Klansman serious and unselfish?" the booming voice asked. "Are you a native-born white, gentile American citizen? Are you absolutely opposed to and free of any allegiance of any nature to any cause, government, people, sect, or ruler that is foreign to the United States of America? Do you believe in the tenets of the Christian religion? Do you esteem the United State of America and its institutions above any other government, civil, political, or ecclesiastical, in the whole world? Do you believe in clannishness and will you faithfully practice same towards Klansmen?"

The night rumbled with solemn "I do's," voices of men empowered with belonging. In the South it was the poor white trash. Who, then, were the devotees here in Colorado?

Frank's sense of danger mounted, and he huddled into his sweater, drew back from the edge of the light.

The small man stepped forward again and set his torch to the cross.

"Klansmen, mortal men cannot assume a more binding oath. Always remember that to keep this oath means to you honor, happiness, and life. To violate it means disgrace, dishonor, and death."

Frank wanted nothing more at that moment than to get out of there. As he made his way past the rows of parked cars, the voices behind him broke into song. Frank couldn't make out the words, but the tune was "America the Beautiful."

❧❦❧

Frank sat in the manager's office of the Stanley, waiting for the call to Liz to go through. The rally had been a show of force, no doubt about it. Frank downed a second shot of the bourbon he'd found in the manor house and drew the back of his hand across his mouth.

Finally, he heard an unsteady "Hello?" and the dread in Liz's voice. No one telephoned in the dead of night unless it was an emergency. But what he had seen in the meadow tonight certainly qualified.

"It's me. Frank."

"Are you okay?" she asked.

"Fine. I just thought you ought to know—" He paused, suddenly seized with the thought that the hotel operator might be listening in. "This thing is mushrooming out of control. You have to promise me to watch your step. I'll be back in Denver sometime the day after tomorrow if I can."

"Frank—"

The door suddenly opened and the desk clerk stuck his head in.

"We'll talk then," Frank said and hung up. The goddamn Klan had invaded his life, and Liz's. The thought of spending tomorrow ferrying the likes of Middleton to Colorado Springs was almost more than he could stomach.

Frank retrieved his rucksack from the desk clerk. He had a two-mile hike in the cool mountain air to the DeHavilland. Sleeping under the stars was just what he needed tonight, but he wished like hell that he'd brought his revolver.

11

Liz arose after a few hours of restless sleep and broken dreams about hordes of hooded men marching around her. She peered through the open window at the pale blue early morning sky and thought of Frank. Something had happened, something serious enough that he didn't feel free to tell her about over the telephone. She was certain it had to do with the Klan. He had said he'd be back the day after tomorrow. But knowing his uncertain schedule, it might be a week or more before she learned what had happened.

She put on her dressing gown and went outside. The morning was rich with the smell of damp earth and the sweet fragrance of Grammy's yellow climbing roses. This time of day, before the city woke up, was Liz's favorite, filled with promise. The grass beneath her bare feet was damp with dew, and the air still cool, though a glance at the yellow-white sun through the trees told Liz another hot day was in the offing. She wished she could hold the world, and the Klan and the murder, at bay.

It was Saturday. Mr. Ware seldom came in on Saturday and never on Sunday. He hadn't assigned her anything until the play at Elitch's. But Harry might be around and bragging about what he'd learned from the police. After a bit of breakfast—orange juice and coffee, she'd go in.

It was just before nine by the time Liz was dressed and in the car. A few eager shoppers stood in front of Joslin's department store, waiting for it to open. Otherwise the streets were quiet. Inside the *Post*, the first-floor offices were closed. Upstairs, the newsroom looked like a tomb. A few reporters, one rewrite man. No sign of Harry Teaks. Or Charlie Collier. The sports-page editor sat behind his desk, feet up, reading the final edition. Liz turned around and went home.

Trading her dress and silk stockings for a blouse and a pair of old slacks, she went to the basement to attack the pile of laundry. The washing machine had always been her nemesis. Half the time, the sheets got tangled in the wringer. To be on the safe side, she washed her underwear and blouses by hand. Wringing them out as best she could, she put them in a laundry basket and lugged it upstairs to hang out on the line in the backyard.

She toyed with the idea of going for a swim at Washington Park, but decided the lake would be too crowded with kids. That night she took the streetcar downtown to the Denham, where she saw *Grandma's Boy* with Harold Lloyd again and was home by nine.

The next morning, she was awakened by church bells. Since Granddad's death, she'd seldom been to mass. She stretched and vowed to change her ways, then fell back to sleep. It was after ten when she finally stirred again. She took a lazy bath, dressed in yesterday's slacks and a fresh blouse, went downstairs, and made a pot of coffee. Out of oranges, she settled for canned tomato juice and a piece of toast. The rest of the day crept by. She brewed a pitcher of tea to ice, and searched the paper for news of the murder, but found none. Later she miraculously ironed a blouse without scorching it and scrambled a couple of eggs for her supper. She hadn't had this much time off for weeks, but the quiet only added to her frustration. Nothing could be accomplished at home.

Monday dawned hot again. Liz had already decided she was going to dress light. To hell with a girdle. Her garter belt would hold up her stockings just fine. She couldn't find a skirt to go with the blouse she had ironed yesterday, so she rummaged in the closet for a clean dress with short sleeves and a V-neck. She thought longingly of the days before Granddad died, when the laundress had come to the house twice a week. Now Liz would settle for being able to send the sheets and towels to Best Ever Laundry. In a perfect world, she'd send the rest—right down to her panties and slips—to Madame Devano's Cleaners.

Liz was at work at nine on the dot. A check at the Classifieds desk showed that no one had answered her ad. A pile of first editions stared up at her from the foot of the stairs.

"White Slavery Suspected in Woman's Murder" ran the headline, with Harry's byline beneath. Emma Volz a victim of white slavery? Where did he get this stuff? Women kidnapped into white slavery were kept in brothels; they weren't living in the Bottoms. Liz read on.

The entire thrust of the story was to excite, not illuminate. She could almost see the thin-lipped wives of Klan members, shaking their heads in horror even as they eagerly read every word. The article only got worse: Phil denying the existence of a speakeasy where four suspected prostitutes had been picked up. Implied was a district attorney who was losing his grip. Every newsboy had probably sold out his papers. The Klan ought to give Harry an award.

Entering the newsroom, she guessed the temperature must already be in the eighties. The room was uncharacteristically quiet. There was no sign of Harry Teaks. Mr. Ware was going over copy. A couple of rewrite men were on the telephone. A scattering of reporters pecked at their typewriters.

She was settling down at her desk when Mr. Ware pushed out of his chair. She watched him approach. From his fierce expression, she could just about read his mind. But she looked up at him with a bright smile of pure innocence.

"Miss O'Brien, I understand you were at the D.A.'s press conference."

Liz let go of the smile. Her friend Harry could always be counted on to keep the newsroom informed. "I was there to give the district attorney a message." She stood up so she could look the city editor in the eye. "The cops involved with the speakeasy or social club—it's not clear which at the moment—are the same ones investigating the Volz murder."

The city editor perched on a nearby desk. "So?"

As long as Mr. Ware would stay and listen, she wanted to talk. "My guess is that unless the D.A. and the police commissioner get a handle on it right now, the Klan will have Phil recalled without a bit of trouble."

Mr. Ware folded his arms across his chest.

"The *Post* has to take a stand, Mr. Ware, and soon, or it's going to be too late."

Liz heard someone clear his throat. She saw Mr. Ware stiffen. The publisher, Mr. Bonfils, was standing in the threshold of his office. She wondered how long he'd been there and how much he'd heard.

Fred Bonfils was the model of a wealthy, successful man: dark hair graying at the temples, slim, impeccably dressed in a beige Palm Beach suit and crisp white shirt that showed off his tan, undoubtedly acquired on the golf course of the Denver Country Club. He and his partner, Harry Tammen, had been con men who'd once worked the carnivals before buying the failing *Post* twenty years ago.

Every time Liz looked into Mr. Bonfils's steel-blue eyes, she was certain morality played no role in his life. There were the usual rumors that he admired pretty young women, and this might be true or she might never have been hired in the first place.

"Ed. Miss O'Brien. If I may have a few minutes." Smiling gravely, the publisher stepped back into his office.

"Be right with you, Mr. Bonfils." Mr. Ware straightened his tie and smoothed the fringe of white hair on his head. Liz followed him into the office, almost ashamed of the city editor's obsequiousness. Ware and Bonfils had had their differences over the years. She'd heard once that about two years ago another local paper had offered the city editor a similar position at double the salary, only to pull out at the last minute and give the job to a younger man. Bonfils had heard about it. Instead of firing Mr. Ware, the publisher had made a big show of generosity and kept him on, though—if rumors were to be believed—at a cut in salary.

Liz glanced around the room as she took the chair Bonfils held for her. The giant polished mahogany desk, the overstuffed dark brown leather chairs, the cream-colored walls, did not reflect the man who stood watching her. She recalled the stories of the way things had been before the *Post* moved uptown to Champa Street. Then the walls of the publishers' office had been blood red. Bonfils had kept a loaded shotgun in the corner behind his desk in case unhappy targets of the *Post's* outrageous journalism had ideas of getting even. Fifteen years ago Tammen and Bonfils hadn't smoothed off the rough edges. If their office had looked like a two-reel western movie, they hadn't noticed or cared. But no more. Even the array of photographs of Bonfils, posed with the nation's greats and near-greats—including President Harding—fit the new respectable image.

The publisher walked around his desk. "Have a seat, Ed," he said as he sank into his high-backed leather chair. Leaning forward, he rested his elbows on the desk and laced his manicured fingers together. "From now on, I want to see any copy—I repeat, any copy—on the Ku Klux Klan."

Mr. Ware swallowed hard, nodded. "Yes, sir." He was sweating profusely.

Bonfils's blue eyes were ice-cold above his benign smile. He turned his gaze toward Liz. "I'm pleased to say I get excellent reports on your theater reviews, and Mrs. Means has commented favorably about your story on the garden dedication."

"Thank you." Liz forced a smile.

The publisher's expression became reflective. "You see, my dear, we are a paper that serves the people. Oh, we have our crusades, of course. Wouldn't have it otherwise. A great newspaper is expected to lead when the occasion warrants. But basically," he looked from Liz to Ed and back to Liz, "as I said, we are a paper that serves the people."

She met his gaze, biting her tongue to keep herself from telling him to take a flying leap. For a moment, the steady ticking of the elegant gold-and-walnut-framed clock on Bonfils's desk was the only sound in the room.

The publisher shifted his gaze to Mr. Ware. "But as you know so well, Ed, we are first and foremost a profit-making institution, not a bunch of do-gooders out to save reputations."

The city editor didn't reply. The reference to the district attorney was plain.

Liz stared bullets at Bonfils and dug her fingernails into her palms. He was a fraud. Everyone in town knew he held hands under the table with every big-time crook in the city while he played nice with polite society. Money was all he cared about. Keep the advertisers happy. No wonder he hadn't come out for Phil Van Cise during the election campaign.

"You understand, I'm sure." Bonfils got to his feet, enabling him to look down at his troops. "I appreciate you both coming in for this little chat, but you must excuse me. I have a meeting." He lifted the straw skimmer—probably bought at Brooks Brothers on his last trip to New York—from the hat rack in the corner. Holding it loosely at his side, he shot a look at Mr. Ware, who had sprung to his feet and was standing as rigidly as an aging man with a potbelly could stand. "If there is any question as to my meaning on the Klan, Ed, I expect you to check with me."

"Sure thing, Mr. Bonfils."

With helpless rage, Liz watched Bonfils stride through the newsroom, clapping a fortunate underling on the back as he passed. Mr. Ware made no move to leave. She could feel his humiliation, his agony. The *Post* didn't deserve a city editor with his standards and honesty. Liz felt like picking up the fancy clock off Bonfils's desk and hurling it at the wall of photographs in hopes a shard of glass would pierce Warren Harding's smiling face.

She studied Mr. Ware. His jaws were clenched as he watched Bonfils depart. Gone was the humble gaze. In its place was such a look of disdain that it almost took her breath away. "Miss O'Brien."

"Yes, sir." Something was up.

"I was just thinking. After the play at Elitch Gardens tonight, there's not much coming up for 'Neighbors' in the next couple of weeks, is there?"

"Not if you say so, sir."

"Good."

What was he telling her? That there wasn't enough work to keep her on? Was she supposed to make herself scarce until Bonfils cooled down? Or did he have some new assignment for her? Before she could ask, he left the room.

12

L iz left the building, her mind still churning. A younger, more quick-tempered city editor might have punched Bonfils in the snoot and quit on the spot. But a man nearing retirement didn't have that luxury. He'd have to save his self-respect some other way. She didn't know what Mr. Ware had in mind, but she was certain it had to do with the Klan, the very story Bonfils had told them to stay away from.

Ed Ware was an astute old guy. His vagueness might mean he was giving her the go-ahead to keep digging. Chances were good that he suspected Harry Teaks was a Klan member. And the city editor knew of her ties with the D.A. and suspected she'd keep in touch with him.

Twenty minutes later she tapped on the open door of Phil's office and walked in. The D.A. was sitting in front of an electric fan, reading an official document.

He looked up. "I finally got the autopsy report. A messenger brought it over a few minutes ago."

"And?"

"The short version: Emma Volz, approximately nineteen years of age, died from a gunshot wound to the chest. The bullet, a .45-caliber, passed through the right chest and cut the pulmonary artery, causing massive internal hemorrhage. The manner of death was homicide."

Liz shivered. Not even Phil's impersonal tone could erase the mental picture of Emma Volz's bloated body sprawled across the bed. "Any suspects yet?"

"Not a one. If she and her friends were hooking, it might have been their pimp."

"I thought of that. But apparently Emma Volz had no priors. The white dress she had on looked like a uniform." And she told Phil about checking at the hospitals. "It's possible she was a maid or a waitress."

"Mmm," Phil responded noncommittally and flipped to the next page. "Listen. 'Judging by the degree of rigor mortis, the state of decomposition, the greenish-brown pigmentation of the skin, the egg hatch and presence of maggots, exacerbated by the temperature, time of death was between ten P.M. Tuesday, June 20, and twelve A.M. Wednesday, June 21. No burns or gunpowder residue or stippling were present." He looked up. "That means the murderer was standing at least sixteen inches from her when the shot was fired."

Phil shook his head. "The exit wound created by a .45 is good-sized and makes a mess. But she hemorrhaged internally. Some of the blood probably was the attacker's. Skin and flesh were found under her fingernails."

"The cops said they'd found a knife. Maybe she and the killer fought, and she stabbed him before he shot her."

"Maybe." Phil frowned, then turned the page and continued reading. "Well now, here's something of interest." He glanced over at Liz. "It seems the victim had recently been pregnant."

"Ginger—the girl I talked to—never mentioned anything about Emma having a baby."

"She could have miscarried." Phil put down the report. "I know you think the murder had nothing to do with prostitution, but I can't rule that out. If the women worked out of the house, it might not have been their pimp but the beat cop who came around to collect protection money. The victim was the only one home. She couldn't cough up any money, he drew a revolver, and—bam!"

"Bentliff and Neihouse are the detectives on the case, Phil. Do you really think they're going to finger a cop?"

Phil leaned back in his chair and eyed her wearily. "I can ask the commissioner to put someone else on the case. But I have to admit: at the moment, I have nothing that amounts to a damn thing."

🐋

Liz sat in the sixth row center of the Elitch Gardens summer theater and forced herself to concentrate on the play, a comedy titled *Boomerang*. The house was packed. As always, the cast was good, the leads from Broadway. But her mind kept drifting to the autopsy report.

She couldn't stop thinking about Emma's pregnancy. A single young woman strapped for money had a hard enough time, but to go through a pregnancy or miscarriage alone would be horrible.

During intermission, Liz stood in the foyer, out of the way of the playgoers gawking at the photographs of famous stars covering the walls, and scribbled down a few notes on the first two acts. The ingenue had flubbed her lines, but she was pretty enough that she would be forgiven. A bell rang, summoning the audience back to their seats. The curtains parted. The third act began.

Liz stared up at the drawing-room set on the stage, but saw instead the blood-smeared bedroom of the little house in the Bottoms. She doubted Bentliff and Neihouse had done any more than a cursory investigation. She stifled a sigh and refocused on the play.

Finally, the curtain came down. Liz was out of her seat and out of the theater before the first curtain call. Outside, the cool air was fragrant with honeysuckle and roses as she passed the nearly deserted penny arcade and found her car in the parking lot. She was home in thirty minutes, wrote her review and phoned it in by eleven-thirty. She was nearly drunk with exhaustion. She hadn't slept well for days. Emma Volz was consuming her life.

❧⳼❧

Later she remembered dreaming that she'd been washing blood out of a dress. But the more she scrubbed, the darker the spot became. She was beginning to cry from frustration when a sharp noise wakened her. She stirred, pulled the sheet over her shoulders. The noise continued. It took her several minutes before she realized it was the doorbell. She opened her eyes. It was still dark.

She felt a flicker of alarm as she sat up, tossed off the bedclothes. Working her arms into the sleeves of her dressing gown and knotting the sash around her waist, she padded downstairs, wondering who could be at the door. Even Western Union never rang the bell at this hour. She switched on the entry hall lights, opened the front door, and saw Phil Van Cise. His tie was askew. His suit was uncharacteristically rumpled. His fine-featured face looked stricken.

"Can I come in?"

The fear shifted to dread. "Sure. Of course." She opened the door wider. "We can go in the library. I'll fix coffee."

He stepped through the entryway. "I wanted to tell you the news myself."

"It sounds serious." Her temples began to throb as she switched on a lamp by the library door and walked over to the couch, indicating that Phil should take a seat.

"Liz, there's no good way to tell you. Patrolman Tim Ryan was found in his garage, dead from a bullet wound. The commissioner called me. I remembered that Ryan was the man you asked to help us."

She shook her head firmly. "There's some mistake."

"Liz, please. It did happen. Probably around midnight. It seems Mrs. Ryan had been expecting her husband home for several hours. She thought she heard his car backfire. She waited for a few minutes, but when he didn't come in, she went out to see what was holding him up. That's when she found him."

"Those bastards!"

"Liz, listen. It was a suicide. His wife found the note in the garage."

"I don't give a damn what was in the garage. Bentliff and Neihouse killed him. And if you can't see that, you don't deserve to be district attorney. Not now, not ever."

He looked at her.

"Tim Ryan was a Catholic, for God's sake. Suicide is a mortal sin. You commit suicide and you can't be buried in consecrated ground. You go to hell," Liz said.

Phil reached out and placed his hands over hers. "The chief is looking into all the possibilities."

She sat very straight, forcing back tears. "They killed him because he was an Irish Catholic who knew something that would prove they were on the take, maybe prove that they'd killed Emma Volz." Her shaky voice faltered. "Tim Ryan was the soundest man in the world—one of the few honest cops this city had, Phil." At that, the tears spilled from her eyes and coursed down her cheeks unchecked.

He gazed at her, his eyes sympathetic.

"And he's dead!" Her voice was nearly a scream.

Phil put an arm around her shoulders and drew her close. Her pain was beyond bearing. In another moment she feared her heart would explode.

"Liz, let me call someone. A priest. A neighbor." He put some-thing in her hand, a handkerchief. "I'll ask the chief to have an officer keep an eye on you."

She jammed the handkerchief against her mouth, shook her head. She desperately wanted him to leave. "Please. Go. I'm all right."

Phil studied her uncertainly before slowly rising to his feet. "If you need me . . ."

A moment later she heard the front door close.

Liz stared out at nothing. She felt strangely detached, disembod-ied, as if she were dreaming again. A dog barked somewhere in the distance. And then the desolation returned, hitting her straight on. Hugging herself so tightly she winced as her fingernails dug into her arms, she saw Tim Ryan's broad, smiling face, his clear blue eyes.

She had killed a kind, loving man who had worshipped her grand-father—killed him as surely as if she'd put the pistol to his chest and pulled the trigger.

Guilt pressed down on her so hard that she could barely breathe. She should have known better than to seek his help. Phil had warned her. Greta had warned her. Mrs. Ryan had known the danger. Tim Ryan had risked everything, risked his life, because she'd asked him to.

Leaning over her knees, her head in her hands, she began to sob.

❦

Liz had had to look at the calendar to know it was Wednesday. Ten o'clock, another hot morning. The sound of the tolling bell grew louder as Liz steered the Buick onto Thirty-fourth Street. Though dressed appropriately in a black silk dress, black straw hat, black shoes and gloves, she felt conspicuous, an interloper. She decided to park down the block from the church to avoid the crowd. Though small and unpretentious, St. Patrick's was a landmark in this part of north Den-ver. Its parishioners were mostly Irish: the men worked the railroad or were policemen like Tim Ryan. The Ryans had lived in the neighbor-hood for thirty years.

The day after Mr. Ryan's murder, Liz had screwed up her courage and paid a condolence call to Mrs. Ryan. Her son, Thomas, had come to the door. A pale, thin man resembling his mother, he had greeted her politely and asked her in. His mother was resting. Four or five men and women sitting stiffly in the front room looked up at her. She nodded hello, but didn't join them. Unable to meet his eyes, she heard Thomas say the mass for the dead would be held the following day, Wednesday. And Liz had felt instant relief at the news. The family must have convinced the Church that there was no conclusive evidence of suicide, or a mass would not have been said.

Walking down Pecos Street toward the church, Liz saw a group of six or eight policemen in dress blues standing by the entrance. Probably Baptists or Methodists, they looked uncomfortable. Inside, the church was hot. Mrs. Ryan, her son and daughter-in-law, and their five children sat along the front pew. Liz sat in the back. The church was filled. Sweat rolled down the priest's face as he led the solemn procession down the aisle toward the altar, the black-draped casket carried by six grim-faced men—none of them in blue.

Liz sank to her knees, clasped her hands in prayer. *In nomine Patris, et Filii, et Spiritus Sancti. Amen.* The priest joined his hands and began the antiphon. The mass proceeded. *Confitebor tibi in cithara, Deus, Deus meus: quare tristis es anima mea, et quare conturbas meus?* Why art thou so heavy, O my soul: why art thou so disquieted within me? Liz ignored the tears slipping down her cheeks.

She whispered the responses. If she'd said them aloud, she would have started sobbing again. She closed her eyes. Tim Ryan—husband and father, proud to be a member of the Denver police force, with all its faults, proud to be a loyal friend of the senator's—had risked his life every day to protect others. He might have spent his waning years enjoying his grandchildren. Instead, she had asked him to snitch on his fellow cops.

At the edge of her consciousness she was aware of the dismal chant *Dies irae, dies illa,* that day of wrath, that dreadful day. Finally, the benediction. The casket was carried out, followed by the family and the priest. It was over but for the burial, which she wouldn't attend. Liz wasn't sure her legs would carry her back to her car. She didn't notice until she was halfway home that the same Model A Ford that had pulled out behind her near the church was still tailing her: Phil's man, looking after her. She should have been comforted, but she wasn't.

Back home, she changed out of her black dress, donned a pair of slacks and a short-sleeved blouse. She had to do something, anything, to get her mind off Mr. Ryan's death. She dragged the lawn mower out of the garage and attacked the four-inch growth of grass. Once, when she stopped to wipe the sweat from her face and neck, she heard the telephone ring. Was Frank back in town? Maybe it was Mr. Ware calling with an assignment, or Phil checking up on her. She didn't care.

Around three o'clock she returned the lawn mower to the garage and surveyed her work with a certain satisfaction. The front and back lawns looked neat and trim. She went inside and brewed a pitcher of iced tea. While it cooled, she took a bath, tossing her sweaty clothes down the laundry chute.

Dressed in a loose-fitting, aging caftan Granddad had brought back from Egypt as a present for Grammy, Liz walked barefoot downstairs, thirsty for tea. A pile of mail lay where it had fallen when the postman stuffed it through the mail drop. She picked up the assortment of envelopes. The usual bills. She was about to toss the entire mess on the table when she noticed the postcard: a photograph of a bronc rider at Cheyenne's Frontier Days Wild West Show.

Liz turned it over, instantly recognizing Greta's labored hand. "Dear Liz. Heard of a Volz who is a cowboy up here. The Grover rodeo is set for the Sunday before the 4th. Yours, Greta." Liz reread the card twice, then pressed it against her chest, filled with wonder at a friend like Greta and the potential, remote as it was, contained in an insignificant picture postcard.

13

The next morning, after her first sleep in days, Liz strode through the *Post's* glass entrance doors, which had been propped open to let in the breeze. She approached the pile of first editions stacked at the foot of the stairs, knowing she'd find a story with Harry Teaks's byline on Mr. Ryan's murder. She steeled herself, leaned down, and picked up a copy. Sure enough, there it was.

"Suicide Hinted in Cop's Death." Just as she'd feared, Harry's story described an aging cop, dead by his own hand, found sprawled in the garage behind his modest home by his equally aging wife. A note and revolver, the same make issued to patrolmen, had been discovered by Tim Ryan's side. The family had refused to comment: good for them. The last paragraph was a quote from the commissioner, saying he would have further remarks after he received an autopsy report and an analysis of the handwriting. No comment from the D.A.

Taken altogether, the mean-spirited piece made Tim Ryan out to be weak man who lacked the courage to face life. Surely the coroner's report would prove otherwise. Liz tossed the newspaper back on the pile and went upstairs.

She was halfway to her desk when she saw the city editor motion to her. This morning his scowl was softened by a paternal look of genuine concern. Only then did it occur to her that he must have learned about her relationship with Tim Ryan.

"I'm sorry. I should have phoned in to explain. I took time off for the funeral."

He continued to frown. He looked tired, hot.

"Harry's wrong. Mr. Ryan's death wasn't a suicide," she said. "It has to do with Emma Volz's death, and the Klan, though I'm not sure how."

"Sinclair Lewis is in town. He's staying at the Cosmo."

The sudden shift in the conversation made her wonder if he'd been listening. "Sinclair Lewis, the writer?" She had to admit she was impressed. Lewis had caused a national stir when his scathing novel *Main Street* was published a year ago. An interview filled with the author's disparaging opinion of small-town America might annoy a few Klansmen. Maybe that was Mr. Ware's intention.

"Nothing against Sinclair Lewis, Mr. Ware, but a friend just wrote me that Emma Volz might have come from around Grover."

"A good distance from Denver." He mopped the beads of sweat on his forehead and rummaged in the wire out-basket for his fan. Finally, giving up the search, he waved her toward the chair by his desk.

"My friend said they put on a good little rodeo up there, just before the Fourth. I realize a rodeo story wouldn't work for "Neighbors." But it might be a good mainstream-America piece." She was making it up as she went, desperate for the chance to establish a connection between Emma and her murderer. "I heard once that the world's first rodeo was held right here in Colorado, in Deer Trail, during the cattle-drive days. In fact, today women are in on the act, even competing in the bronc riding and relay races."

The city editor shook his head. "In Cheyenne, maybe. But sure not at any of those small-town rodeos."

"I suppose not." Liz sensed he was beginning to see the story. Whatever direction it took, she would agree to. "So what about a story from the angle of the cowboys' mothers and sweethearts?"

"I see it more as a humor piece."

"Sounds good to me." Liz had never done humor, but now was a good time to give it a whirl.

"I'll cover train fare to and from Sterling and over to Grover, plus room and board up to three dollars a day. That's it. I want you back here in a week."

"What about Sinclair Lewis?"

"He'll keep." Mr. Ware shot a hard look toward the publishers' office. "This paper needs a good shot in the arm to boost circulation in the boonies. This could be it."

Liz rose to go. Subterfuge, artful lying—whatever you wanted to call it—had transformed Greta's suggestion into a feature story. But it was possible that she and the city editor had just entered into a conspiracy that could prove to be outright dangerous.

14

The train to Grover had been out of the question from the start. Liz needed a car to get around. But the roads in the northern part of the state would probably be little more than wagon ruts. Just to be safe, she stopped by McFarland's Auto and asked Matt McFarland to check the water, the oil, the fan belt, and the tire pressure. A tire inspection revealed worn tread, and after some debate she bought two new ones, reluctantly writing out a check for twenty-four dollars. It was already clear that the three-dollar-a-day allowance Mr. Ware had guaranteed wouldn't begin to cover expenses.

Liz drove home, pulled out her suitcase, and started to pack. She'd be leaving first thing in the morning. Glancing at her watch, she was surprised to see it was quarter to five: Phil's office would be closed in a few minutes. She hurried to the telephone, hoping she could catch him. If she were lucky, the results of Mr. Ryan's autopsy would be in. The secretary put her right through.

Phil said, "Whoever killed Ryan knew what he was doing. The shot that killed him was to the front of the chest, near-contact. But that's also characteristic of suicides."

Liz cut in. "I told you, suicide is out."

"If you'd let me finish, I could tell you that the report also says there were two shots and that the angle of entry is inconsistent with a suicide."

"Of course it was."

"But there's a problem. Ryan's revolver was at his side. In spite of the angle of the shot, his fingerprints were the only ones on the stock. From the smell, it had recently been fired."

"It was his revolver, Phil. He carried it every day. The murderer wore gloves, grabbed the revolver from him—or stole it earlier—and shot him with it. Have you asked Bentliff and Neihouse where they were at the time?"

"Liz, listen to me. I have to have probable cause to bring charges."

"What about other fingerprints?"

"Some were found in the garage. Mr. Ryan's, mostly. His wife's. A few belonged to their son. Nothing else," Phil said.

"Any sign of a struggle?"

"Not so much as the lawn mower out of place."

"I know that garage. It's barely big enough for their Model T," she said. "He must have been murdered in the alley. It's not paved. Maybe you could pick up tire tracks."

"I already asked the chief to have his men check with neighbors who might have seen something."

"Bentliff and Neihouse killed him. Wait and see."

"Liz, I'm doing my best. We'll find the killer. Trust me."

In her heart, Liz doubted the truth would ever come out, though she wouldn't give up hope. Whoever shot Mr. Ryan was protected by that perverse professional loyalty that had been responsible for his death in the first place.

Liz hung up. Blessedly cool air filtered through the open windows. From the growing darkness came the sound of children's squeals and laughter. She remembered summer evenings from childhood, playing hide-and-seek with the neighborhood kids while her granddad and Mr. Ryan sat on the porch, sipping bourbon.

It had been days since she'd watered the yard, and she went outside to set the hoses. Just as she reached for the tap set into the brick wall, she heard twigs snap behind her. Her heart jumped. She whirled to see a tall, slender young man, hatless and in shirtsleeves, standing at the opening of the hedge.

"Miss O'Brien?"

She stared at him. He looked vaguely familiar.

"Jake Steinberg. We met when you came to see Miss Loggin."

Liz's heartbeat steadied. "You scared me half to death."

"Gee, I'm sorry." He gave her a sheepish smile that softened his angular face. "I came about the ad. For the room. It didn't mention your name."

Liz grinned. Fear was replaced with relief that someone she knew had answered the ad. She'd be able to buy coal this winter. "The rent's thirty dollars. With kitchen privileges."

"Fine by me." He dug into his pants pocket and drew out a sheet of carefully folded paper, handing it to her. "In case you need references," he said. "I'm pretty handy with fixing things, too."

Liz couldn't believe her good luck. "How about cutting grass? Not every week. Just when you have time."

He frowned, earnest. "With the hot weather, I'd say once a week at most."

"The room's on the third floor, and you'd have your own bathroom. I'd take a little off the rent whenever you had time to cut the—" She stopped. The neighbors might look askance at her renting a room to a man. But if he lived in the chauffeur's quarters, surely no one would object.

"Actually, the apartment over the garage might suit you better—it's two rooms, a bathroom of its own. It'd be the same rent."

"Sounds great." He grinned.

"It's just that I live in the house by myself. The neighbors can be kind of—"

"No, listen. I understand, Miss O'Brien. I should've thought of it myself. The garage apartment'll be swell. More space than I need. I'll take it."

They shook hands. The deal was done in less than five minutes.

As they stood on the driveway in the deepening dark, Liz explained she'd be leaving town and wouldn't be back for a week or more. If he was in a hurry to move in, he'd have to do it tonight. Jake said he'd be back in an hour. When she asked for the rent in advance, he handed her the cash—just like that. Her financial woes, at least, had been solved.

⚘

The sky was clear blue when Liz drove north out of Denver. It would be eighty-some miles before she'd turn east, another twenty-five to Grover, the town closest to Greta's ranch. Twice as far as she'd driven alone beyond the Denver city limits, and much of it on poor roads. She'd better not be on a wild goose chase.

The morning warmed as she drove. Off to the west, the mountains were soft purple, the tops still capped with white where the snow hadn't melted. By the time Liz reached Greeley—the halfway mark—it was noon. She stopped at the Pioneer Café across from the courthouse, had a ham and cheese sandwich, handed the waitress fifty cents, and went on. Gradually, dried grassland replaced the tilled fields and irrigation ditches. Every now and then, she passed a tiny town, the trees bunched around the houses as if needing protection instead of providing it.

If the map was right, the turnoff to Grover wasn't far, just up the road. But ten miles later, with still no sign of it, she pulled in at the only gas station she'd seen for miles. The sign above the door said "Rockport Post Office."

Inside, a heavyset woman with thin white hair pulled back in a knot was sticking mail into cubbyholes along the wall. Liz asked for directions.

"Next right, up the hill," the woman replied, adding, "You'd be smart to fill up."

Liz looked out the window at the vacant landscape. She was probably right.

She followed the woman outside. A red Coca-Cola cooler sat by the door. Liz pulled a bottle out and stuck the neck into the opener, jimmying off the metal cap. When the woman had finished filling the Buick's tank, Liz handed her a five-dollar bill. Ten gallons of gas at twenty-six cents a gallon, a nickel for the Coke. She entered the costs in her notebook.

Waiting for change, she stood out of reach of the hot wind, in the shade of the overhang by the door. She pressed the cool glass bottle against her cheek for a moment, relishing the feel of it against her skin, then drank deeply. The blades of the windmill across the road turned steadily in the wind.

Liz thought of herself as a westerner, but the empty expanse of prairie and sky that stretched before her filled her with a vague, undefined apprehension. She finished the last of the Coke, slipped the empty bottle into the wooden carton beside the cooler, pocketed her change, and climbed back into the car.

✁

The county road Liz had been searching for turned out to be little more than narrow wagon ruts worn through the carpet of gray-blue grama and buffalo grass. Chalk cliffs—giant slabs of sandstone piled in careless heaps—rose to the north. To the south, stretching directly ahead for as far as she could see was nothing but more grass. She gripped the steering wheel, trying to avoid the ruts, and inched along.

Huge birds drifted effortlessly in lazy circles, riding the air currents of the cloudless sky. She wondered if they were vultures.

Liz bounced and lurched slowly along for another fifteen miles without a single sign of human life. The wind felt like a blast furnace. She questioned her sanity, began to despair that she would ever reach civilization. Then, miraculously, wheat fields appeared on either side of the road. What looked like a ranch house was visible in the distance. Several miles later, she spotted a stout water tower. Where there was a water tower, there was a railroad, and with the railroad would be a town. Grover must be close. Greta's place couldn't be far.

Liz drove past the depot—a two-story, stark-looking frame building painted dark brown—a grain elevator, and the water tower she'd seen. The post office seemed like the logical place to ask directions to Greta's.

The tiny business district was a mix of cement-block buildings and the usual false-front wooden structures. She drove up and down Main Street twice before spotting the "U.S. Post Office" sign over the entrance to the Morris Lumberyard.

Inside, a tall woman with great, pendulous breasts that strained at her cotton dress stood behind the counter. She had the square shoulders and substantial girth of a well-built man. Three rows of post-office boxes had been built into the wall behind her. Liz asked for directions to the Kuhlmann place.

"You kin?" the woman asked, giving Liz an appraising look.

"A friend. From Denver."

The woman's face was expressionless. Her bulk reminded Liz of a huge guard dog.

"I've come for a visit. She invited me." Almost true. "But I lost the directions."

The woman pursed her lips. "Greta didn't say anything about expecting company."

Liz kept smiling. The woman continued to give her the once-over. Finally, she relented. Armed with directions, Liz walked down the block to the Grover General Store and bought several cans of salmon, six bananas, a jar of peanut butter, and a box of fresh strawberries—a house present that Greta wouldn't refuse. She stowed the box in the backseat of the Buick and set out on the last leg of her journey.

15

Liz stopped the car and stared up at the one-story house at the top of the rise, unprepared for what she saw. Bleached by the wind and sun, the unpainted boards had a desperate look about them. A ten-foot stretch of elaborately filigreed wrought-iron fence stood incongruously in front. Small and alone, with nothing to break the wind, the house looked like a shriveled, aging actor standing on a vast, empty stage.

Liz shifted gears and drove closer. The roof was patched with black tarpaper. A shed and a small corral stood off to one side. Liz hadn't expected much, but the bleakness of the setup took her breath away. A girl with a baby was not what Greta needed. If Emma Volz had come from around here, it was no wonder she'd moved to Denver.

As Liz turned into the yard, a young woman, nearly six feet tall, with a thick white-blond braid hanging down her back, stepped out of the door. Her freckled face broke into a smile as she approached the car. Liz introduced herself. The girl said her name was Bessie Lindstrom. Liz pictured her on a dairy farm in Minnesota. She couldn't imagine the circumstances that would make this beaten-down homestead an attractive place for her and her child.

"Greta's told me all about you. She's out fixin' fence. Come in and rest yourself," Bessie said amiably, as if Greta had been expecting Liz all along.

The girl took Liz's suitcase and groceries. They went inside. At one end of the main room was a sleeping loft. A bedroom had been built off the other. An ancient horsehair settee and a rocking chair passed for parlor furniture. Next to a coal stove and a sink were a rickety kitchen table and four mismatched chairs. Beyond the kitchen was a tiny, closed-in porch lined with shelves of jars and cans of liniment and medicines that were probably for the animals. Nothing was out of place. Windows sparkled, the floors were swept.

Bessie walked over to the kitchen table, where an orange crate covered with cheesecloth had been placed. "This here's Cissy," she said, removing the makeshift screening.

Liz looked down at a pretty, chubby baby about three months old, sprawled in sleep.

"She's good as gold. No trouble at all." The girl gave her a nervous smile and rearranged the cheesecloth over the orange crate.

"I'm sure," Liz said without much conviction but wanting to be agreeable. She glanced toward the zinc sink. "Bessie, could I trouble you for a glass of water?"

"You bet." At which Bessie hurried outside and returned with a pail of water and dipper. "It don't taste like much, but it does the job."

Liz plunged the dipper in, drank thirstily. "I see what you mean," she said with a laugh. "A little like iron filings in liquid form."

The girl smiled vaguely and moved the makeshift bassinet off the kitchen table. Sitting opposite each other, they struggled to make conversation for a few minutes. But Liz knew nothing about babies or ranching, so the weather was about all she could think of to talk about. And Bessie didn't have much to add. After ten minutes or so, she got to her feet and excused herself. She had chores to do while Cissy was asleep, she said. She suggested Liz lie down in Greta's room till she came back.

The bedroom was barely large enough for the iron-frame bed and chiffonnier. Bleached flour-sack curtains hung limp at the open window. Liz took off her shoes, eased down onto the narrow bed, and stretched out. The mattress was lumpy. It felt as if it were filled with cornhusks. A fly buzzed overhead. Chickens cackled outside. Liz touched her fingers to her sunburned face and closed her eyes.

ᨠᑊᨠ

It was sundown before Greta, weary to the bone, pulled open the screen door. She'd seen Liz's car. Now the sight of her, gingerly holding baby Cissy, made Greta laugh out loud.

"See? I made it." Liz handed Cissy back to her mother.

Still grinning, Greta glanced around the room. "Well, what d'ya think?"

"The fence really adds something."

The crack was just about what Greta had expected. "Yeah. It's nice. The minute I saw that thing, I thought of you. Story is, the old boy who had the place before me put it up for his wife. But she died anyway."

She and Liz chuckled a little, looked at each other.

"Okay. So it ain't up to your granddad's place. I'll give ya that."

"But it's yours," Liz finished.

"Someday." Greta took off her wide-brimmed hat. "Keep me company while I wash up?"

Liz followed Greta out the back door. "Obviously, I got your postcard. Sorry I just showed up. I guess I should have sent a telegram."

"I figured unless the police found out who murdered that Volz woman, one way or another, you'd be here." Greta removed the washbowl from its nail next to the back door. "How's it goin', anyway? Was the old cop any help?"

Liz looked away.

"That bad?"

Liz nodded, swallowed hard. Tears brimming, she told Greta about Tim Ryan's death. "You warned me, and I didn't listen. Mrs. Ryan as much as begged me not to contact her husband. And now she's a widow."

"Liz, Mr. Ryan did what he did because he wanted to. He could've turned you down flat, but he didn't. It was his choice."

"I know, but—"

"No buts."

Liz sighed, drew her fingers over her eyes, and sat down on the stoop. "Let's talk about you. How's Bessie working out?"

"Fine." Greta filled the tin washbowl with water from the bucket.

"I noticed you were the one fixing fence. I thought she was supposed to be the cowhand."

"She takes care of the garden and the house. I take care of the stock, and what goes with it."

Liz didn't reply.

"Like I say. It's workin' out fine."

"If you say so." Liz leaned back and wrapped her arms around one knee. "So tell me about the Volz you found for me."

"His name is Carl." Greta reached for the sliver of soap on the windowsill. "Liz, if it wasn't fine with Bessie, I'd let ya know."

Liz shrugged. "About Carl Volz . . ."

Greta knew when it was time to move on. "Seems he worked next door—the Lazy J Ranch, a mile east as the crow flies—until last spring, when he decided to take up rodeoin'." Greta pointed toward the clutch of buildings and corrals at the bottom of the hill. "I don't know if he has a sister by the name of Emma. But when Orlo, the old fella who's foreman at the Lazy J, said this Volz might enter buckin' broncs here at Grover, I figured maybe he could be related. You'd have a chance to ask him." She lathered the soap up as best she could, rinsed, and dried with her shirttail.

"You're a marvel. It's the best lead I've had so far," Liz said. "Even at that, I had to sell my editor on the idea of a rodeo story to get up here."

"Well, don't worry. You'll get it. Round here, they call the Grover rodeo 'the best little rodeo in the West.' Mostly it's local boys who compete. But there'll probably be others. Talk is that C.J. Harlan, fella who owns the Lazy J—and half a dozen other places hereabouts— is gonna be the announcer again this year."

"This Harlan, does he live in Grover?"

"Sterling. Twenty-some miles from here. Sells Buick cars, runs a garage, and I don't know what all else. Orlo says Harlan used to run a couple hundred head of Herefords on the Lazy J. But with the price of cattle the way it is, he's cut back. Still keeps the old fella on, though. Out of friendship, I expect. Poor man can hardly get around. Not that it matters. Nowadays there's not much to take care of—a dozen head, as many horses, and some mules and a jack left from an army contract during the war. Every Tuesday like clockwork—sometimes more—a kid named Al Riddle comes out to the ranch with supplies. We'll go over tomorrow, talk to Orlo. Al might be there."

❧❧❧

Later, after supper and helping Greta lug water to the horse trough, Liz was too tired to do anything more than use the outhouse and put on her nightgown. Having talked Greta out of her offer to take the bedroom, Liz spread a makeshift mattress of old blankets across the wide-planked floor at one end of the kitchen. From the loft came the sound of Bessie's soft snores. Liz blew out the kerosene lamp, and for a moment, before her eyes adjusted, the room went dark.

Then, barefoot, she walked over to the open window. The wind had calmed. The air was absolutely still. Bathed in moonlight, the chalk cliffs to the north had a surreal, forbidding look. She leaned against the window frame and thought of the Klan and the Toad a hundred miles south. The chances that Carl Volz was a relative of Emma's were slim at best. And the odds weren't any better that an old foreman or an errand boy named Al might offer any leads. But at this point, she had nothing to lose.

16

Al Riddle pulled into the yard of the Lazy J after a routine drive from Sterling. He'd noticed a slow leak in the truck's front left tire, but his luck—and the tire—had held. Fixing a flat was a fucking pain in the ass. He glanced at his watch. Nine o'clock on the nose. And already hot as hell. He drew a bare forearm across his sweaty forehead, already longing for a tall, cold beer in the back room of Bigby's roadhouse.

And then he saw the car parked alongside the log house.

He knew every Buick in the northern part of the state; this wasn't one of them. Mr. Harlan, his boss, owned the distributorship in Sterling, and Al was learning to do repairs. He could tell the Buick staring back at him was a pre-war model. Al set the brake on the truck, climbed down, and slid the box of groceries out of the bed. Balancing it on one shoulder, he went inside.

Orlo was sitting in the low-ceilinged kitchen in a rocking chair made of elk antlers and cowhide. He was a decent old geezer: gnarled fingers, gimpy leg, half-blind. Al always tried to do right by him. In the dim light Al could see the broad-beamed figure of Greta, the German dame from the place on the hill. She was standing at the stove, pouring coffee. A good-looking woman with nice tits and city clothes sat at the kitchen table. She must belong to the Buick.

"That the delivery boy?" Orlo asked, squinting in Al's direction.

"In person." He looked at Greta. "That your Buick out there?" he asked with a genial smile.

Greta jerked her thumb toward the woman. "Meet Miss O'Brien. The *Denver Post*."

Al whistled softly through his teeth. "A lady reporter. Ain't that somethin'?"

"Miss O'Brien came up for the rodeo," Greta said.

Al cocked an eyebrow, grinned at the thought of the woman in city clothes next to the ranch wives in their cotton housedresses.

He turned to the old man. "Hey, Orlo, what d'ya say to all this?"

"I say it's a good thing you come early this week, 'cause the ladies and me are about out of coffee."

"Do I ever forget ya?" Al went over and placed a hand on the old man's skinny shoulders. "Say now, I sure hope no rustlers have been snoopin' around."

Orlo guffawed at the tired joke. "And if they had, what would you do about it, mister mechanic?" He shot a glance at the woman and Greta. "Al, here, thinks he's some hotshot because one time he brought in some wild horses, and he can handle that cussed jack mule we got."

"Aw, come on now, Orlo. I'm not half-bad," Al said, grinning but serious. He had a way with horses. And the mule. "Listen. You oughta tell the ladies about the old days." He watched the old guy's face light up. It made Al feel good to see it.

"We got the best grass in the world around here," Orlo began, sitting back, relaxed. "Cattle country like none other, if you stick to a cow/calf for every seventy acres. The Arapaho, the Cheyenne, the Lakota—throw in the Pawnee now and again—thought highly of it as hunting grounds."

Greta handed Al a cup of coffee and he nodded his thanks. "What Orlo is tryin' to say is that our boss, C.J. Harlan, is a pretty sharp guy. He could've sold out to some of those farmers who thought this was sugar-beet country. But he didn't. Ain't I right, Orlo?"

"You said it, boy." Al caught a note of pride in the old man's voice.

Greta put the coffeepot back on the stove. "Just before you came, Miss O'Brien was askin' Orlo about Carl Volz."

Al glanced at the reporter. "What about him?"

"You know him?" the city woman asked eagerly.

"Some. From Sterling. And I seen him around when he was workin' here."

"Orlo said he might be at the rodeo tomorrow."

"Might at that."

The woman picked up her coffee cup. "Did he have a sister named Emma?"

"Emma?"

"So you knew her, too?"

"Lady, around here, everybody knows everybody."

The woman straightened ever so slightly. "Emma Volz was murdered in Denver two weeks ago."

"Well, I'll be." Al looked past the reporter, his eyes distant. It had been a Sunday, five years ago, when he'd first seen Emma. She'd been ogling candy through the window of Miller's Sweet Shoppe in downtown Sterling. Fourteen, but tall and already filled out, sturdy from working in the fields, her skin tanned the color of fine leather, her fingernails permanently black from the dirt she could never scrub out.

He remembered how grown-up he'd felt that day, a punk kid of fifteen, in town for the day, a diploma from grammar school stowed in his gear in the bunkhouse on a Harlan farm five miles west. He'd been hired to drive the buck rake instead of pitching hay again. Al didn't think of himself as all that smart, but he'd already figured out that this wasn't a kid's world. A man had to watch out for himself first, others second, or he'd be squashed like a mealy bug in the fields. But a woman was different.

As he and Emma had stood yakking about which candies would melt in your mouth first, he'd told himself she was nothing but a German-Russian kid who smelled funny and was dumber than dirt. That was before he caught the steel glints in her green eyes, before he knew about the hurt. He was proud of his feel for what made people tick. It came from dealing with animals.

Fellows he knew ragged him for hanging around with a dirty Rooshian. Then she'd managed to talk her way into a job as a hired girl for the family who owned the bicycle shop in town. He'd pick her up on her Sundays off, and they'd just walk around town looking at the houses. After a while she told him little stuff about taking care of her drunken old man and her baby brother, like that was what every kid did. It didn't take long before Al decided she was the one who needed caring for. God knows he'd tried.

He and Emma first had each other a year after they'd met. In the dark shadows by the river, she'd told him that her old man had had his way with her when he was drunk and that she was scared, so Al went easy with her. He'd been with girls before, lots of them, mostly older ones who thought he was cute.

As he'd tasted her tears, his hands slowly caressed her breasts, firm and heavy in his hands. He'd kissed his way down to her deep red nipples. Just thinking about them turned him hard as a rock. Her long legs spread, she'd cried out when it was over. The feel of her soon became an obsession that drove him nuts.

"Al?"

He blinked. "Sorry. I was just thinkin' about Emma."

"I know the news comes as a shock, but what you can tell me about her? Who were her friends? Did she have any enemies?"

Al shook his head. "I haven't seen her since last summer. Seems like Carl would be your best bet."

🐦

Emma's death stopped the conversation short. After an awkward si-lence, Al mumbled something about getting back to Sterling and headed for the door. Liz and Greta followed him outside. Al Riddle was a good-looking kid, Liz thought. She could understand how some girls might take to him. Not that tall, but trim, and wide in the shoul-ders. A straw boater sat back on his slicked-down blond hair. Rolled shirtsleeves exposed muscled arms, thick wrists. He was dressed for town, but he had the build for ranch work. Liz guessed his age at about twenty.

As she backed the Buick around, she stuck her head out the win-dow. Al was watching her. She waved, and he grinned and waved back. A nice kid, too, she decided. With a soft heart for an old man. But cocky, like a lot of guys his age. Probably good at pushing his way up in the world.

On the drive back to Greta's, Liz asked about him.

"He works at the Harlan garage in Sterling. He'd like you to think he's a mechanic. But he's pretty much Harlan's errand boy. It's Harlan's money buyin' the groceries for Orlo. The poor old fella hasn't been able to even get up on a horse for as long as I've been here. Al's the real caretaker. He was born not more than ten miles from here. Knows those cliffs like the back of his hand. About every other visit, he takes a ride over there to check on the cattle Harlan still runs. And he feeds the mules."

"He didn't want to talk about Emma, did he?"

"Maybe he didn't have anything to say. Like he told you, Emma's brother is the one you're after. And you'll see him tomorrow."

🐦

The next morning, after a late start, Liz and Greta, Bessie and the baby piled into the Buick and drove the five miles to Grover and the rodeo grounds at one end of Main Street. For comfort's sake, Liz wore slacks, a cotton blouse, and a battered cowboy hat she borrowed from Greta.

A sign made out of oilcloth, long enough to be stretched across the street, swayed in the stiff, hot breeze. Its bright red lettering read "Welcome to the Biggest Little Rodeo in the West." A stream of kids dashed past. Horses neighed. A car backfired. A roar of laughter mixed with yippees and shouts floated in the dry air. Liz's experience with rodeos was limited to the National Western Stock in Denver, held indoors in the dead of winter. Some of the audience came in furs. The Grover rodeo might as well have been on another planet. Made to order for a feature story, she reminded herself.

A group of men—mostly young, in blue jeans and cowboy hats, big kerchiefs around their necks, pointy-toed boots on their feet— stood together, eyeing the horses that milled restlessly inside a large rope corral. At a nearby stand, two women were selling soda pop and balloons. Next to a line of wagons was a new touring car and five or six dust-caked Model Ts. Liz gave them a second look and thought she recognized Al Riddle's pickup, but just then a stubby man with mustache got out of the cab.

Liz turned away and surveyed the scene. The rodeo arena took her by surprise. No wooden grandstand. No solid fence. Instead, the competition took place in a makeshift circle of two dozen cars parked end to end, a crude chute between two of them. The audience sat on blankets spread over the roofs of their cars, or perched on the fenders, or stood in truck or wagon beds.

She looked over at the cowboys, their eyes on the arena, and wondered if Carl Volz was one of them. She tugged on Greta's sleeve and they discussed their options. Greta offered to go over and ask, as long as Liz bought soda pop. She was still waiting in line when Greta returned.

"He's the tall drinka water with the light brown hair."

Liz studied the cowboys.

"The one with the bony face."

Liz's gaze settled on a boy who fit Greta's description. Emma had been sturdy, not bony. Still, bloody and battered as Emma's body had been, Liz was foolish to expect to see any family resemblance. She walked over to him.

"Carl Volz?"

His thumbs locked in his back pockets, he pulled his gaze away from the arena, looked at her.

Liz gave her name. "I'm a reporter from the *Denver Post*. Someone told me you have a sister named Emma. Blond hair. About my height."

The boy's eyes instantly filled with alarm. "Emma's not hurt or anythin'?"

Liz was certain the emotion was genuine. She took his arm. "Let's go somewhere more private."

"Where is she?" Carl asked as he let her lead him out of earshot of the other cowboys.

"I wish there was some other way to break the news, but a young woman named Emma Volz was murdered in Denver nearly two weeks ago."

Carl stared at her.

"The women she was living with have vanished. I came up here for any information that might help track down her killer."

The young cowboy stared at the ground, his jaw clenched.

"I was hoping you could tell me when—and why—she went to Denver. Who her friends were. Anything."

Carl looked up, his deep-set eyes dark, wounded. "I didn't even know for sure she'd left town. I've been on the road. Last I saw her, I'd just come back from Frontier Days in Cheyenne." He shook his head as if wanting to clear it of the nightmare. "She looked good. Happy. Said she'd gotten a job, working for the Harlans as a cook. The pay wasn't great, but room and board and uniform was thrown in, so she could save near all she made."

"Did she have a friend, someone I could talk to?"

"A friend?" he asked, as if the idea were foreign to him.

"Hey, Volz, you're up," a man yelled.

"I gotta go," Carl said.

"I'll talk to you later," Liz called after him.

Next thing she knew, Carl was on his horse in the chute, adjusting his hold on the reins.

"Ladies and gentlemen," boomed the announcer through a megaphone, "you all know our next rider. So give a Grover welcome to Carl Volz from Sterling, Colorado."

A chorus of whistles and cheers erupted as Carl and the bucking horse burst from the chute. Liz crossed her fingers, amazed he was able to concentrate. The spectators continued to cheer when, suddenly, the horse jerked, dug his hind feet into the dirt, and lifted hard, putting space between saddle and rider. For an instant, Carl hung in the air, then slammed down against the saddle. Another jolt and he flew over the horse's head. But unlike the cowboy before him, who had picked himself up and walked off, Carl lay on his side, unable to move.

"Folks, looks like Carl's taken a pretty bad fall. Let's give him a big hand as the boys take him out so the doc can get a look at him."

Clapping accompanied two men as they trotted into the arena with a makeshift stretcher, carefully lifted Carl onto it, and carried him off. The announcer called out the next rider's name, and the rodeo went on.

Liz watched as the men took Carl into the hotel. A man—presumably the doctor—emerged from the feed store and hurried in after them. She wondered if Carl's leg had been broken. Whatever the injury, it might be hours before he'd feel up to more of Liz's questions.

She looked around. Perhaps someone else in this crowd had known Emma. She approached a group of women in sunbonnets, perched in the bed of a truck. This time she wouldn't be quite so direct; she'd take her time, warm up to the real question she had to ask. But she needn't have worried. The women's attention was riveted on the next rider, who had just exploded into the arena on a mean-looking bay.

Left arm in the air, right hand on the reins, the cowboy was making a desperate effort to stick long enough to qualify for the next round. At each turn and twist the crowd groaned. The horse ran close to the cars, turned and kicked a clod of dirt toward one of the women, who merely raised a finger to flick it off, never taking her eyes from the rider, who at this instant parted company with his horse. Almost immediately the cowboy scrambled to his feet and limped out of the arena as a second man on horseback galloped alongside the empty-saddled bronc, reaching beneath it to loosen a strap.

Only then did Liz tap one of the women on the shoulder and introduce herself. Before she'd finished explaining the story she'd been sent to get, the other women had turned around. Liz repeated her story as they eyed her clothes. Liz took down their names. They were friendly enough, a few even eager to answer Liz's questions about the rodeo. Though none of them had sons or brothers competing, they knew most of the riders and had an opinion on every event. They recounted tales of injuries. It was a toss-up as to whether riding bulls or broncs was more dangerous. In either case, a man could have both

his legs broken and his head scrambled and never make enough to
pay the doctor bills. Liz made a show of checking the spelling of their
names, thanked them. Then, finally, as if it were an afterthought, she
asked if any of them knew Emma Volz from Sterling. None did. Trying to hide her disappointment, Liz thanked them again and let them
to get back to the rodeo.

🖋🖋

Across the arena from the chute, C.J. Harlan stood on the truck bed,
megaphone in hand, and stole a glance at his brand-new, spanking-
clean black Buick surrounded by dust-caked Ford trucks and wagons.
He wasn't one to brag, but there were some who said Grover should
be renamed Harlan. His gaze shifted. From here, he had a good view
of the families and the cowboys—his people—enjoying themselves.
It made him feel proud.

He had spotted the woman in men's trousers the moment she
walked up to the arena. Watched her talk to the bony kid who used
to work on one of his places. Saw her interview the Grover ladies. It
was obvious she was a reporter, and from Denver.

Women in these parts wore dresses, or their husbands' overalls—
but only if need be, and not in public. He had to admit she wasn't
bad-looking. Round, full tits beneath the blouse. Nice firm ass.

She must have sensed his eyes on her because she suddenly looked
up at him and smiled. He straightened his white Stetson, jumped down.
The boys immediately cut short their talk, not wanting to miss a thing.

"Miss, if you'll forgive me . . . I couldn't help noticing you with
some of the ladies across the way."

Just as he had expected, the woman introduced herself as a reporter from the *Denver Post*. "I'm here to do a feature story on the
rodeo. From the woman's point of view."

He smiled. "And you couldn't have chosen a better group. I know
all these good people."

"And your name, sir?" the woman asked, pulling out her pencil.

"Why, C.J. Harlan," he said, surprised she didn't know.

He shot a glance at the men grouped around the truck. "Boys, did
you hear that? The *Post*. Grover rodeo's hit the big time. Of course, Jim,
here," he beamed at a gaunt man, "Jim does a fine job with the *Pawnee
Press*. And we couldn't do without the *Sterling Advocate*. But for the
big issues . . . that's where the *Post* comes in." He gave her a full smile.

"Mr. Bonfils and my editor will be pleased to hear that." She took a notebook out of her pocketbook. "Mr. Harlan, you're obviously in the know. I wonder if you can give me a little background on how the rodeo got started here, how you became involved?" She readied her pencil. "If my information is correct, you live in Sterling."

"Tell you what." He held the smile. "There'll be a break pretty soon while they set up for barrel racing. I'd consider it a privilege to buy you a soda or a lemonade. We can sit in the shade over there at the hotel and you can ask away."

"Wonderful. I'll look forward to talking with you."

C.J. clapped one of the boys on the shoulder, climbed up on the truck bed again. The smooth way she looked at him made it plain this woman thought folks around here were a bunch of hicks. But this was his territory. If anyone had a right to take an advantage when it came along, he did.

🖋

While she waited for Harlan, Liz decided to interview some cowboys for her rodeo story, and she found them clustered by the chute. After a few false starts, she found one of them—a big, open-faced kid who turned out to be an expert on the rules—willing to talk to her.

Arms folded and head down, eyes on the tips of his pointy boots, he explained that the rules had changed. This year a bronc rider couldn't wear chaps, had to spur his horse and use a slick saddle with no more than a fifteen-inch swell, and had to start with both feet in the stirrups, spurs against the shoulders.

"A slick saddle?"

"Yeah," he said, as if he couldn't imagine she wouldn't know what he was talking about. Maybe Greta did.

"Are the rules the same for women?"

"There's no women entered in bronc ridin' here. Just barrel racin'."

Liz knew she was way over her head. She struggled for something reasonably intelligent to ask. "Do you ride your own horse?"

"The rodeo committee provides 'em."

She flipped to a fresh page in the notebook. "How about a purse?"

"Finals for bull and bronc ridin' is forty dollars. Same for steer wrestlin'. Barrel racin' is thirty."

More than she'd thought. But only the winners took any money home; the others went empty-handed. The cash came from ticket sales and the ten-dollar entry fee for each contestant. Liz did a quick count of the crowd, put it at a hundred, maximum. Times twenty-five cents came to a total of less than the purse for a single event. Maybe thirty cowboys had entered. They'd have to enter a hundred rodeos just to break even. It seemed like a tough way to earn a living.

"What happens if a cowboy is badly hurt?"

"If it's busted ribs or a leg or an arm, he gets it wrapped up and hopes it heals fast. Otherwise . . ." He shrugged, resigned to the risks of a life he couldn't resist.

"Like Carl Volz."

The boy nodded.

"Did you ever know his sister, Emma?"

The cowboy shook his head, looked inquiringly at his friends.

"She that good-lookin' barrel racer up at Cheyenne?" one cowboy asked.

"I don't think so," Liz said.

The open-faced kid said, "Guess nobody knows her. Sorry."

Liz smiled and thanked him for his time.

But Harlan was still announcing, so she walked over to the hotel. The porch was lined with four chairs, all occupied by fierce-looking women with thin lips and a firm set to their jaws. They looked to be in their sixties. Their gray hair had a yellow cast that had to be the result of the hard local water. They'd rolled their stockings down and spread their knees apart to give any bit of breeze a chance to get under their cotton-print housedresses. Liz asked how the injured cowboy was doing, but no one had heard anything. She went inside. A gnarled little man said the doc was still working on the Volz kid. It didn't look good.

She stepped back outside. A whistle blast announced the arrival of a train. With no chair in sight, she sat down on the edge of the porch. Fifteen minutes later a file of families, picnic baskets in hand, coming from the direction of the depot, trudged toward the rodeo grounds. The sun was straight up. the temperature had to be bordering on one hundred degrees when Mr. Harlan finally strode up, apologizing for the delay.

"I don't know about you, Miss O'Brien, but my whistle's all dried up. If you'll excuse me, I'll get us something cold." He disappeared inside the hotel, returning a few minutes later with two bottles of Cliquat ginger ale.

He surveyed the old women with a smile. "Seems the good ladies of Grover have first dibs on the chairs."

"The edge of the porch is fine." Liz accepted the ginger ale with a smile. It wasn't very cold. The ice in the cooler must have melted. She pulled out her notebook.

Harlan tipped his head back and finished off nearly half his soda in one swallow. "Let's see, now. You say you want to know about the Grover rodeo. First off, it got started about three years ago. And every man does his share, whether it's bringing in the stock or taking tickets."

"And your involvement?"

"Just say I lend support," he said with a smile that revealed a mouthful of gleaming white teeth. He took another long drink, emptying the bottle. He put it down between his feet in the dust of the street. "Like the flag over there. Last year's was shredded by hail. So I arranged for a new one to be shipped by special order." He looked back in the direction of the American flag, flapping atop a pole in front of the Morris Lumberyard. "A stirring sight, isn't it? The very symbol of the American way."

Liz glanced at him. Lately, the phrase reminded her of only one thing: the Klan.

"An inspiration to those who would rise from meager beginnings and make something of themselves." His eyes burned with such fervor that it made her leery. "I'm a self-made man, Miss O'Brien. Proud of it. No one knows better than I do that if it hadn't been for the good people of Weld and Logan counties, people like you see all around you here today, I would never have achieved what I have.

"I own ranch and city properties. I am president of the Sterling Bank, senior deacon at the Presbyterian Church. I live in a lovely house. I'm married to the finest woman in the world. I was a runt of a boy when her daddy, the grand old man of Logan County, Phillip Trotter, gave me my first break. I did every odd job a ranch has, and then some. Mr. Trotter put his faith in me. As did many others. Now it's time for me to pay them back."

Liz had grown up in a household where politics was discussed as often as the weather. She knew a campaign speech when she heard one. The tale of humble beginnings was a tired one, dating back to the days of Andrew Jackson. But apparently, C.J. Harlan thought it effective. She looked up from her notebook and bluntly asked him what office he was running for.

The smile again. "You're a very perceptive woman, Miss O'Brien." A frown replaced the smile. "Friends, Mr. Trotter, business associates— they've urged me to consider public office for several years. The timing seems right. And I am offering my name to fill the vacancy for state senate in District 14. A heavy responsibility, I know. Nonetheless, I can no longer shirk my civic duty, and my dear wife, Miriam, agrees."

Liz dutifully scribbled down his words. She suspected the same drivel had been dished out by Roman senators a thousand years ago. But it wasn't Harlan's campaign plans that interested her. "Mr. Harlan, since you're a lifelong area resident, I wonder if the name Emma Volz means anything to you. Orlo Smith, the foreman of the Lazy J, tells me her brother, Carl, used to work for you. He competed in the bronc riding earlier today."

"Say the name again."

"Volz. Carl Volz."

Harlan smiled. "Sure. I remember his ride. I hope he didn't bust that leg." He nodded at the bottle of soda in Liz's hand. "How about another one?"

She smiled. "Oh, no, thanks."

"You say this Volz worked at the Lazy J?"

"That's what Orlo Smith said."

"Well, you'd best believe it, then. Fine old man. Not many like him these days."

"Actually, I wondered if you knew Carl's sister, Emma."

"I'm afraid you have me on that, Miss O'Brien. You might ask one of the good ladies on the porch." Harlan got to his feet, his gaze now on the rodeo grounds. "Oh-oh. There's Hale Wagner giving me the high sign. Time to get back to work."

"One last question. As a candidate, can you tell me your opinion of the Ku Klux Klan?"

"The Klan?" His eyes were careful.

"It's my understanding that they hope to become a force in the legislature."

"Now, Miss O'Brien, you and I know that no true American needs a mask or a disguise."

"Were you aware that the Klan intends to take over law and order in the state?"

He smiled indulgently. "Let me put it this way. Law and order may be an issue in Denver. Hereabouts, folks worry about the parked cars and the roadhouses where our young girls are ruined and boys go astray."

"You would take that issue to the legislature?"

"God and the voters willing, yes, ma'am." He offered her his hand. "Allow me." She felt its strength as he pulled her to her feet.

"One thing more before I forget, Miss O'Brien. I want to extend a special invitation to my official campaign kickoff. On the fourth. It'll be a big shindig. A barbecue at Sterling's city park. The entire town is invited. We'll roast up some pigs. There'll be corn. Fresh cherry pie. Good old-fashioned American food. If you don't have other plans, come along. It might make another good story for you." He flashed a disarming smile, winked. "And it wouldn't hurt my campaign, either."

17

One elbow on the frame of the open window, Liz drove the Buick out of Grover just as the last apricot-hued rays of sun light slipped behind the ragged frieze of the Rockies thirty miles to the west. She'd gone in search of Carl Volz again, only to discover he'd been taken away, though no one seemed to know where. After that, she'd made the rounds of the spectators, always with the same question: had they known Emma Volz? A few had heard the name, but none had known her.

As dark fell, the air cooled. Blowing against her face as she drove, it smelled faintly of sage. Bessie and the baby were asleep in the back. Greta, seated next to Liz, listened as she related her brief conversation with Carl Volz. "At least I know Emma worked for Harlan. So it wasn't a total loss."

"What'd you think of Harlan?"

Liz shot her a glance. "He sounds like Klan. But I could be overreacting. He talked a lot about the American way. That kind of thing. He's running for state senate."

"Wouldn't be surprised."

"Carl Volz told me his sister had worked for Harlan. But Harlan said he didn't know her."

"It's prob'bly true. With all the farms and ranches he owns, he hires half the county."

Liz turned onto the wagon tracks that led to Greta's place and inched along, the car rocking as she tried to avoid the ruts. Parked in the yard, they got out and shut the doors as gently as they could so as not to wake Bessie and the baby.

Liz stretched, struck by the quiet. Not so much as a cricket chirped. She gazed at the sky, deep black and studded with stars. "Look at that up there. I don't even want to think about murder and the Klan on a night like this."

"It's somethin', ain't it?"

Liz smiled. But then something caught her eye: two points of light coming from the Lazy J. "Greta, look over there. Headlights."

She followed Liz's gaze. "Must be Al Riddle takin' Mr. Smith home from the rodeo."

They watched the bobbing lights.

"I didn't see the truck at the rodeo grounds," Liz said.

"I expect Al brought him over in Harlan's car."

The headlights vanished. Liz figured Al had turned off the engine and was helping the old man into the house.

She and Greta sat down on the back stoop.

"Did I tell you that Harlan invited me to his Fourth of July barbecue?" Liz asked. "He expects me to do a story on him. And I may. I thought I'd drive over to Sterling tomorrow, interview friends or local politicos."

"You're gonna drive home from there?"

"I thought I would."

Greta turned to Liz. "So. What d'ya think?"

"About Emma? Frankly, I don't know what I think. Everyone knows everyone, but no one knows Emma Volz. All her own brother could tell me was that she'd worked for Harlan. And Harlan claims he can't remember her. Poking around Sterling may turn up something. Otherwise, I'm pretty much stumped."

🐦

The next morning Liz hugged Greta, said good-bye to Bessie and the baby, threw her suitcase in the backseat, and drove off. She filled up with gas in Grover and asked directions to Sterling. Only wisps of cloud, delicate as shredded cotton, interrupted the clear blue sky as she drove along the well-used section road. Most of the way, it paralleled the Burlington tracks that led through Sterling, cutting her chances of getting lost.

The landscape shifted from wheat and sugar-beet fields to cactus-dotted rangeland and back again. Except for cottonwoods edging the occasional stream or dry creek bed, there were no trees. She passed through two towns amounting to little more than a main street and a water tower. Finally, the smokestack of the High Plains Sugar factory—

a towering, slender stalk rising from a circle of brilliant green—came into view.

Farmhouses now appeared at regular intervals. She knew she'd reached Sterling when the road became Main Street—hard-packed dirt, glistening with fresh oil to hold down the dust. As Liz drove along, she took in the large white clapboard houses surrounded by flowerbeds, the tidy lawns, the trees, most of them saplings. Emma Volz might have entered through the back doors of these houses to iron clothes or serve meals. The walk to work was no doubt a long one; German-Russian contract workers like the Volzes probably lived in another part of town, on the wrong side of the tracks, several miles away.

The women Liz passed wore flowered voile dresses with neat round collars, hats, white gloves, and silk stockings. The little girls who skipped along behind them were wearing starched cotton dresses, the boys in knee pants rather than coveralls. All things being relative, Sterling was citified.

The hot air had an optimistic feel, exuding prosperity. Sterling looked like a Sinclair Lewis small town where people believed in the future. Where the rules of life were black-and-white. Where nobody argued—at least not in public—and the ugly stuff was kept quiet. But every town had its secrets, and if anyone knew them, it would be the publisher or editor of the local newspaper.

Liz passed a grocery store and a drugstore, signs that she must be approaching the town center. The substantial courthouse was surrounded by well-cared-for lawn. Across the street was a business block. Anchored by the gray stone First National Bank and the Sterling Hardware and Implement Company at either end, the less pretentious establishments—a shoe shop, Proctor's Ladies' Wear, and Benneman's Watch Repair—were yellow or red brick buildings with flat roofs. No sign of a newspaper office.

Main Street dead-ended at Front Street along the tracks. To Liz's right was the smokestack of the sugar-beet factory she'd seen, with sheds and yards nearby. The railway depot was on her left. She spotted the red-and-white Railway Express sign at the far end of the platform. She drove up, parked, and went in to ask directions.

❧❦❧

The *Sterling Advocate* was south on Third Street. Two stories high, yellow brick, with a large plate-glass window. The front door had been propped open in deference to the heat. Liz stepped inside, breathing in the familiar odor of ink, and heard the sound of presses working somewhere beyond a wall that divided the big room. A stout woman behind a counter near the entrance was talking to a customer. She looked over at Liz.

"I'd like to speak to the editor."

"That'd be Will Miller. Last desk on the right."

Mr. Miller was of average height and gaunt, with thinning brown hair and a trimmed mustache. His skin was nut brown and leathery, more like that of a rancher than a newspaper editor. He was hunched over the typewriter, pecking out a story with two fingers. The veins on the backs of his hands stood out like wires beneath the skin.

She stood a few feet from the desk, waiting for a good time to interrupt. The telephone at his elbow rang. He gave it a sidelong glance, sighed, and picked it up. After several minutes, he hung up and scribbled something on a yellow legal pad.

Liz cleared her throat. He looked up at her with brown, intelligent eyes. "Something I can do for you?"

She smiled and introduced herself. What she said next was almost true. "I'm doing a feature story on C.J. Harlan's candidacy for the state senate." She'd get to Emma Volz later.

"Well, now." The editor stood up and brought a chair over for her. Liz noted his cautious reaction.

He sat down again. "It strikes me that a story about a senate race in Sterling is not the *Post's* usual fare."

He looked at her levelly, and she debated how to answer. A small-town newspaper was particularly vulnerable. Harlan and his father-in-law probably owned half the businesses in town, at least the ones that advertised.

"Actually, I was assigned to cover the Grover rodeo. That's when I met Mr. Harlan. He told me he'd be announcing his candidacy at the barbecue he's throwing tomorrow and suggested it might make a good story."

"Might at that. C.J.'s sharp. No doubt about it."

Liz wasn't sure this was intended as a compliment. "Apparently, he's done very well. Ranching, businesses here in Sterling. A regular Horatio Alger."

He pulled a hand down over his mouth, hiding a smile.

"What kind of senator do you think he'll make?" Liz asked.

"Good as most, better than some. He's ambitious. I wouldn't be surprised if he ends up governor someday."

"Any particular issues?" she asked.

"The usual. Eliminate the income tax."

"That's a federal tax."

"In a political campaign, a minor detail."

"Anything else?"

"Raise the tariffs for wheat and sugar beets." He smiled. "I know. That's up to Congress, but it sounds good. Improve the roads. Get freight rates reduced. Oh, and crack down on socialists."

Liz raised an eyebrow at the last. "I didn't know there were any socialists in Logan County."

"There aren't. Unless you count the German Russians, which some do. C.J. told me last winter he'd been all for the decision on the Sacco-Vanzetti trial."

"He mentioned the issue of roadhouses and parked cars."

The editor nodded.

Liz crossed her legs, smoothed her navy blue sharkskin skirt over her knees. "What do you know about the Ku Klux Klan, Mr. Miller?"

He stroked his mustache with two fingers, studying her. "What I do know, I don't like. Why?"

"The Klan's come to Colorado. I was wondering if you've seen it in Sterling?"

"Seen it? No. Heard rumors about it, yes. But so far, no show of white robes and burning crosses. Are you implying Harlan is a member?"

"Is he?"

"To tell the truth, I hadn't thought about it. Why don't you ask him at the picnic?"

"In a roundabout way, I already did. And he hedged. He talked about the roadhouses." She flipped to the next page of her notebook. "There's something else. I understand Harlan hires a good many German Russians in town."

"He can't avoid it. They're the people who work the sugar beets. Oh, a few Mexicans get hired, but the growers prefer the German Russians. Other than Phillip Trotter, Harlan's probably the biggest grower in this part of the state."

"Mr. Miller, you know a lot of people in town. Have you ever heard of a German-Russian family named Volz?"

The editor frowned. "If you mean Martin Volz, sure have. Drunk and disorderly. You'd think there was no Prohibition. But if you want it badly enough, liquor's easy to get, and a good many people around here look the other way. Volz has been a such a fixture in the local jail, I stopped running his name in the police notes."

"Does he have a son and daughter named Carl and Emma?"

Mr. Miller shook his head sadly. "A shame about those two. The girl—Emma—she was one of those kids you see some among her people. I don't think she went past fourth grade, if that. Worked in the fields, trying to take care of her brother and dodge her old man. They say hard work never hurt a soul, but where kids are concerned, I don't believe it."

The presses had stopped. The only sound was the honk of a horn from beyond the open door. Liz saw the indignation in his eyes.

"Did you know Emma was murdered? Shot to death, nearly two weeks ago in Denver?"

"Good lord!" The editor sank back in his chair, squeezed his eyes closed for an instant.

"The police have no suspects. The principle reason I'm in Sterling is to try to find out something about her background that might help the D.A."

"I can tell you her father's a son-of-bitch, if you'll excuse my bluntness, Miss O'Brien."

"Liz. Please."

"Liz." He tried for a smile. "Nobody would hire him on to work sugar beets anymore. Once the boy—Carl—was old enough to work, he and Emma moved out and got a place of their own, though I have no idea where. Old man Volz's meal ticket disappeared. A couple of years ago Emma tried to bring charges against him for assault and battery, but . . ." The editor gave a resigned shrug. "She was underage, and the judge said her father had a legal right to do what he wanted with her."

Liz's pulse quickened. It had never occurred to her that Emma's own father could have been the killer, the man responsible for getting her pregnant. Such things happened. And when she'd left town, he'd been furious. Somehow, he'd found out where she was living, hopped a freight to Denver, hunted her down, shot her. Liz could hardly wait to send Phil the news.

"Miss O'Bri—Liz . . ."

She started at the sound of the editor's voice.

"I hope you're not thinking her father killed her—though the Lord knows he's mean enough to have done it. But he couldn't have. Martin Volz was convicted of aggravated assault with a deadly weapon and sent to the state penitentiary over a year ago."

18

Liz was leaving the newspaper office, let down, trying to decide her next move, when she remembered Al Riddle. Not only had he said he'd known Emma, but he'd impressed Liz as the type who, like the editor, knew everyone in town.

It was nearly five o'clock when Liz drew up in front of the Harlan Garage on the corner of North Fifth and Chestnut. The Buick dealership was next door, the latest model displayed behind a large plate-glass window. Over it was a banner that read "Service to Customers Is Number One." Several cars were lined up in front of the garage, waiting to be repaired. Liz went into the office and asked a man in grease-stained coveralls for Al Riddle.

The mechanic's gaze lingered on her breasts. "He's workin' on a muffler. Want me to get him?"

"No, thanks. I'll wait." She added, for no particular reason, "It's a personal matter."

The man gave her a yellow-stained toothy leer, then leaned through a door and yelled, "Hey, Al. One of your lady friends is waitin' out here for ya."

A few minutes later Al Riddle appeared, wiping his blackened hands on his coveralls. The instant he saw her, he grinned. "Miss O'Brien! I missed ya at the rodeo. What brings ya to Sterling?" He shot the older man a cocky look. "The lady here's a reporter from Denver."

"Oh, yeah?" The man sounded unconvinced.

"Yeah," Al snapped. He looked back at Liz. "I get off work at six. How 'bout you and me goin' over to the Southern Hotel. They serve a swell supper."

Liz smiled, nodded. There was something engaging about Al Riddle.

꧁ꦵꦴ꧂

They sat at a corner table in the empty hotel dining room. Liz ordered
coffee. Al told the young waitress that he'd have the chicken-fried
steak and mashed potatoes, with a slab of apple pie for dessert. He
looked from the waitress to Liz. "Sure you don't want some supper?
The treat's on me."

"No, thanks. Coffee's fine."

The waitress disappeared into the kitchen.

Al leaned toward her. "I happen to know reporters' pay is lousy.
For me, it's easy come, easy go. I got nothin' to tie me down. Money
to burn."

"I had no idea auto mechanics did so well," she said.

Al leaned back, smiled expansively. "Say, I don't depend on what
I make from workin' on cars. No, ma'am. I hustle. I drive Mr. Harlan
around, sometimes to Denver. He sends me there real regular for parts.
I make myself handy. Get my meanin'?"

She shook her head, enjoying his bravado.

"You saw how it is. I help Orlo out at the Lazy J." Al cocked his
head. "He's a good old boy, really."

"That's what you mean by 'hustling'?"

Al looked injured. "That's plenty, if you ask me. And you prob'bly
heard about Mr. Harlan runnin' for office. His business is expandin'.
He needs somebody like me."

Liz dug her notebook and a pencil out of her purse. "What do you
think his chances are for getting elected?"

"Are you kiddin'? He'll win by a landslide."

"Then Mr. Harlan is well liked?"

Al leaned his elbows on the table and glanced furtively around
the empty dining room before he said, "He is and he isn't. See, a man
who's smart, who takes advantage of opportunities, can make people
mad or jealous. Sometimes both. That's how it is with Mr. Harlan. He
was the first man to buy trucks to haul cattle to the railheads 'stead of
spendin' two days on one of them cattle drives. He's up-to-date, and
the old codgers don't like it. Makes 'em look like horses' asses, which
they are." Al inspected the mammoth gold ring on his left ring finger,
then looked back at Liz. "It's dog-eat-dog out there. Take and you
will receive. The Bible even says so."

Liz hid a smile. "I think it's 'Give and you shall receive.' "

Al shrugged. "Same thing."

She suspected that he and C.J. Harlan were two of a kind. The waitress returned with a pot of coffee and filled Liz's cup.

"Steak's comin' right up, Al." The young woman smiled coyly.

"Thanks, sweetheart." He straightened his tie, focusing his attention on Liz again as the waitress retreated. "So what brings ya to the fair city of Sterling?"

"I thought this would be a good place to see what I could find out about Emma Volz. And I remembered you said you knew her."

The waitress reappeared with Al's order and returned to the kitchen.

Al picked up his knife and fork, cut into the steak. "I forget, did I tell ya that I hadn't seen her since last summer?"

Liz took a sip of the coffee, found it bitter, and reached for the sugar. "But before that . . . by any chance, were you and Emma sweethearts?"

"Sweethearts?" He chuckled. "But a fella could do worse," he said, continuing to saw at his steak. "Emma wasn't half bad in the looks department. Fact is, I felt sorry for her. She was one of those Rooshians who had it tough. So I went to bat for her and got her a job workin' at the Harlan place."

"When I interviewed Mr. Harlan at the rodeo, he said he didn't know an Emma Volz."

"Aw, he just forgot." Al shoved a piece of steak in his mouth. In the middle of chewing, he said added, "Anyway, it was the old lady— Mrs. Harlan—who hired her."

Liz reached for the sugar bowl and ladled a spoonful into her coffee. "What can you tell me about Emma's friends?"

"Truth is, I can't think of anybody in particular. Like I said, most everyone knew who she was, but she was a loner, poor kid. Kids like her never stay in school more'n a year or two, so she didn't know many girls, the way most do. She and her old man didn't get along, that's for sure." Al paused, gave her a long look. "Somethin' tells me you've heard all this before."

"Some of it." Al Riddle was shrewd as well as a hustler.

Liz decided to get to the point, and she told him that Emma had supposedly met a hometown friend at a Denver speakeasy just days before she was murdered. "Since you said you drove to Denver for parts, I thought—"

Al held up a hand, interrupting. "Hold it. I steer clear of speakeasies. Mr. Harlan would can me if I hung out in places like that.

Sure, I know where a fella can get a drink. Who doesn't? But if you're thinkin' I was the guy with Emma speakeasy that day, think again."

His indignation sounded almost too righteous to Liz. "Who could it have been, then?"

He shrugged. "No idea." Al stabbed the steak with his fork again. "Labor Day was the last time I seen her."

Liz took another swallow of coffee. The sugar hadn't helped much. She pushed the cup and saucer aside. "Al, I don't want to take up any more of your evening. But I'll be at Mr. Harlan's picnic tomorrow. If you think of anything . . ."

"I'll let ya know. Count on it."

❦

It was nearly seven o'clock by the time she'd tracked down the priest at St. Anthony's and the pastor at First English Lutheran. Both counted German-Russian beet-field workers as members of their parish. But neither remembered Emma Volz. Somehow Liz wasn't surprised. A drunk for a father and the responsibility of caring for a younger brother must have made Emma feel too much of an outsider to show up at Sunday services.

Liz wanted to get a better feel for Emma's life. So she drove past the depot where Emma had waited for the train to take her to Denver, the sugar factory where her father must have worked when he was sober, the courthouse where she'd appeared when she tried to have her father jailed. The lights in the stores along Main Street were dark when Liz realized she still had to find a room for the night, and she drove back to the Southern Hotel.

After some dickering about price, she was given a corner room on the second floor. With the register signed and key in hand, she was headed for the stairs when she noticed the doors to the dining room were still open. The young woman who had waited on her and Al was sitting at a table, folding napkins.

Liz walked over to her and the girl looked up, smiling automatically.

"I'm sorry, miss. We're closed."

"I'd like to talk to you for a moment. Maybe you remember—I was with Al Riddle earlier," Liz said.

"Sure, I remember."

Liz pulled out a chair. "Mind if I sit down?"

"Suit yourself." The waitress shoved the pile of napkins to one side.

"I was wondering. . . ." Liz smiled. "I'm sorry, I don't know your name."

"Fanny."

"I'm Liz O'Brien." She put her handbag in her lap. "Fanny, were you ever a friend of a girl named Emma Volz?"

The girl made a face. "I wouldn't give you two cents for Emma Volz."

Liz stiffened, astonished at how defensive she felt about a complete stranger, and a dead one at that. "What was it you didn't like about her?"

"Where do you want to start?"

"Did Emma steal your boyfriend?"

"If you're talkin' about Al, I'm better off without him."

"How about Emma?"

"You mean were they cozy?" Fanny folded another napkin. "They hung around together some. But they was too much alike. Look out for number one was their motto." She looked up. "Listen, if you want something to eat. . . ."

Liz hadn't realized until just now how hungry she was. "How about just a sandwich? I'm starved."

The waitress twisted around, looked toward the kitchen. "I should've closed the door before doin' the cleanup, but it's so darn hot." She got up. "I'll ask Mrs. Suskin. If there's any left, would you like some iced tea to go with?"

"Sounds wonderful. Thanks."

Liz waited, hearing voices beyond the kitchen door. Ten minutes later Fanny returned, bearing a tray with a sandwich and a tall glass of tea. "Ham's all that was left," she said as she swung the tray expertly off her shoulder and set the food in front of Liz.

"I could eat cardboard I'm so hungry. Ham is perfect," she said gratefully, unfolding her napkin and putting it in her lap. She looked up at the young waitress. "Can you sit down a minute?"

"Better not, but I'll work around here so we can still talk."

Liz bit into her sandwich. The slice of ham was thick and moist. The bread tasted homemade. "Best ham sandwich I've ever tasted," she said with her mouth full.

"I'll tell Mrs. Suskin tomorrow."

Liz took a few swallows of tea, trying to decide how best to approach the subject of Emma's death. "When was the last time you saw Emma Volz?"

Fanny shrugged. "Last summer. Could've been around Labor Day."

Liz broke the news about the murder and Fanny went pale.

"I'm talking to as many people as I can, hoping someone might know something that would lead to her murderer."

Fanny looked close to tears. "Miss, it's true I never liked Emma. But you're not gonna tell the police what I said about her, are ya?"

"Only if it might help solve the case."

"I didn't hate her. I just didn't like her much. I wouldn't do her no harm or have anythin' to do with anybody who would. I swear I wouldn't."

Liz offered an understanding smile. "I believe you. What you told me is just background. Off the record, as they say in newspapers."

Fanny eyed her uncertainly. "For sure?"

"For sure."

Without a reply, Fanny retreated to the kitchen, leaving Liz alone to finish eating. Apparently, there was at least one person in town who believed that Emma Volz wasn't worth risking a job—or anything else—for. After a last swallow of iced tea, Liz got up from the table and walked to the front desk, where she asked for the suitcase she'd left with the clerk.

The air in the small, dark room was stifling. She flicked on the light, walked over to the windows, parted the sheer curtains, and shoved the windows open as far as they would go. Turning, she surveyed the room. A bed covered with a rose-patterned spread, a small desk and chair, a chest of drawers, a rump-sprung overstuffed chair. Through an open door, she saw a small bathroom that might once have been a closet.

Once she was undressed and in her nightgown, she folded back the spread and blanket and crawled under the top sheet, turning off the bedside-table light. Even the sheet was too much and she kicked it off. Staring up into the dark, she reviewed what she knew about Emma so far.

A father in the state pen and a brother on the rodeo circuit. Al thought Emma had been fairly good-looking. He'd described her as a loner, someone he'd felt sorry for. From others, Liz had uncovered someone quite different. Not so much an innocent victim, in the wrong place at the wrong time, as a pragmatist forced to look after herself.

The wail of a distant train whistle intruded on the silence. Liz imagined Emma in a little shack across town on a hot summer night, listening to another train whistle and hearing its seductive call. Ironically, she'd had no way of knowing how far away it would take her.

〜〜〜

The next morning, after breakfast, Liz stopped by the front desk to find out when and where the Fourth of July festivities would begin. "Late afternoon" was the best she got for an answer from the desk clerk, a flabby man with a pale complexion and a vague manner. Plenty of time to hunt down a little background on the Harlan story. She went back to her room and grabbed her hat.

Armed with directions to the Harlan house, Liz drove to the south end of town, pulled the Buick to a stop in front of a substantial-looking house fronted by neatly cut, emerald-green grass and set just far enough back from the road for both privacy and visibility. Fields of sugar beets stretched behind it. It was a typical Victorian: painted white, three stories high, with lacy white wood trim on the porch and an oversized front door with a frosted glass insert. A large carriage house stood off to the left. Smaller structures—one looked like an icehouse—were half-hidden behind a small grove of cherry trees. A graveled drive lined by apple trees led up to the house. Everything was well kept and freshly painted. The entire property advertised success. Nothing else Liz had seen in Sterling compared to it. C.J. Harlan must have a knack for selling cars and trading up in cattle—a rare feat in hard times like these.

Liz was about to drive on when the front door opened and a young woman in a starched white uniform stepped out and began to sweep the porch. After a few minutes, she paused, leaned on the broomstick, and gazed out at the road. Then suddenly she looked over her shoulder, as if someone from inside had called. The girl slowly went back in, closed the door behind her. And Liz imagined how it must have been for Emma.

Liz drove on, passing neat farms with stout barns and silos, acres of fields. Though it was a national holiday, men and women and children were out hoeing sugar beets. Liz felt Emma's presence everywhere, yet nowhere—a person known to many, but as just another German-Russian girl, though perhaps more ambitious than the rest.

Denver had its so-called high society. If there was an equivalent in Sterling, Liz was certain that it didn't include German Russians or Mexicans. The American dream was to strive for more than you were born to. But success was relative. For Emma, it must have seemed that the quickest route out of endless drudgery in the fields was to move to Denver.

❧∭❧

Back at the hotel, Liz took a quick bath in the small claw-foot tub, lay down for an hour. The hot air in the room was still. Beyond the open windows, a firecracker exploded. She checked her watch. Nearly four. She put on her remaining fresh blouse, her navy skirt, applied some lipstick, and set out for the Sterling city park, site of the celebrations.

The sky was bright blue with only a few wisps of cloud to the west. The dirt road was clogged with stop-and-go traffic as cars and trucks mixed with families toting picnic baskets on foot. The closer she came, the stronger the delicious odor of roasting pork became. There was an air of anticipation in the hot, dusty air.

A half-mile from the South Platte River, the park was two acres of mowed weeds edged by an irrigation ditch lined with cottonwoods. Women in starched cotton or gauzy flowered dresses, who looked as if they might live in the white frame houses she'd passed coming into town, were arranging platters of food on tables fashioned from planks and sawhorses and covered with red-and-white-checked tablecloths. Three swarthy, dark-haired men in sweat-stained undershirts, who she guessed were Harlan's hired hands, slowly turned the handles of the spits that held the roasting pigs. Fat dripped onto the glowing coals, sending up a screen of smoke. Huge cast-iron pots filled with water were hung from crossbars. Near boiling, the water would be ready for fresh ears of corn when the meat was almost done. Girls in long-waisted cotton dresses played skip rope. Boys wearing knickers and sporting fresh haircuts chased each other around the base of a flagpole topped by an American flag. Their fathers, in straw boaters or wide-brimmed Stetsons, stood together, off to one side, smoking and probably talking beef prices.

Harlan had said that the entire town was invited. Yet except for the hired hands, the crowd was lily-white, their speech unaccented. The Klan would have loved it.

Suddenly, the loud blast of an automobile horn sounded. All heads turned toward the road, where an open-topped, brand-new Buick touring car rolled to a stop. Liz was not surprised to see Al Riddle behind the wheel, his straw boater tipped at a rakish angle. Next to him was a giant of a man with thick white hair beneath a pearl-gray Stetson. C.J. Harlan was sitting in the back, wearing the white Stetson she remembered from the rodeo. Beside him was a rather pretty woman, presumably his wife, in her late forties, wearing a flowered voile dress and a wide-brimmed straw hat with blue ribbon trim. The lead characters in what was no doubt a carefully orchestrated drama had arrived.

ᘓᕣᕊᕈ

C.J. made no move to get out of the spotless touring car until Al had hurried around to open the passenger door for Mr. Trotter. Only then did C.J. open his own door and offer a hand to his wife, Miriam. Mr. Trotter was already shaking hands when C.J. joined him, leaving Miriam to gab with several women who rushed up to her.

Alert to every cue, C.J. followed behind the old man as he worked the crowd. The head thrown back over a joke called for a laugh, or at least a broad smile. A deep frown and slow shaking of the head were appropriate for tales of cattle lost or a dried-up well. Phil Trotter—mention the name and doors opened. His word and a handshake were better than any written contract. It had taken C.J. close to forty years—from the time he was barely big enough to sit behind a plow—of licking Trotter's boots to get where he was today.

Hard work was the old man's byword. God knows, C.J. had proved himself on that score. Trotter had slowly given him more jobs, responsibilities, testing him. Once, during the dead of winter out in a line camp, C.J. had almost frozen to death. Finally, Trotter invited him to the house for Sunday dinner. C.J. soon became a regular. But he had bided his time, moving his way up, before beginning to court Trotter's daughter, Miriam.

She'd been a slender, shy girl then, anxious to please. The kind who lay under you and stared at the ceiling, never objecting but silently waiting for it to be over. He and Miriam had never had children. For a while, she'd nagged him gently about adopting. It was true that a kid or two would have complemented the image he was building. But he wasn't about to have a mongrel take his name.

C.J. saw the sweating band members done up in bright blue uniforms coming this way. He tapped the old man on the shoulder, nodded toward the musicians, and Trotter went over to them, greeting each by name. Then C.J. gave Jim Dobbins, who doubled as the high school music teacher, the high sign. The band members took up their instruments. People sat down on blankets, ready for the show to begin.

The opening number was "I'm a Yankee Doodle Dandy." Already in a festive mood, the audience sang along with gusto. Next up was "My Country 'Tis of Thee." At the end of the third verse, Mr. Trotter stepped to the fore. The band put their instruments aside. An expectant hush settled over the crowd.

"Friends, most of you have known me all your lives. You've been to my house, eaten at my table."

Smiles. Nodding heads. Scattered applause.

"You also know C.J. Harlan, who came to the Circle D when he wasn't old enough to spit."

Laughter. C.J. smiled. Out of the corner of his eye, he spotted the woman reporter—in a skirt and blouse this time—sitting on a picnic bench. Will Miller from the *Advocate* was beside her.

"I threw everything I had at the boy. Work makes or breaks a man, young or old. C.J. Harlan passed the test. Passed it with flying colors."

More clapping. Some whistled through their teeth.

"Well, you know the story as well as I do, friends." He glanced at Harlan, his famous blue eyes sparkling with what passed for affection. "They tell me you own half of Sterling now, C.J."

He glanced modestly at his boot tops. The old man was a pro.

"But C.J. is more than a successful rancher and businessman, he is a faithful husband to one of the loveliest ladies in all Colorado—my daughter."

Much clapping as he stretched his hand toward Miriam, who came to stand by her father. "With Miriam at his side, C.J. Harlan will fight for the ideals of our Founding Fathers and against those who would turn us into a godless nation." The old man beamed at C.J.

"So today, on the occasion of this gathering to celebrate our great country's birthday, I am pleased—indeed, honored—to announce that I will place in nomination at the Logan County Republican assembly the name of C.J. Harlan for the high office of state senator."

As if on cue, every man, woman, and child in the park stood, clapping and shouting their approval. C.J. shook the old man's hand.

Then, with an arm around Miriam's shoulders, C.J. waved to the crowd. His campaign was off to a good start.

The *Advocate* would give it front-page coverage. But he wasn't fool enough to expect much out of the *Post*. Still, just making his candidacy known outside Logan County was enough for now. The woman served his purpose.

The clapping continued until C.J. signaled for quiet. "Friends, if anyone here is honored today, it's me. Mr. Trotter has taken me into his family, given me his beautiful daughter as my wife. As the Bible says, my cup runneth over."

He looked into one face after another. He had them. "But before we go load up our plates, I want to leave you with a promise. Give me your votes, and I pledge to see that this county—this state—is returned to the American way."

Liz scanned the cheering crowd. They loved it.

"Now, let's eat!" And he and the old man led the crowd to tables laden with food. The band started up again. The mayor gave a speech. A few people gathered up their picnic baskets and headed for their wagons. Most lingered for more free food. C.J. went on shaking hands.

Liz got up from her bench beneath the cottonwoods, dusted off the back of her skirt. Harlan was made to order for the Grand Dragon's purpose. Smooth as syrup. The implication behind his innocent-sounding words was crystal clear to any Klan members in the crowd; everyone else would soon figure it out.

Without his tan, Harlan might have passed for an officer at the local bank. He spoke well. His fingernails were clean. But he still had enough rough edges to suit the local residents. A man that other men would look up to. Interviewing his wife would complete the story. Besides, she was the one who'd hired Emma.

Liz finally spotted Miriam Harlan in the center of a small circle of beaming women. Her own smile looked more like a grimace. Liz walked over to the women and identified herself. "I hate to interrupt, but I have a few questions for Mrs. Harlan." Taking her gently but firmly by the elbow, Liz guided her toward a vacant bench before the women could object.

Miriam Harlan glanced at Liz uncertainly. "Are you sure you don't mean to talk to Mr. Harlan?"

"Never surer." Liz began with standard questions about Mrs. Harlan's activities in the church and community, where she'd gone to school. Once she started talking, Mrs. Harlan relaxed. She'd taught Sunday school, rolled bandages during the war, and was raising money for a new flagpole at the high school.

Liz flipped to another page. "And will you be campaigning with Mr. Harlan?"

"Oh, this business of politics is really for men, don't you think?"

"What about the women's vote?" Liz asked.

Miriam Harlan looked puzzled.

"I mean, how does your husband plan to persuade women voters to cast their ballots for him?"

"Oh, I'm sure C.J. has that all worked out." Miriam Harlan smiled. "You see, my husband takes care of business. And now there's the campaign. It's my job to take care of the home."

"I see."

"That's just how it should be." She must have caught Liz's skepticism because she added, "Some might think that's old-fashioned. But C.J. and I call it God's will."

Liz kept a straight face as she jotted down a few words, then looked up. "If you don't mind, I'd like to shift the conversation."

"Of course."

"Mrs. Harlan, I was told you employed a girl named Emma Volz last summer as a cook."

Miriam Harlan's blue eyes went sharp. "Someone told you wrong, then. Emma was the upstairs maid."

"And that would have been when?"

"Miss O'Brien, I don't mean to be rude, but I don't see what a hired girl has to do with anything."

"I apologize. I should have explained. Emma Volz was murdered in Denver several weeks ago. I'm attempting to get information about her background."

"I'm sorry to hear that. About the murder, I mean. I truly am," Miriam Harlan said in a tone that belied her words. "But I have to tell you that I have no good memories of Emma Volz. I gave that girl a job. A room of her own. And what did she do but up and quit last August, right before my bridge party—which she knew I'd been planning all summer—with no reason, and without so much as a day's notice."

"Do you know where she went?"

"I have no idea. There was talk among the help that she'd gone to Denver. Frankly, I didn't care." Stiff-backed, Miriam Harlan got up.

"I suggest you speak to my husband if you want any further information. Now you'll have to excuse me."

Liz watched her return to the other women. The mere mention of Emma's name had soured a reasonably friendly conversation. Mrs. Harlan had bristled with resentment or anger, or both. Whatever the reason for Emma's departure, if Miriam Harlan knew, she wasn't saying.

As dark descended, kerosene lamps, their wicks glowing white beneath glass chimneys, were set out on the makeshift tables where C.J. Harlan was still deep in conversation with a group of men.

A bat swooped over the treetops as Liz made a last tour of the park. She could go from person to person, asking about Emma, but decided against it. Then she thought of Al Riddle. She had a feeling that he was holding back. If he drove to Denver as often as he bragged he did, he could have run into her, if not at the speakeasy, then somewhere else, or met someone who had. Maybe with a gentle shove . . .

Liz looked around at the dim figures scattered in the dark, but didn't see him. He was probably stationed with the touring car. She walked carefully across the uneven grassy stubble toward the road. As she drew nearer to the line of cars, she heard a man's cocky laugh. Harlan's Buick loomed just ahead. Al Riddle, bareheaded and in shirtsleeves, was perched on one of the front fenders, talking to cronies. The tip of the cigarette stuck in one corner of his mouth moved like an orange firefly in the dark.

As Liz walked closer, he waved. "Hey, if it ain't Miss O'Brien, lady reporter." His friends turned and stared at her as she approached. "Boys, I'm about to get my name in the paper."

The men laughed, looking expectantly from Al to Liz.

"As a matter of fact—if you don't mind—I'd like to ask you a couple more questions," she said.

He glanced at his friends. "Get lost, boys. I'll meet ya over at the pool hall later."

He and Liz watched the men drift off into the dark. When they were well out of earshot, she said, "It's about Emma's murder."

"I figured." He dropped his cigarette butt, ground it out, leaned back against the car.

"That day when Emma was in the speakeasy—"

He crossed his arms. "Hey, I thought I told ya I wasn't there."

"I know what you told me." Liz paused. "Al, I have to level with you. The district attorney wants to solve Emma's murder in the worst way. He has reason to believe that the same cops who came into the speakeasy the day before Emma was killed might be involved in her murder."

"Not good." Al shook his head. Then, as if stalling for time, he fished for the mangled package of cigarettes in his shirt pocket. He shook another one out, stuck it in his mouth, and ran a wooden match across the seat of his pants. Cupping his hands against the breeze, he lit the cigarette. She was willing to wait.

One eye closed against the smoke as he exhaled, Al hitched himself up onto the fender again, leaned back expansively against the hood. Finally, he said, "Listen. You and me's friends. For the record, the last time I saw Emma was in Sterling. But if it'll help nail those cops, I'll let you in on how it was. See, I admit I stop in for a couple of drinks at places once in a while when I drive Mr. Harlan into Denver or go for parts. One of 'em's just off Broadway. That's where I bumped into Emma and saw the cops roust her and her friends."

Liz couldn't hide her smile. Finally, the D.A. would have his witness.

"It was five, six o'clock. I don't see Emma right off. There's a bunch of people at the bar. A lousy band, but better than nothin'. I get a drink, look around. That's when I see her. You coulda knocked me over, I was that surprised. I go over. We start to talk." He nodded, remembering how it had been.

"And?"

"Then wham! In come a couple of cops."

"Were they in uniform?"

"Plainclothes. Said they was detectives. Flashed their badges. Acted real big."

"What did they do?"

Al shot her a look. "They said they had to take us in unless we made it worth their while."

"Then what?"

He laughed. "What else? We paid up. Bartender. The band. Me. The whole shootin' match. Ten bucks a head. Which ain't hay. I can buy me a good suit for that much. Anyway, everybody coughs up except for Emma and her pals."

Liz could hardly believe her good luck.

"Did you catch the cops' names?"

"Nope."

"But you could identify them? The district attorney needs you to testify."

Al dropped his cigarette on the road, rubbed it out with the heel of a shoe. "Not a chance. It's bad enough I told you. If those cops killed Emma and I stand up there and finger 'em, I'll end up a dead man before the day's out."

🕊

Back at the hotel, Liz stood at her window and looked down at the deserted street. Only a dog's persistent yapping interrupted the quiet. Her wristwatch said it was only a little after ten, but once the festivities were over, Sterling had closed down tight.

Tomorrow she would drive back to Denver. But she couldn't sleep until she'd put some order to the information she'd gathered, sorted through the conversation she'd had with Al Riddle. How did it all fit in with Emma Volz? She sat down on the edge of the narrow bed and reached for her notebook. She tipped the shade on the bedside lamp to give herself more light. Leafing through the pages, she began to see a timeline of events, a flesh-and-blood Emma Volz.

Emma had left Sterling late last summer or in early fall. Everyone Liz had talked to—Carl, Al Riddle, the newspaper publisher, Fanny—agreed that she had been a hard worker, savvy, a girl who had grown up with nothing, endured a brutal father, and tried to care for her younger brother. Her last known place of employment had been the Harlans' as a housemaid.

Liz closed her notebook, set it on the bedside table, turned off the light, and undressed in the dark. She still might persuade Al to identify the two cops. As to the Klan, whether they were out here, a hundred miles from Denver, she couldn't say. Certainly, some of the rhetoric was there in Harlan's speech. But his campaign to clamp down on roadhouse booze and heavy petting in parked cars was a far cry from wiping out Catholics and Jews and eliminating big-time crime.

19

The midmorning sun was already hot when Frank pulled open the screen door and ducked slightly to clear the low door frame of the restaurant's back storeroom. Worried half out of his mind about his family, he'd begged off the last two days of his mail run, using personal emergency as an excuse.

Shelves neatly stacked with cans of tomatoes, tin canisters of olive oil, jars of black olives, and sacks of flour lined the walls. A slight breeze stirred the sprigs of drying basil that hung by the window, perfuming the air. He headed for the open door to the kitchen and inhaled deeply. There was nothing like his mother's thick-crusted bread fresh out of the oven, particularly after a week of eating sandwiches and Nebraska café food.

His mother, a white apron around her waist, was bending over the long table in the center of the room, carefully laying out squares of ravioli on snow-white toweling to dry. He walked up behind her. Before he could wrap his arms around her and hug her, she looked around at him with red-rimmed eyes. She was crying.

"Oh, Frankie. I prayed you would come. I think it is the end for sure now."

He placed his hands on her shoulders, turned her gently so that she was facing him. "Mama, it can't be that bad. Sit down." He dragged a chair over. "Rest yourself. Tell me."

She looked past him. "He is out there, talking to Papa."

"Who's out there?" he asked, settling his mother into the chair.

"I listen when I cut out the noodles. He says he can help us now that Mr. Fanzini is arrested."

"Mr. Fanzini was arrested?" Frank felt a flicker of alarm. After Prohibition came in, Dom Fanzini had continued to supply them with the red wine he made in his basement. Every Friday, Papa and Father

Joseph from St. Catherine's would take the streetcar to pick up their orders: a single bottle for Communion, disguised in a paper bag, and several jugs for "medicinal purposes" in a cardboard box for the restaurant. It was poor wine, but it was better than nothing for loyal customers who claimed they couldn't digest their pasta without it. To sell or serve wine was against the law, but people still drank. He thought of the flow of Scotch and French brandy at the Stanley Hotel only a week ago.

Frank squatted so he could look into his mother's eyes and took her small, work-worn hands in his. "When was Mr. Fanzini arrested?"

"When you were away." She sniffed. "Then today comes this other man." Fresh tears coursed down her lined cheeks. Frank dug his handkerchief out of his back pocket and handed it to her.

"What other man, Mama?"

She nodded toward the door. "I told you. The one in the dining room. He's there with Papa."

"Is he a policeman, Mama?" he asked gently.

His mother dabbed at her eyes. "I don't know. Maybe."

He pulled her slowly to her feet and put his arms around her, patting her back. "Stop worrying. I'll go see what's going on."

🏵

The instant Frank left the kitchen, he heard the visitor's voice: deep and rough, that of a man who had spent a lifetime drinking hard liquor. He was sitting at one of the tables, across from Papa. Frank couldn't see the man's face. Whoever he was, he was big—well over six feet—with broad shoulders. Heavyset, he overflowed the wooden chair. One leg was crossed over the other. Relaxed, as if he were paying a social call.

Papa was shaking his head. Shoulders hunched, forehead furrowed, and hands clasped together: he was obviously miserable. Small and slight in contrast to his hulking visitor.

The man must have heard Frank's footsteps because he looked around. The dark eyes above a yellow-toothed smile gave Frank a quick once over, as if sizing him up in a fight. The guy had on a rumpled brown suit that he probably wore year-round. He looked like a cop.

Frank met his smile and crossed over to his father. "What's your business, friend?"

"I was just sayin' to Mr. Capillupo here that I think I can help him out with his problem."

Frank drew a chair close to his father. "What problem's that?" Frank asked, pleasantly enough.

The big man recrossed his legs, and Frank noticed the boots—cowboy boots with silver-tipped toes. Mother of God. He forced himself not to stare. Boots like that were one-of-a-kind. Frank had seen them in the flickering light of a bonfire. The image of the man who had administered the Klan oath—tall enough so that the hem of his robe stopped at his shins, revealing boots with pointy toes capped in silver—was one Frank would never forget.

"Here's the deal—it's Frank, isn't it?"

Frank nodded, increasingly wary.

The big man placed a beefy hand over his knee, kneading it as if to emphasize his strength. "Many's the time I've eaten Capillupo spaghetti. Hell, Capillupo's is an institution. What does it hurt—a little *vino* for special customers? So when the word got out that the feds closed down Dom Fanzini's little operation the other day, I said to myself, 'Joe, you gotta step in and help.'"

"And how would you do that? Sorry, what's the name?"

"Joe. We're friends here. Am I right?" The man trailed his yellowed-toothed smile from Papa to Frank. "You understand it won't be cheap. It may cost ya, but . . ." He shrugged expansively. "It's worth it."

Papa shot Frank a desperate look. "The price is triple, Frank. I can't pay."

"Prices keep goin' up. I've got my own costs. You know how it is," the bully said.

"And if we don't take you up on your offer—Joe?"

"Let me explain like I did to your pa. A word from me and the feds will forget how you've been bringin' in booze here since '17, when the state first went dry, and about your deal with Fanzini."

Frank stroked his chin. He'd had his run-ins with crooked cops before, but not cops who belonged to the Klan. First it was Maria. Now the entire Capillupo family. Frank didn't need a scorecard to know that the shakedown was only the beginning of what would soon become a reign of terror. Face it. There was no trench deep enough to hide from these animals. The only way out was over the top, with guns blazing.

"A hundred bucks." The bully got up, and Frank caught sight of the revolver in his belt. "Cash every Tuesday night. Starting next week."

Frank watched the cop stride out the door, letting the screen door slam behind him. The Capillupos had never paid protection money—not to the local mafioso who roamed Little Italy or to the police. They sure as hell weren't going to start with the KKK.

20

Liz slowed as she turned onto Washington Street and checked her watch. One-thirty. She'd left early. Still, she'd made good time, in spite of the horrible roads from Sterling. Her stomach growled, reminding her that she'd skipped breakfast. She was thinking about what might be in the cupboard as she pulled into her driveway and caught sight of the large circle of blackened grass.

She yanked on the emergency brake, bolted out of the car, and ran toward the center of her front lawn. Dropping to her haunches, she ruffled the blackened patch of grass in search of embers that might set off another fire. But the stubble was cool to the touch. She stood, drew a shaky breath.

Ever since her interview with the Grand Dragon she'd half expected that sooner or later the Klan would come after her. When they managed to have Maria Capillupo fired, Liz was sure it was only a matter of time. But a burning cross? If they had intended to frighten her, they were doing a very good job.

She glanced toward the garage and thought of Jake. From his vantage point in the apartment, he might have seen the Klan in full regalia. He was such an earnest young man; he might even have rushed out to try to stop them.

Her hands flew to her mouth. It had never occurred to her. Jake Steinberg was a Jew, as much a Klan target as she was. And there was a covenant against Jews living in this neighborhood. The burning cross had been a warning to them both.

Imagining the worst, she raced to the garage, pushed open the side door, and took the stairs to the apartment two at a time.

"Jake!" She burst into the room, expecting to see his bruised and battered body stretched across the bed. But the bed hadn't been slept in. Nothing was amiss. Maybe he had seen the Klansmen and managed to slip downstairs and out into the dark. If anyone knew what had happened to him, it would be his boss, Mildred Loggin.

✺

The moment Liz stepped into the reception area and saw the secretary's red-rimmed, bloodshot eyes, she knew something was very wrong. An instant later, Mildred Loggin appeared.

"Ah, Miss O'Brien. I didn't know how to get in touch with you. I take it you discovered your front lawn. I received the same treatment. Fortunately, I wasn't home, either."

"And Jake?"

"He's at Denver General. The Klan did its best to kill him. And from the seriousness of his condition, they still might succeed."

"What happened?"

"I'm not sure, but from what I was told by the police, he must have rushed out like a damn fool to keep the fire from spreading. The Klan jumped him, broke both his arms and his ribs. The doctors say there is a skull fracture. The damage was probably done by blackjacks. According to the nurses, he hasn't regained consciousness."

Liz sank into the nearest chair. "Who found him?"

Mildred Loggin's mouth twisted into an ironic smile. "The police. Seems one of your neighbors telephoned to complain about the noise. Can you believe it? The Klan is burning a cross on a neighbor's lawn and beating the hell out of a man, and someone complains about the noise!"

"It's my fault," Liz said.

"I'm not sure that matters now."

"I knew it was against neighborhood covenants to sell to Jews, but it never dawned on me that renting a room to one would be a problem." She let her breath out slowly. "If anything happens to him . . ."

"It already has, Miss O'Brien."

Liz stiffened.

"But don't worry. There's plenty of stupidity to go around. Jake Steinberg is a lawyer, a Jewish lawyer, who knew damn well about your neighborhood covenants. If he didn't, he should have." Miss Loggin walked toward the door. "I'm going over to the hospital. You can come with me if you wish."

✺

Denver General was an aging three-story stone building south of Cherry Creek, rising up from a neighborhood of shabby rooming houses. The hospital's patients were the poor and injured people of Denver whom the police picked up. Respectable citizens never ventured through its door. Liz had been inside only two or three times, on assignment.

The cloying smell of disinfectant permeated the cool, dark hallways. The wooden stairs sagged and creaked beneath her feet as she and Miss Loggin went up to the men's ward on the second floor. They asked a white-capped nurse at the nurses' station if they could visit Jacob Steinberg.

She gave them a careful look. "Are you members of the family?"

"Friends," Miss Loggin said before Liz could answer.

"Then, I'm afraid . . . Doctor said no visitors."

"Can you at least give us a progress report?" Miss Loggin asked.

"His injuries are severe, but youth is on his side." From beyond the door to the men's ward came a plaintive voice calling for water. The nurse stood.

"Mr. Steinberg will be all right, won't he?" Liz asked.

The nurse gave Liz a professionally sympathetic smile. "The next few hours will tell. But it wouldn't hurt to pray," she said, and disappeared through the door.

Mildred Loggin turned to Liz. "You needn't wait. I called Jake's parents when I was contacted by the police. They're probably on their way over now."

Liz nodded, glad for an excuse to leave. Waiting at bedsides made her feel like a ghoul. If Jake needed anyone now, it was his family.

"But come by the office later this afternoon, if you would," Miss Loggin said. "We need to talk. And by then we may know more about Jake's condition."

Outside in the brilliant sunlight, Liz couldn't shake the image of the charred circle of grass. Jake could have been doing something innocuous one day, like cutting the lawn, and introduced himself to a passing neighbor, who told his wife about the young man with the Jewish name at the O'Brien place. And his wife told . . . who? Good Lord, neighbor spying on neighbor, then standing back, silent, to await the ensuing violence.

With considerable effort Liz pulled herself together and drove downtown to the *Post*. It had been nearly a week since she'd left Denver. Mr. Ware would expect a full report. As she walked into the newsroom, she saw nothing had changed: the sound of men's voices, the banging of typewriters, the incessant shrill of ringing telephones.

She glanced at Harry Teaks's desk. If anyone had the skinny on the cross burnings, he would. But his desk was clear, and there was no sign of him.

She looked across the room to see Mr. Ware frowning at her. She walked over and took the chair next to his desk.

"You don't have the sense God gave a demented cockroach, renting a room to a Jew."

Liz didn't admit mistakes easily. "You heard."

"Harry told me."

The city editor heaved a great sigh, pushed to his feet, and walked toward his favored thinking spot—the watercooler. She followed him, as she knew he expected, feeling the eyes of her fellow reporters. Mr. Ware must have felt them, too, and he glared back. There was a reluctant stirring. The click of typewriters slowly resumed.

At the watercooler, Mr. Ware stuck a paper cup under the spigot and filled it, drinking the contents in one gulp. He tossed the cup in the wire wastebasket and led her to the open fire escape door, with its view of the alley.

She waited. Below them a peddler pushed a cart full of rags. Now and then he stopped to investigate trash bins by the buildings' back doors, pulling something out now and then and adding it to the mound of rags.

She pulled back her shoulders. "Mr. Ware, if you're thinking of firing me, I won't go quietly."

He didn't reply.

"Has Mr. Bonfils said anything?"

"Not yet."

"Surely, two burning crosses in a single night must convince him the Klan isn't something we can just ignore." Liz said. "In the Klan's grand plan for Colorado, I'm a nobody, but it's obvious that this outfit pays attention to details. It certainly won't tolerate a woman—a single Catholic woman at that—working for a major newspaper and running around the state asking questions. The burning cross was only a warning.

"So, a Catholic woman here, a Jew there. And before anyone realizes what has happened, the Klan will control Denver—in fact, the entire state."

Mr. Ware contemplated her with that familiar look that told her he was way ahead of her. But it didn't stop her.

"As a matter of fact, I met a man up in Sterling—C.J. Harlan—who's running for the state legislature. I interviewed him. He's sharp, as ambitious as they come. Worse, he has KKK practically tattooed on his forehead. For all I know, he could be a confidante of the Grand Dragon. Lord only knows how many more like him are out there. They're magnets, drawing in the lost or disgruntled like so many iron filings."

Sighing deeply, Mr. Ware drew a huge handkerchief from his back pocket and mopped his perspiring forehead.

She swallowed hard. "As far as the Volz case is concerned, I've always thought some of the police are KKK. The detectives who shook down the speakeasy are probably among them. The Klan's agenda suits their purpose—getting rid of the D.A. If they didn't kill the Volz woman, they most certainly killed Patrolman Ryan."

The city editor shifted his gaze back to the alley, and she held her tongue. But after a few moments, she grew impatient. "I got the rodeo story. I think you'll like it."

He still didn't reply.

"After Harlan is nominated, I'd like to do a story about him and use the interviews and his Fourth of July speech as background."

Mr. Ware glanced back at her. "Did I mention that you don't have good sense?"

"Yes, sir, you did."

"It's true." She couldn't read his look. "Nevertheless, since you have the rodeo story, you might as well hand it in."

"Yes, sir." She braced herself for reassignment to the society page, at the very least.

"Then for Lord's sake stay out of sight for a while, at least until I figure out the lay of the land."

❧❧❧

The secretary told Liz that Miss Loggin was waiting for her in the library. Without so much as a hello, she waved Liz to a chair across the long mahogany table and lit up a cigarillo.

"Any word from the hospital?" Liz asked.

"Jake's holding his own. That's about all the nurse will say. I'd follow her advice and light a candle for him, if I were you." Miss Loggin pulled a thick file folder toward her. "Jake left extensive notes. I want to go over them." She drew deeply on the cigarillo and then removed a stack of papers from the folder, squinting at the pages through the smoke. "Here. He says he went to the Northside substation on June 18 at my request to secure the release of four women being held for questioning. He talked to the two detectives—Joe Bentliff and Ed Neihouse—who brought the women in. The detectives claimed the women's records—solicitation and prostitution—were sufficient grounds to book them. Jake insisted on talking to the women alone. They told him they'd only been having a drink. Of lemonade. In a social club."

Liz said, "Jake also mentioned that Emma ran into someone from home. I met the man in Sterling, and he corroborated what Jake told me, except that the man said it was a speakeasy."

Mildred Loggin acknowledged the information with brisk nod, tapped the silvery ash from the cigarillo into the ashtray at her elbow, and flipped to the next page. "Again according to Jake, the women stated that the detectives demanded payment of ten dollars from each person on the premises. When the women refused to pay, the detectives took them in." She looked at Liz. "Nothing new about cops on the take in Denver. What *is* new is their connection with the Klan. The two in question are members, of course."

"Don't we need proof?" Liz asked.

"It'll come. For now, I'm going on instinct and experience. The way I see it, the Klan is the detectives' insurance policy. Van Cise campaigned to eliminate crooked cops from the force. His career hangs on this case. He has to nail the detectives and Emma Volz's murderer, which is turning out to be a difficult task. If he fails, he may well be recalled, the Klan will replace him with their own man, who'll look the other way and allow the detectives to go scot-free. Their extortion racket will continue, and God knows what else will go on."

"Like the cross burnings."

Miss Loggin nodded. "Fortunately, the Klan isn't very bright. They chose the wrong women to intimidate."

Liz had to smile.

"But back to the police. I agree with your hunch that the detectives at the speakeasy were involved with the Volz murder—and probably with the death of the Irish Catholic policeman." Miss Loggin sat back. "The point is this, Miss O'Brien. Despite what you may think about some of my clients, they have no more use for the Klan than we do. Partly because the Klan intends to muscle into their territory."

Liz pursed her lips.

"You're surprised I would admit such a thing, aren't you? Well, consider this: my clients know better than most that once the Klan gets members elected to the bench and the state legislature and controls the police and the city councils, habeas corpus and due process will be things of the past. My clients will be victimized just as surely as the so-called honest citizens. Count on it."

The older woman paused, picked up her cigarillo. "So. I'll admit I find that what I am about to suggest more than a little awkward. Phil Van Cise is and always will be a nincompoop. I'm sure he has little use for me. And I don't really care. But the two of us must join forces to put a stop to this insanity."

"I couldn't agree more," Liz said, astonished at Miss Loggin's offer.

She ground out the cigarillo and pushed the ashtray aside. "Well, then. Don't just sit there, Miss O'Brien. Go tell him so. I have a law office to run."

❦

It was nearly six when Liz arrived at the D.A.'s office and found his secretary adjusting the cloth cover over her typewriter, preparing to go home.

At the sound of Liz's heels against the hardwood floor, she glanced over her shoulder, smiled. "He's still here. Go on in."

The instant Liz tapped on the door frame, Phil looked up from the pile of papers on his desk. "I've been trying all day to get hold of you. Come in. The commissioner told me about the Jewish kid and the crosses. I understand he was a roomer at your place?"

Liz nodded, rubbed the back of her neck. She felt a full-bore headache coming on. "A cross was also burned on Mildred Loggin's lawn."

"I heard."

"I just came from her office with a message." Liz repeated the attorney's proposal. "What'll I tell her?"

"Tell her thanks. I may call her."

"*May* call her?"

"If I need her."

"You think fighting the Klan is a one-man show?" Liz asked, astounded.

"It is as long as I'm the object of a recall."

"What's gotten into you? Are you afraid Mildred Loggin is going to hold a press conference and sully your sacred reputation with an offer of her support? Because if you are, you're stupid."

He gave her a frosty look.

"I realize you're handling all this yourself now, but you may be interested to know that I've found you a witness." She told him about Al Riddle. "He says he won't testify. He's afraid the cops will get to him. But you might talk him into identifying them from a lineup."

"That won't be necessary. I'll have him subpoenaed." Phil leaned back in his chair, smoothed his hair back with both hands, a satisfied smile spreading across his face. "God, Liz, this is great news! I'll have this Volz thing wrapped up in no time."

She eyed him wearily—he was arrogant one minute, ebullient the next. She wished she shared his optimism.

21

It was nearly eight, past dinnertime, when Liz pulled into the driveway and saw the Nash parked out front. Her heart did a little leap. She'd thought that Frank had gone back to his regular delivery schedule. The moment she stepped out of the car, he was beside her, gathering her into his arms and holding her so tight she nearly gasped. Whatever had brought him back to Denver wasn't good.

"The Klan's after my folks now," he said into her hair.

She pulled away. "Are you sure?" Whatever had been between them before they'd parted last week wasn't important anymore. "Come inside. I've got some iced tea in the fridge." She saw his dark anger and reconsidered. "Better yet, why don't I go get something from Granddad's cache in the cellar?"

"I'll go." Frank disappeared down the back stairs. A few minutes later he returned bearing a dusty bottle Liz recognized as one of the last bottles of French cognac. She went to the cupboard in the pantry and got two brandy snifters from the top shelf. The glasses were dirty, a testimony either to her poor housekeeping or to her priorities. Whichever it was, a thorough washing was in order before anyone drank from them. She reached for two jelly glasses instead.

"I decided to contact the feds and make a deal," he said as he opened the bottle. She held out the stout glasses, and Frank poured a generous splash into each.

"It was that or take matters in my own hands, which isn't the way to go." He told her about the man who had come into the restaurant—a cop, Frank was sure, intending to blackmail his father. "And the second I spotted those boots, I knew he was the guy I saw in Estes Park at the Klan initiation."

"The night you telephoned."

He nodded. "Big—six feet six, two hundred fifty pounds—wearing the same boots, with silver tips. Said his name was Joe. No last name."

"The description fits Joe Bentliff. He and his partner are investigating the Volz murder. I've been told they took payoffs at the speakeasy where Emma was picked up the day before. I'm not sure I ever noticed his boots, but he always seems to wear a brown suit." She sat down heavily in the nearest kitchen chair, took a generous sip of cognac and felt the amber liquid travel a fiery course down her throat. "In case you didn't notice, the Klan burned a cross on my front lawn last night. And on Mildred Loggin's."

"Jesus! Does the D.A. know?"

She nodded, and brought Frank up to date. "Phil truly thinks he has everything under control now that he has a witness. Wait till he hears about another police shakedown."

Frank took her hands in his. "At least we'll have the feds involved."

Liz wasn't sure that was much help. "Did they know about the wine you served?"

Frank's answer was a wry smile.

"What does your family get out of your cooperation?"

"That's being negotiated. The feds weren't going to give anything. I thought my flying might be worth something, but when I trotted it out, I discovered they were way ahead of me. They even knew my schedule. They've had their eyes on us for a good long while, I suspect."

"So?"

"They want me to track big operators."

"Let's go out on the porch. It's too hot in here." She took his hand and led him out through the dining room and onto the screened porch.

"I don't know whether you remember, Liz, but when Colorado went dry, most of the illegal stuff was locally made. In backyards, out in the sticks. As a matter of fact, some of the stills were up north in the Pawnee chalk cliffs near Grover. They used the sugar beets. Booze came in by the bottle then. Now it's coming in by the gallon and bottled in Denver. The feds know this because they're finding a uniform product. All the signs say the little man is out. The investment's too big, the risk too high."

Frank walked to the end of the porch and back. "The Treasury men say the trail begins in Canada, leads down through Montana and

Wyoming via Cheyenne, and eventually ends in Denver. But in the last year, they've noticed a change. Denver's supply has increased, and it's coming in bulk. The Treasury wants me to keep track of any patterns I see."

She said, "What if the stills in those chalk cliffs had started up again? With all the German Russians around there who loathe Prohibition and still raise sugar beets . . ."

"They'd have to be small-time. What the feds are after is a big operation with big money behind it. Midwest money, probably." He undid his collar button and pulled off his tie.

"I wouldn't discount the cliffs, Frank. The fellow I told you about—C.J. Harlan—and another man named Trotter are doing very well indeed. Trotter's acreage is huge, and Harlan's not far behind. He owns the ranch next to Greta's place, right up against the chalk cliffs. And he's got businesses in Sterling and the surrounding little towns."

Frank looked unconvinced.

"As low as prices are, Harlan couldn't be making much on cattle. And his other businesses certainly can't be all that prosperous. Yet he drives a new car, has a big house. He doesn't throw money around. He's too smart for that. He could be just the man you're looking for."

"Not according to the Treasury."

"That's because they don't know about him. Harlan's running for state senate. I'm almost positive he belongs to the Klan, which came out for Prohibition. Can you think of a better cover?"

"How would he get the booze out? The roads are poor at best. I doubt if there are any near the cliffs," Frank said.

"Harlan owns a Buick distributorship. His gofer, Al Riddle—the fellow who may testify about the cops—picks up parts in Denver every week. Maybe . . ."

Frank shook his head. "It'd be a lot cheaper to ship by rail."

"But that would mean loading it on the train, unloading at the other end. Too many people involved who might figure out what was going on."

"In other words, you think this Al guy is a runner."

"Yes." Liz took another sip of brandy. "Though he probably isn't the only one." She pictured the straw boater tipped back on his head, the swagger in his walk. "I think he's decent enough, but he's young. Small-town life has got to be dull for him. And running booze could be the excitement he's after."

Frank's face slowly filled with a wide grin. "Honey, you may just have something. Wait 'til I tell the Treasury boys."

"But what if we're wrong? Al may be running booze all on his own, without Harlan's knowledge. As many ranches as Harlan's said to own, there's no way he could keep up on their daily operations. With a legitimate reason to visit the Lazy J regularly, Al could pick up whiskey being made in the cliffs nearby. The caretaker is nearly blind. It would be easy."

Frank looked unperturbed. "Either way, the Treasury will see that Riddle could be the key to the big operator."

Liz frowned. "Except . . . the D.A. is counting on Al Riddle to testify. If he's a runner and the Treasury takes him in, our only link to Emma's murderers will be gone."

Frank put his hands on her shoulders. "Liz, the next time Riddle comes to Denver, he'll be in the D.A.'s jurisdiction. If he's carrying booze, the D.A. will have him just where he wants him. Doing time in a federal facility is no joke. Al Riddle will cop a plea and testify. You'll get your murderer. Depend on it."

He got up, stretched as if a great weight had been lifted off his shoulders. "I'm going to call my contact. In the meantime, how does steak at Zeke's sound?"

22

Frank parked the Nash next to the phone booth outside Shorty's Pool Hall on Larimer Street. The din from inside would discourage eavesdroppers. It seemed the safest way to contact the feds. After four rings, a man answered. Frank identified himself, explained that the matter was urgent, and outlined his plan to pick up Al Riddle. Frank was told to hold.

As he waited, he turned and saw Liz in the car. She was watching him, and he gave her an encouraging smile. A voice finally came back on the line. A man with brown hair, wearing white shoes and red socks and carrying a paper bag, would meet him at City Park Lake tomorrow morning at nine o'clock. The line went dead.

Frank hung up and walked to the car, shaking his head in disbelief. He felt like a goddamned spy. Wrong. He *was* a goddamned spy.

⧞

The lights were still on, but a Closed sign hung in the window of Zeke's Steak House when Frank rapped on the glass-fronted door. After a few minutes, a waiter emerged from the kitchen, ready to send whoever it was away. But one look at Frank and he opened the door, greeting him like a long-lost friend.

Frank clapped him on the shoulder, enjoying the benefits of his lingering fame as a former star for the Denver Bears. He introduced Liz. The waiter ushered them to a table, the whole time talking about the Bears' record. The preliminaries dispensed with, Frank ordered T-bones, medium rare. The waiter disappeared.

As soon as they were alone again, Liz fixed him with worried eyes. "This business of meeting a man with red socks sounds a little dramatic, don't you think?"

He breathed in the faint scent of her perfume. "The way I see it, I do what I'm told." He kissed her fingertips. "Maybe you should fill me in on what else you discovered at Greta's."

"Emma Volz grew up in Sterling. She and Al Riddle knew each other. Whether romance was involved, I couldn't really tell. She was German-Russian—a Rooshian, he called her. I suspect there's an iron-clad pecking order in Sterling, with German Russians at or near the bottom. Anyway, she'd worked since she was a kid. Her father was a drunk. He's in the pen. Her brother's on the rodeo circuit and didn't know his sister had been killed. The last time he'd seen her was last summer. Al Riddle claimed he got Emma a job at the Harlans'."

"I talked to Mrs. Harlan. I might be reading something into it, but I got the sense that Emma may have been pregnant when she quit or was fired and went to Denver."

"You think Harlan might have been the father?"

Liz gave a little shrug and idly twisted the stem of the water glass. "He certainly would have had the opportunity. But somehow it doesn't fit. The man is too smooth to jeopardize all those ambitions."

The waiter appeared with their dinner. The steaks were just the way Frank liked them—charred on the outside, pink inside. They must have weighed a pound each. There was barely room on the plate for the mashed potatoes and green beans.

His mouth watering, Frank picked up his knife and fork, cut into the slab of beef, took a bite, and sighed with satisfaction as he chewed. Then he noticed that Liz hadn't touched her food. "Aren't you going to eat?"

"I was just thinking. If there's a connection between Emma Volz's murder and Harlan, it's Al Riddle. He already admitted talking to her at the speakeasy the day before. All I have to do is pick up his trail after that."

ᾧᾠ

The next morning, Frank arrived at the lake in City Park half an hour early. He got out of the Nash and lit a cigarette. His was the only car. It was too early for the families who came to feed the ducks and swans. The air was still cool, the blue sky cloudless. Off in the distance, the shadowy, deep blue fringe of mountains edged the western horizon. Across the road, a fat robin hopped over the grass, pausing occasionally and cocking its head, alert for a worm. A brilliantly plumed blue jay shrieked in the elm overhead. If he hadn't been so nervous, Frank would have enjoyed the setting.

On the dot of nine, he saw a Ford coupe coming his way. The car parked about twenty feet from his, next to the path circling the lake. The man who climbed out was slender, clean-shaven with nondescript features. He wore a gray pinstriped suit that bagged at the knees and a well-worn fedora over light brown hair. Except for his white shoes and red socks, he was completely forgettable. He was carrying a brown paper bag.

Frank reached through his car window and retrieved the bag of bread crumbs he'd decided to bring at the last minute. He and the other man ambled to the edge of the lake. The man took a handful of bread cubes from his bag, tossed them over the water. Frank did the same. They watched the swans and ducks glide toward them.

"Nice day," the man said, without looking at him.

Frank tried for a smile. He wasn't sure how to proceed.

"The basic plan is fine, but we think it would be better to stay clear of the runner himself," he said. "More important is the time and day of the deliveries made, we presume, at the parts store. We'll take it from there."

"What about air surveillance?"

"We'll leave the details up to you." The man tossed another handful of crumbs at the birds, then walked to his car and drove off.

🕊

Two hours later Liz stood beside Frank in the hangar's small office and studied the well-creased maps—a 1920 railroad map and a topo map—spread across the battered desk. She'd been at him for hours until he gave in, admitting the logic that she should become directly involved with the Treasury's plan. She knew the territory around Grover, she said, and Frank didn't.

"The Harlan ranch is visible from Greta's house. I won't go near Al. I won't have to: I'll have my binoculars. I'll be able to keep track of his comings and goings. Where do you want me to phone you?"

"At the restaurant. If I'm not there, ask for Maria." Frank frowned. A lot rested on nabbing Al Riddle in the middle of a run. Frank didn't like involving Maria, but there was no way around it. And he worried about Liz. If she actually stuck to her plan, fine. The damn trouble was she might get it into her head to do more.

Liz placed a hand on his neck, massaging it gently. "Relax. I'll show you where Greta's place is on these maps. You'll know exactly where I am."

He glanced at her soft, smiling lips and knew he was beaten. "Okay. Put your finger on the spot."

"It's five miles northwest of Grover." She leaned over the topo map, traced a finger along the sheet. "Darn. These lines drive me nuts."

"They indicate elevation."

Liz looked up, grinned, and stuck out her tongue. Frank had seen her in action before. Give her a challenge and caution was thrown to the winds. "Let's see." She bent over the maps. "Half the length of my thumb is about an inch, which would mean Greta's place is right there."

Liz placed an index finger on a sliver of white space between ridge lines, then squinted. "And here: I think this is the road I use after I turn off the main drag between Greeley and Cheyenne."

Frank circled Greta's ranch with a red wax pencil, found the same spot on the railroad map, put an arrow next to the state highway where it joined with the county road to Grover.

Liz leaned stiff-armed on the desk and turned her head so she could see the bright red DeHavilland biplane parked in the center of the hangar. "Frank, I've always wondered—how do you know where you're going at night?"

He saw the worry in her eyes, smiled. "Honey, fliers are like sailors. They use the stars."

"But what if it's cloudy?"

He and Liz left the small office and walked toward the plane. "We carry a flashlight so we can check the map. The Post Office contracts with farmers at regular intervals along the route to set bonfires. We have emergency landing fields." Explaining the process, he realized how crude it sounded. It was. "By next year they're supposed to have rotating electric beacons and boundary markers. The new model DeHavilland will have illuminated instrument, navigation, and landing lights. The works." Frank put a hand on a strut.

"Can't you get a new one now?"

"Even if the money was there, the Treasury wants everything to look normal, like nothing has changed. That means flying the same old plane."

Liz gazed at the wing above them. "Even so, I think you should get Mr. Humphreys to buy a new one."

"He just bought this one." The hot breeze blew a piece of trash through the open hangar doors.

Liz trailed after him as he checked the carburetor and the spare tire under the fuselage. "I thought he wanted to impress potential investors," she said.

"He does," Frank said, inspecting the landing gear. About a month ago it had broken on the right side. He checked the repair, which had replaced steel with wood. It looked firm. He climbed up on the wing and eased into the front cockpit. He flicked a thumbnail against the glass on the booster-pump gauge, twisted around and checked the fuel tank between the cockpits.

"Frank?"

He pushed himself out of the seat.

"I should be going."

He jumped down, pulled a rag from the back pocket of his coveralls, and wiped his hands.

"I want to get up to Greta's before dark."

"Good idea." He walked her to the Buick, parked in the shade next to the hangar. "Remember. Phone me at my folks' place the minute you get a fix on the guy."

Frank slammed the door as she settled behind the wheel and pushed the starter button. Once the engine settled down, he poked his head through the open window and kissed her. The warmth of her lips on his made him want to pull her out of the car and make love to her. Instead, like a damn jackass, he was letting her risk her neck for him. "Don't take any chances, Liz."

"Ditto." She shifted into first.

Frank watched her drive away until all he could see was a plume of dust drifting off in the wind. Only then did he walk back to the hangar.

23

Twilight was fading into full dark when Liz finally turned onto the wagon tracks that led to Greta's house. Before she left, she had written a note to Mr. Ware, saying she was following up on a new lead and would be back in a couple of days.

As she drew closer, Liz saw the kitchen windows aglow. Greta and Bessie were probably having supper. There wouldn't be leftovers, and Liz was hungry. She hoped some of the peanut butter she'd brought a week ago was still left.

As Liz cut the engine, the back door opened and Greta stepped outside, framed in the light. "Guess who?" Liz called.

Grinning, Greta leaned back through the doorway and yelled for Bessie, who appeared a minute later, baby on one hip.

Liz clambered out of the car, gave Greta a quick hug, and smiled at Bessie.

"Well, what are ya waitin' for? Come on in and tell me the latest." Greta turned and headed back inside.

Liz eyed the empty supper plates on the kitchen table. "If you have any peanut butter left, I'll make myself a sandwich first."

"Don't look at me. Ask Bessie," Greta said.

"There's a little left. I put it away 'cause Greta said you might be back."

Liz looked at Greta and laughed.

"And I was right, was't I?" Greta carried the plates to the sink. "I gotta finish feedin'. When you're done eatin', I'll show you my porkers and we can talk."

Twenty minutes later, Liz picked her way across the dark yard on the way to the shed, pausing periodically to gaze up at the star-filled sky and the sliver of moon in their midst. No sounds of traffic, no barking dogs, not even a crying child. Only the whine of mosquitoes interrupted the quiet. The tranquil setting made it difficult to imagine that a bootleg operation connected with the Klan could be just a few miles off.

A lantern hanging from a hook in the center of the shed threw a wavering light over the white-faced milk cow placidly chewing hay. Greta looked up from mucking out the stall as Liz walked in. "Go take a look at my babies while I finish up here."

Liz dutifully inspected the pigs—porkers, as Greta called them. "What would you like me to say? That they're fat as pigs?"

"Go ahead, laugh. But you're lookin' at money on the hoof." Greta put the pitchfork aside. "Okay. Now tell me what's goin' on."

Liz started with her conversation with Al Riddle after the barbecue, when he'd admitted to seeing Emma in the speakeasy and paying off the cops. "He could be a key witness for the prosecution. But that's only the beginning. The Treasury is after a big bottling operation. They think it may be in Denver. Frank's agreed to help them find it. There's a good chance that the Klan is involved."

Greta leaned against the shed, folded her arms. "And you're here because they think the stuff's being made around here and Al is runnin' it."

"Exactly. The way I see it, no one pays any attention to Al's coming and going. It's part of his job. Delivering groceries, feeding Mr. Harlan's mules every week."

"Sounds about right," Greta said.

"Frank will do surveillance from the air. I'll be keeping track of Al here on the ground."

Greta lifted the lantern off the hook. "And it wouldn't hurt if we took a look around the cliffs ourselves. Anybody asks, I'll tell 'em we're chasin' stray cows."

～∭～

The following morning dawned bright and windy. Liz traded her slacks for a pair of Greta's Levi's. It was Monday—the day before Al Riddle's weekly visit to the Lazy J. The plan was to spend the day checking out the cliffs along the Lazy J, but only after they had Orlo Smith's permission: trespassing was a dangerous activity. Greta seated beside her in the Buick with a plate of buttermilk biscuits on her lap, Liz drove over to pay the foreman a call.

The moment they drew up to the ranch house, the door opened and the old man hobbled out.

"Mornin', Orlo," Greta called. "It's Greta. Miss O'Brien's back for another visit. We brought over somethin' for your breakfast."

Orlo came closer, squinted at the plate Greta held out the car window to him, and inhaled deeply. "I do believe them's biscuits."

"Bessie's best," Liz said.

They followed the old man inside, and he motioned them to the rough-hewn kitchen table, where he set the plate of biscuits. Removing the blue-and-white-checked napkin, he sat down and tucked it in the neck of his sweat-stained union suit.

"Say, Greta, go over to the cooler and get that butter you brung the other day. Biscuits are no-count without it. Seems like there's some preserves left, too."

Finally, with the butter and a jelly glass of wild plum preserves lined up next to the plate, Orlo reached for one of the lightly browned biscuits. For the next few minutes the only sound in the low-ceilinged room was the old man's sighs of contentment as he ate. Finally, he paused, looked across the table at them. "Ain't you girls havin' any?"

"We brought them for you," Greta said.

The old man beamed, reached for another biscuit. "Greta, that girl of yours can cook. You can tell her I said so."

"Bessie'll be obliged." Greta and Liz exchanged glances.

The preliminaries over, Greta said, "Orlo, a couple of my beef are missin'. Got through a hole in the fence, most likely. I was hopin' you wouldn't mind if I looked around your place for 'em."

Orlo Smith wiped his butter-smeared mouth with one end of the blue-checked napkin, chuckled. "I shoulda knowed them biscuits weren't free."

"Me and Liz thought we'd ride over today before it gets too hot."

The old man glanced at Liz. "Sure enough? You city girls ride?"

She laughed. "Let's just say we hang on."

Orlo guffawed, enjoying the little joke, and Liz felt a tug of guilt. They were using this lonely old man, betraying his trust, just as Al and, perhaps, C.J. Harlan were using him.

✢

Staples, pliers, and fence stretcher in her saddlebag, Greta took the lead on the roan, with Liz not far behind on the mare. From the instant she'd pulled into the saddle, the animal's ears had flattened against its head. One look, one whiff, and every horse instantly recognized her terror. She'd never understood how anyone could fawn over an animal nearly six feet high as if it were a house pet.

Liz pulled the wide brim of Greta's battered hat low against the glare of the midmorning sun. The wind was steady and from the east. Cauliflower-shaped clouds were moving fast across the blue sky. By now the Lazy J ranch house was on the other side of the ridge, out of sight. They rode single-file toward where the fence that divided Greta's property from Harlan's dead-ended at the buff-colored cliffs. The closer they came, the more uneasy Liz grew.

Greta reined in. Stiff-armed, she leaned one gloved hand against the roan's rump and waited for Liz. "We can go through here." She flung her left leg over the roan's withers, jumped down, and got her tools out of the saddlebag. She pulled the staples that held the strands of barbed wire from the adjoining fence posts, let them drop, and motioned for Liz to ride on through. Then she swung up in the saddle and followed behind on the roan.

Liz reached back and dug out the binoculars she had wrapped in a yellow rain duster tied behind the saddle. Craning her neck, she inspected the irregular piles of sandstone that formed the cliffs. "I hate to admit it, but I'm beginning to get cold feet."

"You wanna go back?"

"Not yet." Liz trained the binoculars on a windmill and a small corral with a cabin and shed a quarter of a mile or so away. "What's that over there?"

"A kinda line camp. Where Harlan keeps his mules. Maybe we should go take a look." Greta nudged the roan into a trot.

As they neared, Liz saw a water trough, a haystack next to the shed. The cabin was small, not much bigger than her bedroom in Denver. On the other side of it well-worn wheel tracks led back over the rise toward the main ranch house and outbuildings. Some cattle and a half dozen mules drank at the trough. From a distance the mules could be mistaken for horses, but their long faces and ears and lack of manes set them apart.

"Hello, the camp," Greta called, cupping her mouth against the wind. They waited. No answer or sign of anyone. Liz felt a wave of relief.

Greta reined the roan toward the water. The animals at the trough raised their heads, curious about the interlopers. A few drifted away. She and Liz slid off their horses and led them to the trough.

As the mare drank, Liz stared at the cliffs rising behind the shed. "Where do you suppose the fuel and sugar beets and stuff are stored?"

"At the still. Or maybe Al brings it in each week and puts it in that cabin."

"It's pretty small," Liz said doubtfully, handing the binoculars to Greta, who stowed them in her saddlebag.

The mules had moved to the shade of the shed. The remains of the hay thrown down earlier that morning lay strewn around them.

"Who do you suppose feeds the mules every day?" Liz asked.

"Orlo can't get down here. So it would have to be the fellas workin' the still."

A mule with a deep brown coat looked at Liz and Greta with huge brown eyes and began to bray. What began as something that sounded like a baritone horn slipped into a grating squeak. Another mule took up the call. The braying reverberated against the cliffs.

Liz glanced nervously toward the cabin. But no one appeared. Whoever lived there was deaf or gone. She inspected the shed. A pitchfork and shovel, a line of tack hanging from the wooden pegs. She went over to the tack. "What's all this for?"

"The mules." Greta came over, fingered the gear. "Looks first-rate. Double rigs, good wide tie straps. Even an extra cinch girth. These babies are meant to handle weight. I'd say the mules carry in the beets and the wood or coal, then bring out the booze."

"But where is it stored?"

They both gazed at the little cabin. And, with more than a little trepidation, Liz led the way across the hard-packed yard and knocked on the door. When no one answered, she cautiously lifted the latch and went in.

What she saw was not what she had expected. A bunk covered by a blanket was built into one wall. Next to it, on the floor, was a small humpbacked trunk. A calendar graced by smiling girl with bobbed blond hair and skirts raised above her knees was nailed to the wall above the bunk. A shirt and a pair of pants hung neatly from hooks. An orange crate tipped on its side to serve as a cupboard contained a few cooking utensils and some cans of tomatoes and beans. A rough wooden table and a single chair had been placed on a cracked piece of linoleum rug next to a coal heater. Clearly, whoever lived here had settled in—or that's how it was meant to look.

"Neat as a pin. Even a plank floor," said Greta.

"But not a box of booze or a sack of sugar beets."

Frowning, they surveyed the room.

"If it were bigger, it would probably have a cellar," Liz said.

Greta eyed the coal heater, which sat on a square of sheet metal. She and Liz exchanged glances. "What d'ya say?"

"It won't hurt to see." Liz grabbed the handle on one side, Greta the other, and with some grunts, they managed to lift the heater enough to move it off the square of sheet metal. It was no problem to push aside the linoleum rug. A round iron handle had been sunk flush against the plank floor. Greta grabbed hold and gave it a hard tug. Straining, she pulled up a trap door.

Liz peered over the edge into the darkness but couldn't see much. She jumped down onto the dirt floor, careful to keep her head low. Her eyes adjusted to the dim light. Forms became visible. "Greta! I found the sacks. And gas cans. One, two, three—ten of them."

"Empty or full?"

Liz tried to move one of the cans, leaned closer and sniffed. "Smells like alcohol to me." She felt one of the lumpy gunnysacks. "Could be the beets."

"Where's the coal?"

Liz felt the others. She had shoveled enough coal into her grandfather's old furnace to recognize the shape of the lumps. "It's here, too." She grinned at her friend. "Give me a hand up."

With particular care, they left everything exactly as they had found it, took one last look around, and left.

The wind had picked up, the clouds had the look of rain. "We better get on back," Greta said.

"What about the still?"

"You only found ten cans. That's gotta mean it's not much of an operation. Maybe it's not the place we're lookin' for," Greta said.

"It's one of them, though. There could be another dozen operations stuck in the cliffs all along here. Catch Al in the process of delivering supplies or bringing out the booze here, and he'll lead the Treasury to the others."

Greta shot her a doubtful look as she pulled up into her saddle, gathered the reins.

"Al can't be so loyal that he'd keep his mouth shut and go to jail willingly while the rest of the operation goes merrily on without him."

Liz struggled onto her horse and trained her binoculars past the corral. One hundred feet away were the cliffs.

"Could be anyplace in among those cliffs with an opening wide
enough for a cow or a mule. I'm beginning to think Frank's flyovers
won't help much. The still is probably so well hidden that there's no
way he'd see even a hint of it from the air."

"We need to look for mule manure. Spot the trail with the manure and the Treasury will have their still."

Liz couldn't hold back a smile. "Greta, you forget. I'm just a city
girl."

"Mule is little brown apples."

They nudged their horses to a walk.

"Greta, your father brewed beer. Besides the wood or coal for the
fire and sugar beets, what did he need?"

"Water."

"Of course. I should have thought of that."

Greta eyed her sardonically. "Liz, if you think we're gonna go up
every one of these draws lookin' for a spring, think again."

"Orlo gave us permission to hunt strays. That's what we're doing,"
Liz insisted.

"We could have our heads blowed off. Me, I wanna stay alive. I
say we find the mule manure and call it a day."

So they retied their hats against the wind and followed a sandy
trail sprinkled with cow pies and dried mule manure leading from the
corral. Less than a quarter mile later the trail turned into a draw.

Liz studied the hoof-marked path worn into the soil. It seemed to
beckon to her, despite the danger. She looked at Greta inquiringly.

"We're not goin' in there."

"Okay." Liz studied the cliffs looming overhead. "Is there a way
we could get up on top?"

"You mean on the butte?"

"If that's the top, yes. We could see the smoke from the still's fire
from there and tell how far back it is."

Greta eyed the darkening sky, then looked at Liz. "You're set on
this, are ya?"

"Well, not set on it. But . . ."

"Then we better get a move on."

🙢🙢🙢

The ride up onto the butte was agonizingly slow, the way steep in places, the trail narrow, switching back and forth. Keeping her head down against the wind, Liz clung to the saddle horn, giving the mare its head. The ground underfoot was rocky and loose. The horses stumbled several times. It seemed like a week had passed before Liz saw the top, and she leaned forward as the mare took a last lunge onto flat land.

The sky was black as they urged their horses to a trot, riding east along the edge of the treeless butte. Liz bounced along, her spine hammering against a saddle hard as concrete, envious of how easily Greta moved with her horse, as if she were sitting in a rocking chair. Liz tried posting, as she'd done in an English saddle years before, but her motion somehow didn't fit the horse's. She stood in the stirrups until her legs gave out.

Finally, mercifully, Greta glanced back at Liz and reined in. "This is open range, but we might as well be on Harlan land. I think we oughta go north here and follow along the top of the cliffs."

Guiding their horses close to the edge, they looked for any signs—they weren't quite sure what—of a bootleg operation. A roll of thunder echoed across the sky. The eerie gloom, or maybe days of relentless, drying heat, made the grass look gray. Then, ahead, where the butte's ragged edge curved like splayed fingers, Liz noticed a large patch of bright green. Water vapor. She kicked the mare to catch up with Greta.

"Look out there." She had to cup her mouth against the wind to be heard.

Greta reined in, looked toward the edge of the butte where Liz pointed. "The grass. See how green it is."

Lightning speared the gray-black sky. Several seconds later, thunder rumbled across the butte like a cannon's boom. The mare sidestepped, laid its ears flat against its head. Liz drew in the reins, terrified that the animal might bolt.

"I want to get closer," she yelled.

Greta regarded the sky. "I dunno. Right now we got a choice. Get killed by lightning or bootleggers."

But they continued to ride side by side, fighting to hold their nervous horses to a walk as they drew closer to the bright green grass. Liz couldn't see a chimney or stovepipe, but she was certain that a still was close by. She got off the mare and handed Greta the reins.

Leaning into the wind, Liz approached the fingers of rock, dropped on her haunches. The air felt moist, warmer here. She thought she could smell coal smoke.

Another blade of lightning was followed almost instantly by a crack of thunder. Liz stood, grabbed the mare's reins from Greta and pulled into the saddle.

Grim-faced, sitting the roan as it did a nervous dance, Greta shouted, "We gotta go."

Still Liz hesitated, trying to fix this place and its location in her memory, noting where the grass was green, where she had smelled the coal smoke. Suddenly, she heard men's voices beyond the wind. Her heart lurched. Greta held her horse still. She must have heard it, too. Liz thought the voices were growing louder.

Then, just as suddenly, the sky opened up. The rain came down in sheets, driven sideways by the wind. Liz held her hat brim down to shield her eyes, searching for a glimpse of whoever might be out there. The rain turned to hail. She felt the knifelike stings against the back of her hands, cutting through her blouse. The tiny crystals became thumbnail-size. She flinched as they struck. Now there was no holding the horses.

"Take your feet out of the stirrups, hang on, and let her go," Greta called.

And they raced back across the butte, Greta's head bent low along her horse's neck, Indian style, Liz desperately clinging to the mare's mane, the men's voices lost but not forgotten in the fury of hail.

24

The next morning dawned clear, the air fresh from the rain. It was Tuesday, Al's usual delivery day at the Lazy J. Yesterday, they'd made it back to Greta's, bruised and battered and soaked, pausing only long enough to repair the break in the fence. Whether the wild ride had turned up anything the Treasury could use remained to be seen. As planned, a few minutes before nine, Liz stood in Greta's yard and aimed her binoculars toward the ranch.

She didn't have long to wait before Al's truck turned in. She caught the license plate number easily, then shifted the binoculars to the truck bed, with its slatted sides. Inside was a box of what looked like groceries, several gunnysacks, and gas cans similar to those she had seen in the cellar. She began counting them, some fallen on their sides, some upright. Unsure of the number, she counted again. Still, she needed a closer look to be certain. She lowered the binoculars and ran toward the Buick.

Fifteen minutes later, Liz drew into the yard of the Lazy J and parked next to Al's truck. She climbed out, quietly closed the car door. If Al or Orlo appeared, she would say that she had come for Greta's plate and napkin. She made a show of brushing off her skirt and smoothing her hair as she peered into the truck bed. A dozen gunnysacks, ten cans with no distinguishing marks, exactly like those she and Greta had found. Al must have taken the box of groceries inside to Orlo.

Suddenly, a door opened. Liz whirled and saw Al in the doorway of the ranch house, grinning at her.

"Hey, the lady reporter again. I thought I heard that old clunker of yours pull up."

"Good morning," she said, her heart racing.

"Orlo was just sayin' you and Greta was over yesterday with biscuits."

"We were, yes. In fact, I came to pick up the plate and the napkin," she said, covering her nervousness with a smile.

"I hear you was also out huntin' down some cows."

She held onto her smile. "I haven't been on a horse for years. I can hardly walk today."

The direction of the conversation made Liz distinctly uneasy.

"Well, hey. I know right where the plate you're after's at," Al said, holding the door open for her as she went inside.

Orlo was sitting at the kitchen table, a half-eaten plate of eggs and sausage in front of him. Al must have been cooking.

"The reporter lady's back for her plate," Al said.

"And napkin," Liz added.

Orlo chuckled. "I figured it'd bring one of you girls back."

Liz was conscious of Al, arms folded, leaning against the sink, watching her.

"You can bring me over some more of those biscuits any old time," the old man said.

"I'll tell Bessie." Liz smiled, and looked from Orlo to Al. "Well. I have to go. It was good to see you again."

But Al followed her outside. "So what brings you back to these parts?"

"When I got back to Denver and told my editor about your boss running for state senate, he thought it could be a good feature story," Liz lied as she climbed behind the steering wheel. "What about you? Isn't this your day to head for Denver?"

"Sure is." He grinned at her, leaned on the window ledge, his face close enough for her to see into his guileless blue eyes. "If you can keep a secret, I'm hopin' to take in a Bears game while I'm there."

"Sounds like fun," she said, smelling the sweet scent of his hair pomade.

Al straightened, walked over to the truck, leaned into the cab to adjust something, then emerged, crank in hand. Inserting it in the front of the engine, he gave the handle a couple of quick, sure turns until the engine caught.

He came back to the Buick. "Ya know, someday I'd like to hear how you and a farm girl like Greta got hooked up." He flashed that cocky grin of his again.

"You might not believe it," she said.

"Might not at that," he replied as he climbed into the truck cab, shifted gears. His hands on the steering wheel, he stuck his head out the window. "Say, don't forget that plate and napkin you came for."

Liz swallowed hard, gave a little laugh. "So I did." And she opened the car door and went inside again.

〰

Back at Greta's house, binoculars in hand again, Liz walked past the corral to the shed, where she hoped to get a better view of the line camp's corrals and the base of the cliffs where they'd found the trail with mule manure. Frank only needed the day and time of Al's departure for Denver. But how much more impressive it would be if he could also pass on her account of seeing Al loading the truck with booze. But the angle was wrong. Disappointed, she headed back to the house, dragged a kitchen chair outside, and settled down to wait.

It was over an hour before the dust-covered hood of Al's truck crested the hill and rolled slowly back past the corral to the ranch house, stopped. Liz shot to her feet. Adjusting the focus, she saw Al climb down from the truck and go into the house.

Liz swung the binoculars to the truck bed, counted. The sacks were gone. And instead of the jumble of cans were two neat rows—tied down and easy to count this time—twenty in all. A few minutes later, Al reappeared, climbed into the truck, drove out through the gate and turned right, toward the Denver-Cheyenne road.

Liz yelled through the screened door. "Bessie! Tell Greta I'm going into Grover."

Flooring the gas pedal, Liz maneuvered the Buick along the top of the deep ridges worn into the road, careened around the corner at the junction, nearly tipping over but not slowing until she pulled up in front of Morris Lumber. The screen door banged behind her as she strode inside, where the proprietor was waiting on a customer.

"I'm sorry to interrupt," Liz said, breathlessly. "But could you tell me where I'd find the telephone exchange?"

Mrs. Morris glanced past the customer, smiled in recognition. "Use my phone if you want. It's in the back."

"Thank you, but it's a private conversation. About my job," Liz added because it was partly true.

"The exchange is in the next block. At the back of Bunker's feed store. Olive Bunker's the operator. But it's no more private."

Liz waved good-bye, ran out the door and down the block, across the street to the feed store. Slowing her pace to a fast walk, she went in. Three farmers lounging around the counter looked over at her, startled by her sudden appearance. She smiled and headed toward an open door at the back of the store.

Pausing to catch her breath, Liz was relieved to see a switchboard and a substantial-looking woman with thinning brown hair seated in front of it. Her broad shoulders beneath a short-sleeved cotton house-dress hinted at years of forking hay and milking cows. The instant a light flashed on the switchboard, she thrust the plug into the connection with such authority that the fat on her upper arm jiggled.

Liz waited until she had connected the caller.

"Mrs. Bunker?"

The huge woman swiveled in her chair and regarded Liz with small, penetrating dark eyes.

"I'd like to make a long-distance call on a one-party line." Liz paused, remembering to smile. "It's a private matter."

"Do I know you?"

"I'm Liz O'Brien. We may have met at the rodeo. I'm a friend of Greta Kuhlmann's."

The heavy woman blotted the sweat beading her forehead with a small lace-edged white handkerchief. "You're the reporter."

"Yes."

Olive Bunker glanced over her shoulder toward the switchboard, then looked back at Liz. "There's a phone in the store, but folks would hear you."

Liz strained for patience. It had been nearly an hour since Al left for Denver.

"Long distance, you say?"

"Denver."

"It won't be cheap."

"I understand that."

Liz was just about to risk a conversation in Olive Bunker's presence when the older woman said, "Tell you what."

Liz felt hope returning.

"You give me the number, I'll connect you. While you're talking, I can go help Mr. Bunker with customers for a couple of minutes. I don't get many calls. If one should come in, ignore it. They'll try again later."

Frank answered on the second ring. The connection was so bad that Liz could hardly hear. And she had to shout as she quickly reported Al Riddle's departure time, point of origin, and license plate number. She was glad Mrs. Bunker had thought to close the door. Before Liz hung up, she told Frank that she planned to start back to Denver by late afternoon.

25

Frank put down the receiver, feeling Maria's curious gaze. He turned and looked at his sister. Maria was the rock of the family, with a head for business, the one who could calm their excitable father with a hug. Once a jokester, her jokes had been few and far between since she'd been fired. She spent her days at the restaurant, keeping the books, pretending she didn't care, but the fire was gone from her eyes.

"What's going on, Frank?"

"You have to keep this quiet."

She scowled.

"I'm doing some work for the Treasury."

Maria's frown deepened as he explained the plan to trace the liquor coming into Denver.

"If I'm not here, they'll ask for you."

" 'They' being the Treasury?"

"Or Liz."

Maria sat back, folded her arms over her full breasts. "Is that all you want from me? To take messages?"

"For now, yes." He put his arms around her, smelling the camomile tea she used to rinse her thick black hair. "Remember. The folks mustn't know."

❧

The Denver Buick distributorship was in a sprawling new building—concrete with a checkerboard of windows—in the middle of the wholesale area, next to the railroad tracks. A good spot for shipping, Frank realized.

With both car windows rolled down to catch any breeze, Frank slumped in the driver's seat of the Nash and drummed his fingers on the steering wheel. He checked his watch again, frowned. Five o'clock. He hoped like hell that nothing had gone wrong. Riddle had had plenty of time to get to Denver. Frank had given the Treasury boys Liz's description of the truck and the time Riddle had left the ranch. They knew the truck contained gas cans full of booze. The way Frank had put it together, Riddle would deliver the booze at the Buick dis-tributorship, or someplace near it.

Frank scanned the doorways of the nearby buildings for signs of Trea-sury men but didn't see a soul. The D.A. had wanted in on the arrest; Frank hadn't seen Van Cise but figured he was somewhere around, likely with handpicked cops. The stage was set. Only the villain was missing.

Frank told himself that Riddle could have stopped by a speakeasy for a drink. The truck could have broken down. Then, just as Frank was about to give up hope, a Model T truck that fit the description of Riddle's rolled by and pulled up to a supply dock.

Instantly, men appeared from everywhere and converged on the truck. A blond fellow whom Frank presumed was Riddle was ordered out of the cab. If he was worried, he didn't show it. A Treasury man pointed to the truck bed. Riddle shrugged. The D.A. stepped for-ward. Riddle said something, and the D.A. replied with gestures. They walked to the truck bed. It appeared to Frank that Riddle had agreed to a search.

He watched the Treasury men examine the gas cans. Ten of them. But Liz had specifically said she'd seen at least twenty. Nose to the spout, a Treasury man took the top off one and poured out a sample. Scowls. Frank didn't need to be any closer to know the liquid flowing out of the can wasn't hooch.

The D.A. and a Treasury man moved away and conferred. Riddle watched, a smile on his face, relaxed. After several minutes, the D.A. and the Treasury man came back and said something to him. Riddle grinned, got in the truck, and drove away. It was over. Not a drop of booze. Someone or something had tipped him off.

Dejected, Frank got out of the Nash and walked over to the D.A. "It wasn't Riddle?"

"Oh, that was Riddle all right. You just screwed up. Those cans were full of gas."

Frank felt the black gaze of the Treasury man. The possibility that he thought Frank had purposefully given them a bum steer flashed through his mind.

"We'll get him next time," Frank said.

You sure as hell better, the Treasury man's look said.

Frank walked back to the Nash. Somehow that cocky sonofabitch had outfoxed them. Liz had said she'd counted ten cans of booze in the cellar of the cabin. Frank was certain she had told him that when the truck left Harlan's place, she'd counted twenty cans, neatly tied down. What had happened to the other ten?

Frank got in the car, his mind churning. Liz had seen twenty cans all right, but what if only half of them had been full? That way when Al delivered the booze, he'd still have ten more to fill with gas later as a cover. That done, he'd come to the Buick place to pick up parts, all very legit. Maybe go to a speakeasy for a good time, as Liz said he'd done the night he'd bumped into the woman who'd been killed.

Frank rubbed the bridge of his nose, closed his eyes in thought. Somehow he had to get back in the good graces of the Treasury. Verifying Riddle's routine was vital. A visit to the gas station at the north end of town might be a good start.

⚘

The man overseeing the gas pumps was heavyset with red hair. Deep half-moons of sweat stained the underarms of his blue work shirt. An oil-stained rag hung out of the back pocket of his coveralls.

"You in charge?" Frank asked pleasantly.

"That's what they tell me," the man said, taking the nozzle of one of the gas lines off its hook. "Want me to fill 'er up before I close for the day?"

Frank hadn't thought about getting gas. "I guess so. Sure." He watched the gas level in the glass tank lower, then stop. "Say, I've been looking for a fellow and thought he might do business here. Blond. Twenty or so. Drives a Model T truck. He usually carries a dozen or so cans that need filling."

The red-haired man returned the gas nozzle to its hook and screwed Frank's gas cap in place. "A lot of trucks come through here."

"He's a regular. From out of town. I think he comes to Denver every week."

The man pulled out the dirty rag and wiped his hands. "Blond, you say?"

Frank nodded. "Good-sized guy. A talker."

The man's thick lips curled into a half smile. "I bet I know who you mean. Works for a garage up north someplace, he told me once. Always comes in for gas in the afternoon. You just missed him. He was here a couple of hours ago. Said he was gonna pick up some parts and go to the ball game."

"Sounds like him," Frank said and gave the man a dollar for the gas. Climbing back into the Nash, Frank was certain that today Al Riddle was not headed to a speakeasy or a ball game but on his way north. The encounter with the Treasury men and the D.A. was clear evidence that someone was on to him. And who more likely than Liz, the reporter from Denver, whom he had seen just this morning?

Riddle would go after her, maybe kill her before she could do any more harm—to him or his boss. Frank had to get to her first.

26

Liz leaned over the steering wheel, squinting against the fierce rays of sun streaming directly into her eyes. She guessed it must be close to eight. She'd intended to leave sooner. Driving in the dark was always tricky; the Buick's headlights weren't the best. And she was anxious to get home. With the late start, she wouldn't reach Denver until at least eleven, which would mean putting off a follow-up call to Frank until morning.

By now, if all had gone according to plan, Al would be in custody, the Treasury would be satisfied that Frank had held up his end of the deal. And Phil would have worked out a valuable plea bargain requiring Al to testify when Emma Volz's murderer finally went to trial.

Liz held up a hand against the sun, about to pull off the road to wait for sunset, when she heard a car engine. She glanced in her rearview mirror but saw nothing. The sound grew louder and louder. Then she spotted it—a truck—coming at her head-on as if she weren't even in the road. The driver must be drunk. She fumbled frantically for the horn. The truck kept coming, about to ram into her when, instinctively, she yanked the steering wheel to the right. The Buick bounced violently as the wheels caught in the ruts. She struggled for control, but the car pitched on its side. Terror-struck, she felt it roll over and then abruptly settle to a stop.

Several minutes went by before Liz realized she was lying against the roof. She felt a sharp pain in her forehead and something warm dripping into her eyes and flowing down her cheeks. Blood. Her blouse was torn. Her arms were slashed with cuts from the broken windshield. She reached up and carefully explored the bridge of her nose, felt a shard of glass, and pulled it out. She tried to move her legs, but something was pinning them down.

She remembered the truck. She prayed the driver had stopped, and she called for help. Several moments went by. She called again, and heard someone moving about. Her hopes soared.

❧

Al Riddle poked his head through the shattered car window and saw the reporter upside down, wedged against the steering wheel. She was bleeding heavily. "Well, lookee here."

"Al? I thought—"

"That I was in jail?" He saw the fear in her eyes.

"You've got to help me." She winced. "I'm hurt."

"That's too bad. It really is."

"I'll vouch for you."

He shook his head.

"Al, it's the money men behind the operation the Treasury is after. If you help me, they'll go easy on you."

"Last I heard, bootleggin' was a federal offense."

"The D.A. will work something out. I know he will." She sucked in a quick breath as if she were hurting badly, licked her blood-caked lips. "Al, at least go for help."

"Sorry."

"You could get away. Go to Montana, Canada even. The cops would never find you."

Al looked over his shoulder toward the road. If he read it right, as fast it was getting dark, he'd be the last to come along tonight. Tomorrow was a regular workday. No reason for folks to go into town and pass this section of road. It would be days before anyone found her.

But he couldn't take any chances. He drew the revolver out of his belt, wrapped his finger around the trigger.

"Al, don't!" the woman pleaded, trying to move out of his line of sight.

His arm outstretched, he fired. The explosion ripped through the evening silence. The woman slumped, lay still.

He waited for a moment, but she didn't move. He backed out, avoiding the shattered glass, and climbed the embankment. As he walked slowly back to the truck, he noticed that the prairie was already losing its details in the growing dark.

27

Liz felt herself fade in and out of consciousness. She wasn't sure how long she'd lain there in the dark. Her shoulder felt as if it were on fire. She sobbed in frustration, then ran out of strength to do even that.

Time passed. Her lips moved in a prayer, "Hail, Mary, full of grace. . . ." She felt a terrible need to sleep, but she fought against it, fearing she might never wake up. Another wave of pain washed over her, and she was sliding toward blackness when she heard a sound, faint at first, then growing louder, until there was no mistaking the steady hum. An airplane engine. Hope raced through her. It had to be Frank up there, looking for her.

She reached toward the dashboard, groping for the light switch. If only the headlights would work. She found the knob, pulled. Her heart jumped as two pale yellow beams spread into the darkness. Minutes went by. The sound of the airplane faded, in its place absolute stillness. She pushed the knob back against the dashboard to conserve the battery and went back to praying. Then she heard the plane again, in the distance, but coming closer. Frantically, she felt for the knob and yanked it toward her. Again the feeble lights cut through the night. She was wondering how long the battery would last, when she heard a thud, then an engine racing, and, finally, the crunch of footsteps on dry grass.

"Frank!" she called out. But her voice sounded so feeble she was afraid he might not hear her.

A flashlight beam filled the car's interior, blinding her.

"Liz, thank God."

Tears of relief trickled down her face. "I knew you'd come."

"You're bleeding," he said, alarm in his voice.

"Al Riddle tried to kill me, but his aim was off."

"You'll be okay. We're going to get you out of here." Frank yanked at the driver's door, but it didn't budge. He gave it another mighty pull. It gave a little. He tried again, and this time it opened. Leaning inside the car, he pushed on the dashboard, trying to lift it off her chest. She gasped with pain.

"I need a lever to get this off you. I'm going to see if I can find a fence post."

Long minutes went by. She felt her strength ebbing as she waited. Then there he was, lugging a ragged post.

"Success. But I need you to help. I'm going to wedge this under the dash. Once it's in there nice and firm, I'll lean down on it and raise the dash off your legs. On my count of three, you've got to try to work clear." His encouraging smile gave her strength. "Ready?"

She did her best to return his smile. "Ready."

With a grunt, Frank shoved the post under the dash. "Okay." He glanced at her. "One."

On "Three," Liz squirmed, winced at a jolt of excruciating pain as she tried to work free. But she was only able to move a few inches.

"I'm stuck, Frank."

"Let's give it another try."

This time Liz placed her hands behind her. Ignoring the pain, she leaned her hands on the roof—now beneath her—and gingerly pushed herself backward, away from the dash, trying to avoid the scattered bits of glass, until she was able to squirm through the door to freedom.

As Frank gently helped her to her feet, she leaned against him, feeling so lightheaded she thought she might faint. Now that she was out of the car, she could see the shadowy outline of the DeHavilland across the road.

Frank touched her bloody shoulder. "You need to get something against that."

"My slip's all I have. I'd tear it off, but I don't think I can do it."

"Let me." He bent over, pulled up her skirt. "I know this isn't very gentlemanly, but here goes."

She felt him tug against the slip, heard the sound of fabric ripping. Straightening, he folded the length of white silk into a square and handed it to her. "Press this to your shoulder." He scooped her up into his arms. "Now we're going to get you home."

When they reached the plane, Frank carried her to the back of the lower wing and lifted her up onto it so that she was next to the front cockpit. "Stay put. I'll help you climb in."

The jar of his footstep against the wing was an agony. The pain in her shoulder shot to the tips of her toes. She let out a gasp when he helped her into the cockpit.

"Good girl. The worst is over," Frank said. "I've got to strap you in, and I want you to use my helmet. I'd give you my goggles, but without them I can't see where the hell I'm going."

Liz heard him adjusting instruments in the cockpit behind her before he jumped down to the ground. A moment later the engine caught and the propeller began to slowly revolve. The plane rolled forward, about as fast as a man could walk. Frank ducked under the wing, jumped up onto it and into the rear cockpit. In a second the plane surged forward, and Liz braced herself as it bumped and raced over the uneven ground, then turned its nose into the wind. In seconds it left the ground and soared into the air, guided only by the light of the half moon. Her eyes half-closed against the wind, Liz felt the plane bank as gracefully as a giant red-tailed hawk. She strained for a glimpse of the prairie below to bid a last good-bye to the crumpled Buick. But the headlights had died out, leaving only darkness.

🌾

The night sky was fading into dawn when the DeHavilland taxied to a stop in front of Bud Humphreys's hangar. Frank cut the engine, jumped down, and wedged the chocks against the wheels before he helped her down. The flight had revived her a little, but her shoulder throbbed fiercely. It was almost as difficult to get out of the cockpit as it had been to get in. Frank had to carry her to the small office inside the hangar.

"Who's your doctor, Liz?" he asked as he lowered her onto a dusty, tufted black leather divan.

"Richard Dickens," she said, stifling a gasp of pain. "But I don't think you should call until you've checked with the Treasury."

"To hell with that."

"Frank, I'm lying down now. I'm not going to die on you any time soon." She smiled up into his worry-lined face. "Another hour. Then you can call Dr. Dickens."

"I don't like it."

"Frank, you're wasting time. The sooner you call your Treasury contact, the sooner I can get fixed up."

It wasn't more than fifteen minutes after Frank put in the call that a Ford drove up and a man in a nondescript suit got out. Frank went out to greet him and led him into the hangar office.

Liz on the divan, Frank perched on the edge of the desk, the Treasury man quizzed her about the accident and what led up to it. He wanted to know everything: Al's pattern of operation at the Lazy J, how she and Greta had found the booze in the cellar of the line-camp cabin, the ride on the butte where they'd discovered signs of a still.

"We appreciate your assistance, Miss O'Brien. You certainly held up your end. But we cannot afford another fiasco like the one last week," the Treasury man said. "This time we'll station men along Riddle's route to Denver. We'll track his every move until he leads us to the bottling plant. If he's smart, he'll cooperate and divulge the names of the money men behind the operation. If not, he's headed for a federal facility."

"Won't he be wary and change his route?" Liz asked.

"Probably. But we'll be watching him. Further, I doubt very much that he'll tell his boss or bosses—whoever they are—that he was almost nabbed during his last run. So they'll expect him to continue to make deliveries. As long as he thinks you're dead, Miss O'Brien, he may even grow careless."

"Can I contact my boss at the *Post?*" Liz asked.

"Not for now. Of course, we'll arrange for groceries to be brought to your house. The rest will probably do you good."

"What if Al Riddle goes back to my Buick and finds me gone?"

"We'll send someone up from Greeley today. Both you and your car will be gone—your body ostensibly taken to the Greeley morgue, the car towed away," the Treasury man said.

"The bullet that missed me is probably lodged in the car somewhere, maybe in the front seat," she said.

"We'll check that out, of course. And set up a surveillance of the Harlan property."

"Just so you know, my friend Greta Kuhlmann's place is on top of a little rise with a good view of the ranch. Frank can show you where it is on the map."

28

Greta was brushing down the roan, wondering whether Al Riddle was in jail, when she heard an auto coming up the hill. After finding the booze and coming across what could be the still, Greta wasn't about to take chances. She went to the shed, where she kept her rifle. Checking the magazine and the chamber to be sure they were full, she walked out to the yard, rifle at the ready.

The auto turned out to be a truck. Dust-caked, but newer than a rancher around here would drive. It might belong to Harlan. She tightened her hold on the rifle. A fellow with blond hair beneath a battered tan Stetson climbed out. He wore Levi's, an old work shirt, and pointy-toed boots. It occurred to her that he could be one of the cowboys Harlan occasionally hired to chase cows.

"Somethin' I can do for ya?" she asked casually, walking toward him slowly. He was good-sized with broad shoulders.

He smiled at her. "Is this the Kuhlmann place?"

"Sure is." The Kuhlmann place. The words had a nice ring.

"Then you must be Miss Kuhlmann."

He didn't sound like a cowboy. "Greta's the name."

The smile held, and his gaze slid toward the rifle. His eyes were the color of the cornflowers her mama used to grow. For no reason other than a gut feeling, she asked, "You like pigs?"

"My dad had pigs at our place outside Encampment."

"But you yourself don't take to 'em."

The grin held. "I'm a cow man myself."

Greta grinned back, not surprised that a Wyoming man would choose cows over pigs. Yet his easy manner with her was unusual. He was no tongue-tied cowboy when it came to women. From his smooth hands, it'd been a spell since he'd mended fence. She suspected he'd gone to college. She loosened her grip on the rifle. "I didn't catch the name."

He reached into his back pocket and drew out an official-looking card. "Bob Sitka. Department of the Treasury."

Greta inspected the card. It looked real enough. She looked up at him. "Did you get Al Riddle?"

"Not yet. That's why I'm here." He told her about the botched bust and how Al had attempted to kill Liz. "We want him to believe he was successful."

"But Liz is okay, isn't she?"

"As far as I know, Miss O'Brien is doing fine."

Greta put the safety back on the rifle. "So where do you come in?"

"I've been ordered to keep an eye on the Harlan place until Riddle's next run, which, if he follows his routine, will be Tuesday."

"You got a place to stay?"

He glanced at the truck. "A sleeping bag."

"You can bunk in the house if you want."

"I'd appreciate that."

"Bessie will call supper after a while. We wash up outside the back door."

Bob Sitka gave a quick tug at the brim of his Stetson. "I'm obliged."

🐎

Sitting at the kitchen table two hours later, Greta noticed that Bessie had changed her apron and combed her hair. Coming from a family where eating was a necessity and how you approached it wasn't important, Greta especially appreciated Bob's nice table manners. During her years in Denver, she'd learned you could put food in your mouth without shoveling it in like you were stoking the furnace. It was a whole lot nicer to watch.

Baby Cissie was usually shy with strangers, but she latched on to Bob like she'd seen him every day of her life, babbling her baby talk at him, squealing when he paid attention to her. Bessie fussed over him like he was the king of England. Greta paid it no mind. The novelty of a man around the house would soon wear off.

Finally, he said, "Ladies, as far as you're concerned, I'm an old family friend who stopped by for a week or so to visit."

Bessie looked confused. Greta had meant to tell her what was going on.

"We don't go into town much. Unless you show your face, nobody's gonna know you're here," she said.

He smiled. "Just thought I'd mention it."

She passed him the pitcher of milk. "If you need my story, I come from Windsor, near Greeley. Papa has forty acres in sugar beets. I got four sisters and brothers. Mamma was born in Russia. Bessie works for me. She's from Nebraska."

He nodded. "I've got it. Thanks." He refilled his glass with milk.

After supper Bob Sitka moved his truck next to the corral like he was part of the family and planning to stay a while. He set up his watch post in whatever patch of shade he could find and settled in, binoculars trained on the Harlan place.

The next day he mucked out the shed for Greta. He got up on the roof and patched the tar paper. But whatever he did, he always kept one eye on the Lazy J. Sunday he asked her at breakfast if he could mend fence for her.

"If I go with ya," she replied, "nobody will ask questions."

He rose, pushed his chair back against the table, and reached for the hat he'd left on the peg by the door.

They saddled up. She stowed the bag of staples and the wire pull in her saddlebag, went into the shed, and got the rifle and a handful of shells. From three days of watching Bob whenever he left the house, she knew a revolver was stuck in his belt.

They followed the fence line dividing her place from Harlan's, just like she and Liz had done. She told him about visiting the line camp, about the mules and the coal. She pointed out the trail where they had spotted mule manure. This time she paid more attention to the weather. But today the sky was clear. What wind there was kept down the horseflies. Two hours on the trail, she wished she'd packed a lunch.

Bob Sitka was a good man on a horse, and the mare did its best to please him. When he spotted a loose wire, he got off and fixed it, just like they'd supposedly come to do. But they kept going, so that by noon they'd wound their way around the cliffs and were up on the butte, cutting across the sage and grass at a good easy gallop toward the edge where she and Liz had spotted the patch of green grass. As they came up about a hundred yards from the place, she motioned for him to rein in.

"It's over there." She pointed. "You want to take a look?"

He stood in his stirrups, staring at it. "This is close enough, but when we get back, I want you to draw me a map."

29

Liz spent the first two days after the accident in bed, sleeping fitfully. The bullet had only grazed her shoulder, but the room spun when she got up to relieve herself. She had to hang on to the bannister the first time she went down to the kitchen for a cup of tea and a little something to eat. She began to believe Dr. Dickens when he told her she'd lost more blood than she realized. But the pain in her shoulder slowly subsided. And the cut between her eyes showed signs of healing.

Frank came over every evening with the day's newspapers and a few groceries. Once his mother sent over an envelope containing dried herbs—Frank wasn't sure what they were, though they smelled like sage and basil—that she claimed had curative powers when mixed with tea.

He was loving, solicitous—asked how she was feeling, scowled at the bandage. But he didn't know any more than she did about what was going on. No one had informed him about the progress of the surveillance at Greta's or whether Al had returned to the scene of his crime. One night, after Frank had left and she'd crawled into bed, she realized that their recent conversations had never once touched on Emma's murder. It was almost as if all that had been forgotten.

By the fourth day, Liz could no longer contain herself, and she called Phil Van Cise.

"Liz, good to hear your voice. That was a close call you had up there. How are you feeling?"

"As if I've been cut off from the rest of the world."

The D.A. laughed. "You don't have a thing to worry about. Everything's falling into place."

"Does that include the murder investigation?"

"Actually, yes. You'll be pleased to know that the bullet the cops dug out of the plaster in the bedroom was from a .45, just like the coroner's report said."

"That's it? That's all you have? What about fingerprints?"

"Unfortunately, the prints the cops lifted don't match anybody's that we have on file."

"But once you pick up Al Riddle—"

"If you're thinking Riddle might have been the murderer, forget it. The bullet the Treasury boys retrieved from the roof of your Buick was a .32-caliber, from a Colt pocket auto."

Liz inhaled deeply.

"Liz?"

"Still here. It's just that . . . what kind of pistols do the police carry?"

"A Colt police positive .38. Which takes care of the theory that it was a cop."

Liz gazed across the entry hall at the sunlight streaming through the dining room windows. "So the case is at a standstill."

"We're working on it."

"And in the meantime, the Klan is gathering up its eight thousand signatures and will have you recalled and out of office. And then guess what?"

He didn't reply.

"The case will be buried as deep as the victim is. Because whoever the Klan handpicks to replace you won't care one small hoot who killed a German-Russian girl in the Bottoms. In fact, he'll probably say she had it coming."

"Liz, listen. Just as soon as I get this Riddle thing wrapped up, I promise—"

The anger was mounting inside her. "You're running out of time, Phil. Your promises aren't going to stop the clock. And so far, if Tim Ryan's shooting is any example, they don't solve murders either."

"That's not fair, Liz."

"Maybe not, but it's true." And she hung up.

Seething, Liz pushed through the swinging door of the pantry, slamming it against the wall, and strode into the kitchen. She glared at the refrigerator, the stove, cupboards, unable to remember what she'd been after. All she could think about was the Klan and its timetable. So far, events were right on schedule.

The Treasury had every reason to believe a good-size bottling operation existed in Denver, yet its whereabouts was still a mystery. The ghastly murder of a young woman had been committed, and not a single substantive piece of incriminating evidence had been discovered. To all appearances, the D.A. and the police were incompetent. The last report she'd read, the infamous Law Enforcement Association had come up with nearly five thousand signatures on the recall petitions, and no wonder.

She was seized with the urge to do something, anything. So she went down to the basement and the billiard room. Second only to his study, the billiard room had been her granddad's favorite retreat. It had been months since she'd even opened the door. The room smelled stuffy, unused. She pulled the slender chain attached to the overhead light. Directly in front of her stood the majestic table made to her granddad's specifications, all but hidden beneath the protective covering of old bedsheets. On impulse, she yanked them off, then rummaged for the box that held the two cue balls and the red ball. After she'd found it, she placed the balls on their respective diamonds, then chose one of the long cue sticks lined up in the wall rack where her granddad had left them seven years ago.

She leaned over the green felt-covered table, wincing as she awkwardly rested the tip end of the cue along the middle finger of her left hand. She lined up her first shot, tapped the white ball, which hit the bumper, recoiled, glanced against the red ball, missed the second white ball, and rolled to a stop.

Her head began to clear. And she thought of Ginger, the elusive long-legged, red-haired girl in the faded blue dress. The neighborhood snoop, the neighborhood snitch. For a dime she had come up with the number of women who'd up and left the morning of the murder, and in what make of car. Then she had vanished, taking with her the missing information that only she could provide about what had gone on later that afternoon and evening.

Liz straightened, put the cue stick aside. Her efforts to find the girl had failed. Yet, barring the possibility that Ginger had moved, Liz believed she was still out there, waiting to be found—if only on her own terms. But this time it would take more than a dime, an ice cream cone, and a handful of operetta tickets.

Liz turned off the overhead light, hurried upstairs, and rummaged for the empty grocery boxes she had stowed in the closet by the back

door. She took four of them up to the study with her, and with diffi-
culty managed to rip them apart. She held up the pieces of brown
cardboard, satisfied with their size. Fountain pen would never show
up against the brown cardboard. Crayons were what she needed.

Then she remembered Maria Capillupo often lettered the signs
announcing the restaurant's daily specials. And Liz reached for the
telephone on the desk.

"Maria, it's Liz."

"Frank's in the kitchen. Hold on."

"Wait. I need to know if you have any crayons."

Silence. "Crayons?"

"Red, blue, orange—something bright that people will notice. I'm
making signs."

"What kind of signs?"

"Reward signs."

"Oh." A pause. "Maybe you better talk to Frank."

"Fine. But do you have any?"

"I think I can find some red and green."

"Perfect."

"I'll get Frank."

🦋

Liz sat beside Frank in the Nash and directed him to the street in the
Bottoms. Stowed in the rumble seat was a box containing the crude
posters she had made and several hundred flyers a friend of Frank's
father's had printed up for her at no charge. At her feet was a hammer
and a can of nails.

"I still don't think the kid's going to bite," Frank said.

"One hundred dollars is quite an incentive. It's far more than her
father—if she has one—makes in a month."

"Even if she steps forward, how can you be sure she won't just
make something up?"

"I can't. But she's the only link we have, Frank. I've got to try."

Frank frowned. "I'll bet a hundred bucks is about every cent of
savings you have. The police department ought to come up with the
dough. Or, at the very least, the D.A."

Liz patted Frank's knee. "It'll work out." Liz saw Emma's house up
the street, its green front door still sealed by a yellow police notice.
"Let's start right here."

Frank pulled over to the side of the road, turned off the engine, and sat back. "I can't talk you out of this?"

"Nope." She got out, opened the rumble seat, and removed the box of flyers and posters. She liked the effect of the bright red block letters, edged in green. "$100 Reward for Ginger (Last Name Unknown) In Exchange for Vital Information. Call Capitol 4451, Day or Night."

Liz and Frank surveyed the houses. No sign of anyone. Just like that fateful day nearly a month ago. The neighborhood might as well be deserted. They walked over to a light post and she handed Frank a poster. As the thud of the hammer reverberated through the quiet, Liz said a little prayer that Ginger was out there somewhere, listening and watching.

❦

It was close to five o'clock when Frank finally pulled the Nash into Liz's driveway. It had taken all afternoon, tramping each dusty street in the heat, nailing up the posters and passing out the leaflets. The looks Liz got were either suspicious or cynical. The people in the Bottoms knew that money—certainly that much money—was never given away without serious strings attached. Several women assured Frank that they were Ginger and asked him what they really had to do for the money. But Liz hadn't expected a warm reception committee.

Liz opened the car door, glanced at Frank. "Come in. I think the afternoon calls for a celebration of sorts. I have a feeling we're this close to Emma Volz's murderer. I'll even fix us an omelet."

"Honey, don't get your hopes up too high." He leaned over and kissed her. "Actually, a cold beer would really hit the spot."

"A splash of brandy is the best I can do."

He kissed her again, this time more thoroughly. "You smell good."

She pushed him away. "You lie through your teeth. I need a bath and a change of clothes."

She heard the weariness in his laugh. "Actually, an omelet sounds good. I don't suppose you have a green pepper and an onion?"

"An onion, for sure. A green pepper, I doubt it."

As they stepped inside the house, the air was close and warm, and Liz went around opening windows as Frank explored the refrigerator.

"You were right, no green pepper," he said when she walked into the kitchen.

Liz shrugged. "Water's what I need at the moment." She took a glass out of the cupboard, went to the sink, and turned on the cold-water tap. She enjoyed good food, but preparing it took more patience than she generally had. If she had any sense, she'd marry Frank tomorrow and have the problem solved forever: he was an excellent cook.

She downed two glasses of water, glanced over her shoulder at Frank, who was getting out a pan.

"Frank, what will happen if the Treasury messes up with Al Riddle again?"

He placed the pan over a burner but didn't turn on the gas. "I don't even want to think about it."

"A mess-up will finish Phil off for good. I know you can't stand him, but this isn't about personal feelings anymore. He needs our help," she said.

"What about my family? Don't they need help?"

"Frank, it's not an either-or. It's your family *and* the D.A. This is the Klan we're talking about.

"So let's think about it. We know booze is being made on at least one of Harlan's ranches. We know Al takes it to Denver every week. What else?"

Frank yanked off his tie and loosened his shirt collar. "Riddle tried to kill you. Out of self-protection or out of loyalty to his boss, who knows?"

"Okay. Now what about Harlan? Ambitious. Successful. Not at all what he wants you to believe he is. A Klan member."

"You don't know that," Frank said.

"Not with certainty, but the signs are all there." Liz got out two glasses and the remains of the bottle of brandy and poured enough to cover the bottoms of the glasses, handing one to Frank.

"So for the moment, let's say we have a Klan member who's making enough booze to fill ten twenty-gallon cans once a week and shipping it to Denver. Now all we have to do is figure out where it's bottled."

Liz stared across the kitchen, then looked at Frank, who, apparently, had lost interest in supper. "When I did that interview with the Toad, he told me the Klan was going to open headquarters on Fourteenth and Glenarm. I went there. There was no sign, but I went in. It was set up to look like a clinic, but it smelled funny. Musty."

He looked at her hard.

"The Klan headquarters is the bottling plant. In the basement. Either that or it could be the place next door and they're connected by a tunnel."

She could tell by Frank's expression that he was taking the idea seriously.

"If you wanted to hide an operation that entailed bottling illegal whiskey, where better than under the skirts of the Klan, particularly with all their talk about law and order? The Grand Dragon is a doctor who had his license yanked. He and the others would steal the gold out of their grandmothers' teeth if it furthered their cause. Harlan is dealing with the devil."

"I don't know, Liz. All we have is pure conjecture. Including the stuff about Harlan. The Treasury won't buy it."

"What can they lose? If I'm right about the headquarters being the bottling plant, they'll at least have Al. And I can't believe he'll willingly go to federal prison for his boss," Liz said.

"Your friend the D.A. will make a deal for his testimony about the cops. Riddle won't serve a year. And then he can go right back into business with Harlan's blessing."

"So you won't even call your contact?" Liz asked.

"Did I say that?" Frank tossed down the last of his brandy, set the glass on the drain board, and went to the front hall and the telephone.

A few minutes later he was back. "Jesus! He as much as laughed at me. Said didn't I know the Klan had always supported Prohibition."

"Did you tell him that's why it's such a perfect cover?"

His brown eyes bitter, Frank sat down heavily in the nearest kitchen chair.

"We should have talked to Phil first. I know he would have agreed with us, and then he could have convinced the feds," Liz said.

"Well, we didn't."

"I'll call him now," Liz said.

"No, you won't. I will."

30

Monday morning. Hot and dry. Greta was out in the corral, picking the mare's hooves, when she heard Bob Sitka holler. He'd been keeping an eye out for activity at the Lazy J through his binoculars. From the sound of his voice, he'd seen something important, and she raced to the front of the house.

"Riddle just pulled in. He's got ten cans in his truck. And he's a day ahead of schedule," Bob said.

"You watch, there'll be twenty of 'em when he comes back from the line camp."

Bob kept the binoculars trained on the ranch house.

"What's happenin'?" Greta asked.

"Al just went into the house."

Ten minutes went by.

"Here he comes. He's going down to the corral," Bob said.

"He'll throw some hay and then get in the truck."

More waiting.

"That's what he's doing, all right." Bob shifted the binoculars slightly. "There he goes over the rise. Can't see him anymore." Bob lowered the glasses.

"I'll get you a cup of coffee. It'll be a while before he comes back."

It was two long hours before Al reappeared.

"Hey. Here he comes," Bob said. "But he isn't stopping."

"He always stops."

"Maybe so, but not today." Bob adjusted the glasses. "He's through the gate and he's turning left."

"Left? Left is toward Grover and on to Sterling. Al always turns right toward the state highway."

"Well, he's changed his mind again. And I've got to get to a phone."

"What if we see Al in Grover?"

"Not a chance. Al has business on his mind. He won't stop."

"It's gonna take him a good hour—maybe longer—to go all the way to Sterling, and at least another three hours to Denver," Greta said.

"But he must think it's a whole lot safer."

Greta drove with Bob Sitka to the telephone exchange to keep up the appearance that he was an old friend on a visit.

She introduced Bob to Olive Bunker as a family friend from Encampment. The older woman nodded, taking Bob's measure as she did with everybody. Greta liked Olive. She had a toughness mixed with basic kindness that Greta admired. She also had a good feel for people. Greta suspected Olive wasn't fooled.

Bob said he'd like to make a call to Denver, and she told him he had his choice: use the phone in the front of the store or go back to the exchange. To Greta's surprise, he said the front of the store would be just fine, and he gave Olive the number.

Greta stayed near enough to hear, examining a pair of chamois work gloves, even though she saw by the price tag that they were way out of her reach.

"Hello, Fred? Bob." Pause. "Everything is set. The order just went out. But the route's by way of Sterling." Another pause. "Well, good talkin' to you." He returned the earpiece to its hook alongside the receiver box and glanced at Greta. "Anything you need to pick up in town?"

Greta returned the gloves to the shelf. "Nope."

Bob turned to Olive, who was leaning against the door frame of the exchange, her arms folded over her ample bosom, and he tipped his hat. "Good meetin' you, Mizz Bunker."

She smiled, nodded. "Same here."

Once they were settled back in the truck, though, Bob shed his easy manner and just drove, not saying boo, the whole way back to her place. It wasn't until he had parked in her yard and was climbing out of the truck that he finally told her what she'd been busting to know.

"I'm to seize the line camp and the still."

"What if Al gets away?"

"One way or the other, we'll get him."

"But he went a different direction. That means he's already suspicious. He might have warned whoever's up there at the still," Greta said.

"I guess I'll just have to wait and see, won't I?" He was already walking toward the corral, and Greta followed along.

They worked well as a team. Bob saddled, adding a scabbard for his rifle, and Greta worked the bridle on the mare.

It was only ten minutes before he pulled up onto the mare's back, eased into the saddle, slid his rifle into the scabbard, and adjusted the reins to his liking.

"You better get those fellas," Greta said, looking up at him.

"That's the plan."

"This place is my home, Bob. I don't take much to havin' boot-leggers as neighbors."

31

It was almost noon and time for lunch. Frank had been awake most of the night, frantic with the thought that the bottling plant might not be at Klan headquarters after all. Thank God the D.A. had gone along with Liz's scenario. But Van Cise had only been able to persuade the Treasury to assign a few men to the area. If the plan went sideways, the Capillupo restaurant would be history and the D.A. all but out of a job.

Maria was just putting a plate of cheese and bread on the kitchen table when the phone by the cash register rang. Frank hurried to answer it.

"Frank Capillupo?" He recognized the voice of his contact.

"Speaking."

"The plans have been altered. You're to go immediately to the district attorney's office to receive further instructions." And the line went dead.

Frank slowly hung the receiver back on the wall, not sure what to make of the message. Al Riddle wasn't due in Denver until tomorrow.

⌇⌇⌇

All the way over to Van Cise's office, Frank tried to figure out what was up. Last night the Treasury hadn't bought in on the Klan headquarters idea. Yet now they were ordering him to the D.A.'s office. Al Riddle might have changed his routine and decided to deliver the booze a day early. Or maybe the surveillance man assigned to Greta's had been told to nab Riddle with the booze and not risk losing him once he hit Denver.

Frank pulled the Nash up to the curb in front of the Justice building, cut the engine, got out, and straightened his tie. Shoulders squared, he marched upstairs to the D.A.'s office. He was in the process of convincing himself that he'd go along with whatever Van Cise and the Treasury had in mind, when the secretary informed him that Mr. Van Cise had been called out of the office. He wouldn't be back for at least an hour. She invited Frank to take a seat.

Jamming his hands in his pants pockets, he didn't know what to think. Too nervous to sit, he walked over to a little hole-in-the-wall on Santa Fe that made great tamales. But when the steaming plate was placed before him, he was so distracted he couldn't eat. And he returned to the D.A.'s office.

Van Cise still wasn't back. Frank was reduced to trying to read a year-old copy of *National Geographic*, all the while watching the stairs. He stole yet another glance at his watch. Two-thirty. If Al Riddle kept anywhere close to his usual schedule, he would arrive in Denver in an hour.

Then, just as Frank was about to telephone his contact again, he heard heavy footsteps, and Van Cise appeared at the top of the stairs. Done up in his Palm Beach suit and starched white shirt and a blue silk tie that was probably handmade, he looked like something out of a haberdashery ad instead of a hard-hitting D.A. Frank didn't bother to get up.

"Sorry about the delay," was all Van Cise said. "Your car or mine?"

"Mine's right in front." Frank was relieved the D.A. seemed to mean business. And as the driver, Frank figured he'd be in charge.

As they walked downstairs, Van Cise said, "If past performance is any indication, Riddle should be showing up anytime."

Frank nodded. "Has the Treasury changed its mind?"

"That's what I was working on the last hour, with only limited success."

"Does that mean we're still pretty much on our own?"

"You, me, and the Denver police department, yes."

Frank glanced at Van Cise, who flashed a sly, satisfied smile. "I couldn't let the boys in blue take all the glory."

❧❧❧

Nothing seemed out of the ordinary along the block between Fifteenth and Fourteenth on Glenarm. Shoppers were walking under the buildings' awnings to keep out of the sun and heat. A streetcar clanged as it rattled east on Fifteenth toward Broadway. Frank cruised by Klan headquarters. A casual observer would say the place was closed. Frank turned into the alley. The only sign of life was an old man picking through a trash barrel. Taken altogether, it was just a sleepy Monday afternoon in summer.

Seated beside Frank, Van Cise stuck his elbow out the open window. "If I could just get a solid fix on this crowd. They're like fucking chameleons. One minute they burn crosses on women's lawns, the next they scream about law and order." He shot a glance at Frank. "Don't know whether you heard, but they've already drummed up five thousand signatures against me."

Frank shook his head in sympathy, his eyes fixed on the traffic.

"Tell you what. Drive over to Chidum's Drugstore in the next block," Van Cise ordered. "I want to make a call."

Frank steered the Nash through traffic and pulled up in front of the drugstore. The D.A. got out and strode inside. A few minutes later he was back. "I wanted to give the Treasury boys one more chance. It's time to park this. We should be on foot from now on."

Frank slipped the Nash into a space around the block from Klan headquarters. They walked at a steady pace but didn't hurry.

At the entrance to the alley that backed the Klan's headquarters, they scouted around for somewhere to conceal themselves. A narrow space between two buildings was the most likely spot. Checking quickly for any observers, they ducked into the alley and took up their posts.

The weed-filled space, stinking of urine, was strewn with rusting tin cans and refuse. Five, then ten, then fifteen minutes went by. Frank inspected the windows and doorways of the other buildings for signs of the Treasury. Nothing stirred. A truck turned in at the far end of the alley. Frank tensed. Then gears ground and the truck slowly backed out again and rejoined traffic.

Van Cise shot Frank a questioning look. Frank shrugged. If the truck's driver had been Riddle, he'd smelled a rat. But it might not have been Riddle at all. The D.A. was leaning out into the alley, when another truck nosed in. Instantly, Van Cise slid back out of sight.

Frank's heart pounded in his ears. He wondered where the hell the police—or the Treasury boys—were. He heard the truck stop. Frank took a quick peek. The truck was parked next to the Klan's delivery door. A blond guy he recognized as Riddle climbed out of the cab, glanced up and down the alley. Apparently satisfied it was safe, he knocked on the delivery door, and it opened.

The, out of nowhere, figures with guns drawn appeared on neighboring rooftops and out of doorways. Frank wondered how he could have missed them. Two men burst into the back of the Klan storehouse with shouts of "Police!" Two others climbed up onto the truck bed, filled with a collection of gas cans.

"Hands on your head, Riddle," one shouted. "You're under arrest for violation of the Volstead Act."

A photographer's flash went off, and Riddle blinked. But he did what he was told. And as his hands went up, a faint smile twitched at the corners of his mouth, as if, once again, the joke were on them.

32

Liz, prowling barefoot, paused for a moment at the entrance to the living room. She couldn't seem to sit still. The room was filled with antiques that Grammy had chosen years ago with ultimate care. Against the far wall was the Chippendale secretary she had found in Boston. Bathed in afternoon light, its mahogany shone like chocolate satin. Hanging next to it was a magnificent, gilt-framed Albert Bierstadt mountain landscape. The entire room was beautiful, a showcase. Yet right now it had a suffocating feel as she waited for the phone to ring, bringing the missing information that might affect her entire future, perhaps the future of Denver.

A slight breeze stirred the sheer fabric at the tall windows, sending a whiff of air against this awful July heat. From outside came the steady squirt of the sprinkler Liz had set on the front lawn; she decided to go out and move it.

Dressed in her slacks and a loose-fitting overblouse, she opened the front door and stepped out. She had called the D.A.'s office at about three, only to be told by his secretary that Phil had left with Mr. Capillupo. Something unexpected must have come up. Had Al Riddle sniffed a rat and moved up his delivery schedule? So much depended on catching him this time.

Mr. Ware had put his faith in her. He could have fired her, but instead he had backed her trip to Grover and still held her job open. She realized it had only been a day since she and Frank had put up the posters, but timing was critical. If Ginger never materialized . . .

The cement front walk was hot against her bare soles, and she quickly moved onto the grass. She was contemplating how best to grab the sprinkler without getting wet, when she saw her.

Liz's heart stopped. She looked again. There was no mistake. The red-haired girl, walking along the sidewalk with a proud, businesslike stride, as if daring someone to tell her to run along. Her hair was long and straggly. She wore what looked like the same faded blue dress with an uneven hem, and on her feet were strange-looking brown shoes a couple of sizes too large. The world might see a street urchin. To Liz, Ginger looked like an angel.

"Ginger?"

The girl stopped, fixed Liz with a wary look.

"How'd you find me?"

"Simple. I figured it was you from the poster. I looked in the phone book. The number was the same. What's so hard about that?"

Liz had to smile. She walked across the lawn, dodging the arc of water from the sprinkler, to the sidewalk where the girl stood. "I can't tell you how grateful I am that you came."

"It's a joke about the hundred dollars, right?"

"Oh, it's no joke. Believe me." Liz glanced back at the house. "Please come in. I'll bet you're hot. I've got some iced tea. I think I have some lemons for lemonade, if that sounds be better." Liz heard herself babbling.

Ginger eyed the house suspiciously. "This your place?"

"It was my granddad's. Please come in. I'll get you the money, and we can talk."

Ginger followed her inside. As she closed the door, she noticed the girl steal glances at the dining room and the living room on either side of the entry hall. "Pretty fancy."

"I'm glad you like it," was all Liz could think to say. "Let's go in the kitchen. Right down the hall is a bathroom if you need one."

"That's okay," the girl said casually. "How many rooms you got in here, anyway?"

"Bedrooms, bathrooms, a study—all together? Fifteen or sixteen, maybe."

Ginger made no reply, but stopped and inspected a photograph of Liz's granddad. "Who's the old geezer?"

"My granddad."

"He musta had a dozen kids to fill this house."

"Actually, he only had one. My father. He died in the war."

Ginger nodded solemnly and followed Liz into the kitchen.

"Who-ee!" The girl looked around her. "It's as big as our whole place."

Liz opened the refrigerator door, glanced over her shoulder at Ginger. "Is iced tea okay?"

"Sure." The girl pulled out a chair and sat down at the kitchen table, making herself at home.

Liz took two glasses out of the cupboard and filled them. "Do you like sugar?"

"You bet."

Liz brought the glasses and the sugar bowl to the table. "Help yourself. If you'll excuse me, I'll go get the check."

"What am I gonna do with a check?"

Liz stared at her. "Well, I thought—" But she hadn't thought. A girl in the Bottoms probably couldn't cash a check. "I don't have that much cash on hand. But I can give you what I have and then—"

The girl ladled several heaping spoonfuls of sugar into her glass of iced tea. "Go get it at the bank. The sign said a hundred dollars."

Liz smiled at her weakly. "I'm afraid the banks close at three o'clock." She glanced at her watch. "And it's nearly six."

The girl shrugged.

"I have a friend who can help. I can't reach him right this minute, but when I do, I'm sure he'll get it to me quick as a wink." Liz sank down on the straight-backed wood chair across the table from the girl. "The information I hope you can give me is terribly important."

"That's what the sign said, yeah."

"It's about Emma Volz, the woman who was murdered in the house with the green door."

"I figured."

"I tried to get in touch with you before. Did you know that?"

Not looking at Liz, the girl took several gulps of iced tea.

"Wait here. I'll call my friend. And I'll get my purse."

Liz found thirty-four dollars and fifty-two cents in her purse. Using the telephone in the study, she called the Capillupos. Maria answered. Frank had left before lunch. She didn't know when to expect him. Liz asked her to have him call as soon as he returned.

Back in the kitchen, Liz placed the bills and change before the girl, who proceeded to count it. "You're short sixty-five dollars and forty-eight cents."

"I'll have the remainder soon."

"A hundred dollars. That's the deal," the girl said, pocketing the bills and the change.

Liz took off her watch. "Here. You can have this until I get the rest of the money. It's gold."

The girl studied the watch, turning it over, holding it up against one ear. Then she put it around her thin wrist and buckled the strap in place. "So what's so big that you're willin' to fork up a hundred bucks?"

"The district attorney and the police are looking for witnesses who might have information that will lead them to the person who killed Emma Volz." Liz sat down opposite the girl. "Ginger, the minute we met that day, I could tell that you notice what's going on in the neighborhood. You told me about the other women who left. You even remembered the kind of car that picked them up."

The girl gave Liz an even look.

"I don't blame you for being reluctant to speak up. For all you or anyone knows, the person who killed Emma Volz could still be in the neighborhood."

The girl didn't blink an eye.

"Any information could be important. Something you saw that day after the other women left . . ."

Ginger folded her arms. "There was a big, new Buick."

Liz held her breath for an instant, then exhaled. "And?"

"It stopped in front of Emma's house that night."

"Did you catch the license number? See the driver?"

The girl slowly moved the sweating glass of iced tea in a wide circle. "A fella got out."

"Young, old?"

"On the old side." She glanced up at Liz. "He was wearin' a cow-boy hat. It was white. Looked brand new."

C.J. Harlan. It had to be. Liz felt her heart racing. "Would you recognize him if you saw him again?"

"Might."

"How about the license number?"

Ginger fingered the watch and rubbed the face with her thumb. "Twenty-three dash twelve nine three."

Relief flooded over Liz. "I want to write that down. Just a sec." Liz ran out to the entry hall, grabbed the pad and pencil she kept by the telephone, dashed back to the kitchen, and scribbled down the number before she forgot it.

Ginger glanced at the refrigerator. "Say, you got anythin' to eat in there?"

Liz sprang to feet as if she were weightless. "Let me look." She opened the door, peered inside, and saw the remains of the pound of cheddar cheese Frank had brought three days ago. "How does a melted cheese sandwich sound?"

"That's all you got?"

Liz held the cheese up to her nose, sniffed. "I'm not much of a cook."

"Sure. A cheese sandwich is okay." The girl got to her feet and began to pull open the drawers and cupboard doors, inspecting the contents.

Liz took the loaf of bread out of the breadbox. Ginger's information came with more than a dollars-and-cents price tag attached, that much was clear. "Did you see anything else that day?" she asked over her shoulder.

"What d'ya mean?"

"Or hear anything?"

"Not that I can think of." The girl stood beside her. "I like butter on my sandwiches."

"It's in the refrigerator, if you'd like to get it out." Liz doubted Ginger ever saw butter in her house, much less had it spread on a sandwich.

A moment later Ginger plunked down the plate with a cube of butter on it.

"How long did the man stay at Emma's house?"

"A while. I dunno. It was gettin' dark and Ma called me to get back home."

The shrill ring of the telephone came from the entry hall. "That might be my friend. I'll be right back." Nearly running to answer the call, Liz felt as if the door to the cage had just sprung open. And the key had been worth every cent.

33

O nly a few minutes after nine and the day was already a scorcher. But Liz had more than the heat on her mind as she strode into Phil's office. When she had called him last night with the news about Harlan, his reaction had been a satisfied "That does it," and something about tearing up recall petitions. She hoped he'd come down to earth by now.

At the sound of her footsteps, Phil looked up from the edition of the *Post* he was reading. "Great photo of Riddle with his hands in the air, don't you think?"

"But not a word about the Klan," she observed ruefully.

"An oversight." He tossed the newspaper aside. "I'm calling a press conference this afternoon. Four o'clock. You should be there."

"How about a preview?"

"First, I'll announce that the Treasury man assigned to locate the still on the Lazy J not only found it but placed two men under arrest."

"With Greta Kuhlmann's help."

Phil nodded, a little absently, she thought. "Naturally, I will remind the boys that we have the runner in jail. And then I'll tell them Denver's finest searched Riddle's truck and found the .32 he used to try to kill you."

Liz pulled over a chair and sat down.

Phil continued. "Then I'll announce that the assistant U.S. attorney will file a request in the name of the U.S. attorney asking the grand jury to bring in an indictment of violation of the Volstead Act against him. And I'll tie in the Klan, of course."

"I hope you're prepared for them to deny any association with the bottling operation."

"Deny all they want. The evidence is as clear as it can get. Best of all, I handle any state violations that occurred in my jurisdiction." Phil's frown eased into a smile of satisfaction.

"When do you get to the Volz murder?"

"Ah! That'll be the frosting on the cake."

"Which reminds me, Phil. Finding your witness cost me a hundred dollars."

"Don't worry about it." Seemingly oblivious to anything so mundane as her bank balance, he went on. "Not an hour ago we verified the license plate number as Harlan's. And I've asked Judge Buck in District 8 to issue a search warrant to comb Harlan's house and property for the .45."

"Are you going to put Riddle on the stand? Because if you are, I can't imagine that he'd testify against Harlan."

"Then you're in for a pleasant surprise. When I paid him a visit this morning in his cell and he discovered we had him on attempted murder, he couldn't talk fast enough. As it turns out, it was sheer chance that Al went to the speakeasy that afternoon and bumped into Emma Volz. He'd dropped Harlan off at a political meeting at the state capitol. It was hot, Riddle was thirsty, and he knew the place. He saw Emma, bought her a drink, and she blurted out the whole story: how Harlan got her pregnant—she even claimed he'd raped her—and then how he paid her barely enough to cover doctor bills and train fare to Denver. She miscarried and couldn't work for a while. She was about to be thrown out on the streets when she read a squib about Harlan running for state senate. That's when she got the bright idea of blackmailing him—money she claimed he owed her anyway. So she wrote Harlan a letter, demanding five hundred dollars or she would ruin him."

"Emma told Al all this?" Liz asked.

"Yep. Maybe she thought he'd help her. Who knows? Anyway, seems Harlan promised to come up with the money. Once Riddle heard that, he knew his boss had come to Denver for more than a political meeting. But Riddle turned a blind eye. He didn't want to get involved."

"That's Al. For a while, I could almost believe he cared for someone besides himself." Liz cocked her head reflectively. "But Harlan . . . He probably thought he was invulnerable, that the Klan would protect him. And they just might. That's the irony."

Phil shook his head. "Anyway—according to Riddle—the day after he bumped into Emma in the speakeasy and the cops took her and the other women in—"

"The day of the murder."

"Correct. That morning at the Cosmo Hotel, where Harlan was staying, he tells Al that he can have the day off but to leave the car. So Al takes the streetcar out to Merchants Park to the Bears–Oklahoma City ball game. He doesn't see his boss again until the next morning, when he gets himself over to the hotel and drives Harlan back to Sterling," Phil said.

Liz imagined the situation. "So while Al was at the ball game and maybe having a drink or two afterwards, Harlan drove down to the Bottoms and killed Emma."

"If it weren't for the knife, it'd be a textbook case of premeditated murder," Phil observed cynically. "Unfortunately, with the knife as evidence, the defense may try argue that Harlan went to Emma's to pay her off, and for some reason, she attacked him, and he shot her in self-defense."

"Will a jury buy that?"

"Not as long as I'm the prosecutor."

Liz fought back a smile. As vexing as his bravado could be, it was part of Phil's charm.

"However, what I can't control are the papers. Particularly that rag you work for," he said.

"And you know Harry Teaks. It'll be the rape and incest, a loose woman, the infamous Bottoms." Liz shuddered.

Phil eyed her. "What about you?"

"Actually, I have some ideas." She stood. "In fact, I'm on my way right now to see whether my editor will go for them."

"Before you leave . . ." Phil got to his feet, dug into his back pants pocket and drew out his wallet. After a moment of searching, he pulled out a gold coin and handed it to her. "For you. It's an 1890 twenty-dollar gold piece. The same year I was born. My father gave it to me as a good-luck charm before I went over to France."

Liz hesitated for an instant before she took the coin. On one side was the American eagle, on the other the head of Lady Liberty, a coronet gracing her curls. Liz looked at Phil. "I can't accept this."

"I have four more at home for you, but they're 1907s."

"Phil, I mean it. Your father meant you to have this."

"And now it's yours."

❦

An hour later Liz walked past the rewrite desks of the newsroom and nodded in response to a few desultory hellos. Floor fans whirred uselessly against the hot air that drifted through the open windows.

She swept her dark hair off her perspiring forehead and prepared herself for what lay ahead. Last night after she and Frank had made love, they'd admitted to one another that Harlan's conviction was far from a sure thing. And whether Bentliff and Neihouse ever went to trial for killing Tim Ryan was another question. The Klan was just warming up. Yet in different ways, both she and Frank intended to see it to the end. For her part, she'd already broken rules, gone against unstated *Post* policy not to rock the boat. Now she was about to confront Mr. Ware and ask to rock that boat a little harder.

The city editor was at his desk. His tie was loosened. His paunch strained the buttons of his shirt. Sweat glistened on his wrinkled face and balding head. He reminded Liz a little of an ancient Buddha. He was bent over the front page of the first edition spread across his desk.

She cleared her throat and he looked up.

"Why was there no mention of the Klan in the story about the raid?" There was no sense beating around the bush.

The click of typewriter keys slowed. Liz could feel the eyes of every man in the room.

"Would have been if we'd had any background."

She stared at the editor. Unless her ears deceived her, he was opening the door to an exposé of the Klan, risking his retirement.

"You'll have it. For starters, there's the interview with Harlan and his speech on the Fourth. There'll be his trial. And Phil isn't going to forget the Ryan murder," she assured him, hardly able to suppress her excitement.

"I also want the lowdown on the beating that Jewish kid took."

She sat down. "His name is Jake Steinberg. As far as I know, he's still in the hospital."

"Then go to the hospital," Mr. Ware said. "And nose around to find out what other campaigns the Klan is backing. Top to bottom. The Senate, the governor, mayor, judges, right down to justice of the peace and dogcatcher. You'll need help. I'll assign Collier. He's honest and dependable, not apt to go off half-cocked."

Liz wanted to hug the dear old man.

"And I want you to bring me a daily tally on how the petitions to oust the D.A. are faring." Ware's voice was stronger than it had been for months. His eyes were shining.

"I warn you. I'm not going to give up on this," Liz said.

"Didn't think you would."

Liz regarded the aging city editor fondly. "I grew up here. This city—this state—means too much to let a bunch of vicious bigots swindle people out of their dreams." She straightened, inched her chair closer to his desk. "What would you think of a front-page interview tomorrow with the Grand Dragon at his headquarters—complete with photos?"